A

PERMANENT

EXILE

Also by Aseem Kumar Giri

Imposters at the Gate: A Novel about Private Equity

A

PERMANENT

EXILE

Aseem Kumar Giri

Tusk Publishing Inc.

Tusk Publishing Inc.

PUBLISHING

Copyright 2008 Tusk Publishing Inc.
ISBN 978-1-60502-003-7

Library of Congress Cataloging-in-Publication Data available upon request.

First Edition.

Tusk Publishing books may be purchased for educational, business or sales promotional use.   For information, please write to main@tuskpublishing.com.

www.tuskpublishing.com

Publisher's Note

You will notice on the front inside flap of the cover a BIN™ number.   This
is the work's *Book Identification Number*.   Please use it to register on our
website <u>www.tuskpublishing.com</u> to receive additional benefits and services.
We hope you enjoy this work.

This book is dedicated to my grandparents, parents, godparents, parents-in-law and the millions of others who have left the comfort and familiarity of their places of birth in search of a better life for themselves and their posterity.

This is a small token of gratitude for your sacrifices.

CHAPTER ONE

May 2007

Arun Gandharni left his house at seven that morning, continuing with piety the practice he had adopted religiously over two months ago of walking through his neighborhood. He had adopted this new routine as a direct result of the incident. He liked the space he was able to create for himself on these walks. As his body wandered about from street to street, it was as if his mind were a dog on a leash, a vehicle being pulled by a tow truck or a railcar guided by a locomotive. His mind was forced to follow suit – forced to navigate the myriad thoughts occupying him, enabling him to identify, categorize and organize his inner cerebral meanderings. He was a mental and emotional mess without these strolls; a road atlas without any labels, grid or index.

The jaunt had done its trick. On this morning, prior to arriving home, he stopped by the florist. He purchased a single rose to take home to his wife. It was his birthday today, but he preferred being the one giving the gift. He knew it would make her smile. He walked into his house with relative peace of mind, feeling invigorated and ready to face the day's hurdles.

That equipoise was quickly disturbed when he caught sight of his wife. She was hugging herself, arms wrapped around her seven-month ripe belly, leaning against the kitchen counter. Of the two lives that Arun gazed upon, one of them, the visible one, looked as if she had been crying.

"It's in the paper," she surrendered. The sense of devastation in her voice was difficult for Arun to bear. It was the sound of defeat. He swallowed hard. He placed the rose on the island counter-top that now stood in between him and his wife. She noticed the flower; the outer edges of her eyes drooped slightly, revealing that she was touched by the gesture. Her eyes quickly returned to their normal position, an acknowledgment that this was not the best time to comment on it.

The home phone rang. Radha twitched involuntarily when she heard it. Arun looked at the phone and saw that it was his sister-in-law, first noticing his wife's maiden name of Bhardpuri and then the initial A for Anjali. Arun saw that Radha had observed the caller ID as well. Radha stood still. Arun didn't bother pressing the 'talk' button. Perhaps she was just calling to wish him a happy birthday.

"She's the one who found the article," Radha said to him. The grim resignation that continued to permeate her voice grated at him. He had not wanted that to happen.

It seemed unfair thought Arun. There was supposed to be an unwritten rule, or perhaps it was just general belief, he decided, that the world needed to be kind to you on your birthday. People, circumstances, fate, should all yield on that one day. But that wasn't the case after the incident, as if the laws of the universe had abruptly changed. He could have used the relief; his system had been going through a bit of emotional and cognitive overload, over the last two months, since the incident.

"I'll be right back," Arun called over his shoulder as he went back out the front door. Radha knew where he was going. They ceased having a paper delivered at home; as if events of the outside world didn't matter anymore. While crossing the road, Arun heard the sound of tires screeching and a horn blowing. Startled, he turned, jumped back from the road, and mouthed an apology to the riled driver who sped away shaking his head in disgust.

Arun realized that just because his world had stopped, it didn't mean the rest of the world had followed accordingly. Arun could feel his heart beating faster, and he felt like a meteor had just dented his head. A shock went through his body again, as if the words he was now recounting from Radha had triggered a flash of lightning through every cell of his constitution. He felt like he was controlling an involuntary bowel movement.

He walked to the convenient store two blocks away. He went to buy the paper. He felt relieved as he saw that it was buried on the third page. *Who was he kidding*, he realized; the third page was not buried, it was glaring.

"US ATTORNEY LAUNCHES INVESTIGATION INTO FORMER GOWIRE SYSTEMS GENERAL COUNSEL"

And then he saw his name in print. That's when the cold sweat began. Soon he felt the extra weight of his clothes, heavy from the moisture collecting about his neck, back and armpits. He began to see white, as if the sun were exploding in front of him, blinding him. His knees gave way and he fell to the floor. It was a clean execution.

● ● ●

With the help of the checkout clerk, Arun got to his feet. He wondered how long he had been out. He walked out the door, after purchasing the paper, and embarked on another walk, as if he had not been out yet for that day.

He was faithful to these excursions during times of mental duress or turmoil – devoted to laying out anew the neighborhood of his mind. Like a skilled cartographer, he could chart the avenues he most relished and stroll up and down them. He could avoid the gulleys and thoroughfares that had been providing him discordant heartache or anguish. He could traverse different experiences and emotions he had been having, pass-by and re-live positive encounters he had recently had and avoid the potholes and pits of negative events. He liked to saunter down the boulevard of "Time With his Wife and Children", as if window-shopping. He preferred dashing through the alleys of "The Incident", "His Parents", and "Fear", like he was running from danger. He would maneuver this map of his psyche, as if hunting for treasure, and emerge, where the X marks the spot, right where he wanted to be.

Or so that was the plan. Some days, it wasn't physically possible to walk far enough to re-align those intersecting lanes, roads and trails. Some days it was just too tough.

He arrived home. The house he and his wife had bought several years ago had competing design concepts. Parts of it were flashy; other areas had a more muted elegance. Radha wanted to be reserved, Arun showy. From the street, the two-storey house looked like it was the grandest on the block, and probably the neighborhood. It was in a woody enclave of Los Angeles, halfway between the ocean and the towers of Century City. As Arun approached his house today, suddenly a number of flaws came into focus: the brown patches on the lawn, the chipped paint on the siding and the missing shutter boards by two windows. The overall look and feel from a distance gave credence to a once grand stature, one that matched the solid foundation of the household; on close inspection, however, it betrayed the nature of the prevailing times. *How much could change in two months*, pondered Arun.

He caught sight of himself in the hall mirror as he walked in. He observed his short black hair combed to the side, his elongated face ending in a pointed chin, his high cheekbones complementing his pronounced forehead that framed his large eyes. At six feet he was above average in height compared to his fellow ethnic Indians and a good eight inches taller than his wife.

He kept his fainting episode in the convenient store from Radha. He had grown more talkative lately; when he first started these walks, he was completely quiet upon his return. In the beginning, when Radha had asked him how the weather was, he had responded that he didn't know. A month later she asked if the large tree on Manning Avenue had bloomed yet. He said probably not. He had thought he had been down that way, but he couldn't remember. Two days ago she wondered if the Randall family was away – had Arun seen any cars in the driveway? No, he confirmed.

Radha hadn't moved from the kitchen. He was suddenly worried that she should sit down. Sadness didn't suit her face, he decided; she had been fortunate enough to be born with a nose, chin and jaw line that looked sculpted by an artist. There was no room for tears on that canvas. She kept her hair long, which suited her oval shaped face. Like him, she had high cheekbones and an even more pronounced forehead. Her eyes matched his in size, but her expressiveness with those eyes was always more emphatic compared to him – her eyes would grow wider when she was surprised or squint smaller when she was unhappy. Above all, her eyes were inviting. There was an allure to them that grew beyond sexual attractiveness to signal the presence of a kind, caring soul, someone who could be trusted to be good to the people with whom she interacted.

Radha's round belly was all the more noticeable because of her petite frame. Prior to getting pregnant, she had been a lean one hundred ten pounds. Although she had been born and raised in the UK, her family was from India originally. Nonetheless, because of her very fair complexion, people would at times confuse her for being Persian, Turkish or even Italian.

The phone at home rang again. Radha answered it this time. He could overhear Anjali asking repeatedly to speak to him. He didn't want to.

Radha's mother Parvati phoned shortly thereafter. Arun respectfully declined talking to her as well.

Two hours later, Anjali showed up in person. She first hugged Arun. Arun could feel the emotion rising inside him. He opened his eyes wide to evaporate the moisture that was beginning to pool together. He didn't want to do this in front of her or in front of Radha.

"Happy Birthday," were the first words she said.

It was a reminder for Arun. He had forgotten. Arun responded by holding her more tightly.

"Don't worry," she said, "We'll get through this."

He pushed back and looked at her. It was a look of incredulity. He didn't know if he should trust her or not. Was she sincere? Did she really intend to help? Could she really be relied upon?

He remembered the conversation that he had with Radha on the matter, shortly after the incident occurred. "Family cannot be relied upon," was Arun's firm conclusion.

"Yes, they can, Arun," Radha had pleaded, "not all families are the same."

Perhaps Arun would have to concede that Radha was right. The sound of his wife's voice brought him back to the present.

"I think we should talk to my parents about this," Radha had just finished saying.

"Are you kidding?" retorted Arun, "Your father's reputation is at issue here."

Radha looked at Arun and stated matter-of-factly, "Mum can provide us with a lot of support."

"They probably still don't even know. They are all the way in the U.K.," argued Arun. "Why would we want to inform them and deal with all of the fallout related to that?"

"Radha is right," said Anjali. She added grimly, "Also, they already know."

Arun turned to face Anjali.   He closed his eyes, grimacing as if in pain.

"Don't be so mortified, Arun.   Look, in Radha's condition it would be good for her to have additional comfort.   Mum won't judge you, she will just want what is best for you," Anjali expanded.

"I am so embarrassed about this," Arun exclaimed.   He was trying to control the rising swell of anger building up in him.

Radha gave him a hug.   "Don't worry.   Telling our parents will actually be helpful to us," she implored.

Arun held his wife close to him, maneuvering around her stomach, and let out an exasperated sigh.   As he had often done, he ran his hand through her hair.

"I can't do it," he confessed, his voice barely a whisper.

Anjali's cell phone rang.   "Right.   Now look, the only reason I am going to answer this, is because I know it is Mum," she stated, as she held the phone up in the air to emphasize the point.   Holding his wife eased some of the tension Arun had been feeling, allowing him to reflect on other matters.   Arun would always smile when his wife or her sister betrayed with their accents their having been raised in the U.K.   He managed a smile.

"Yeah, Mum.   He's here.   Would you like to have a word?"   Anjali looked up at Arun as she spoke.

Arun reluctantly took the phone.

"Happy birthday, my son."

"Thank you, Mom," said Arun with strain in his voice.

"Don't worry about anything.   Everything will be all right."

"Okay."   He handed the phone back to Anjali hurriedly and walked away.   So, it was true, she knew what was going on. At that point for Arun, shutting his mother-in-law out was easier. He approached the window overlooking the front yard.   He

7

wondered how his own parents would react. He had just seen them a few weeks ago at Nandini's sixth birthday party. He didn't want to go back to the three-year period of silence that he had to live through between him and his parents. It took his father having a heart attack for the family to come together again. But even at that time, his mother had managed a two-minute call every year to wish him happy birthday. It was as if she were acknowledging the sanctity of the day. He scrunched his forehead. He tried to look away from Radha. She would always say that she knew when he thought about his parents because he always scrunched his forehead. He didn't want her to notice him.

I'll probably hear from them later today, Arun thought. They always called on his birthday. As the sun forfeited the sky to the moon, Arun had still not heard from them. *Maybe they will call later,* he consoled himself.

He waited until midnight. He went to sleep without hearing from them. The twenty-four hours of the day of his birth had passed and the people responsible for it, alive and well and a mere three hundred miles away from him had not reached out, for the first time in forty years, to acknowledge the event. Arun shifted his body on the bed. *Looks like a period of silence is upon us again.* He turned to face his back towards his wife so that she couldn't see his scrunched forehead.

It all began two months ago with the incident. Or perhaps the story started long before that.

CHAPTER TWO

May 1967

Arun was born shortly after Rajiv and Meena arrived in the US. They knew they were expecting when they made the journey. Meena's command of English was not superb, and the doctors in California at that time, even in the Bay Area, had not grown as accustomed to seeing people of different nationalities in their delivery rooms. This made it hard on both sides. The delivery was taxing, but things seemed to fall in place when the questions stopped and nature was allowed to run its course. Rajiv tried his best to cope.

"Mr. Gandharni, you tell us when your wife would like an epidural to relieve the pain," the doctor had informed Rajiv.

"I not knowing..." was Rajiv's response, delivered hesitatingly. He cleared his throat. He was squinting his eyes and shaking his head, almost apologetically.

"An epidural..."

Rajiv tried to listen more carefully.

"...to relieve the pain."

"Everything is okay?" asked Rajiv.

"Yes," replied the doctor, "but if your wife needs an epidural, let us know."

"But everything fine?"

"Yes, Mr. Gandharni."

Rajiv turned away as the doctor walked out the door. He looked in the mirror facing him. For the first time he wondered what his child would look like. He took stock of himself. Rajiv was physically short in stature with a wiry thin frame. He stood only five feet four inches tall. His face was elongated, and it appeared as if the skin were pulled very tightly across his face. His jaw line and cheekbones were sharply delineated. His eyes were a bit sunken. It gave him the appearance of being consummately sad. He decided that he didn't want his child to look like him.

Matters grew more complicated for Meena. Nurses would ask her regularly about the pain.

"Very pain. Very pain," would be her constant response.

Meena's five feet three inch tall body looked smaller amongst the taller nurses, Rajiv observed. She still had a pleasantness about her face, round eyes and a pointed nose. She had some minor scarring on her face, clustered about her cheekbones, like miniscule divots, that had been the result of acne. She always kept her hair braided back.

"Would you like an epidural?" the nurses would ask. Meena would look at her husband, and Rajiv would wear a blank expression.

After several hours, the doctor approached Rajiv. "The baby is breached."

"I don't knowing," came Rajiv's soft-toned response. He again squinted his eyes and shook his head.

"The head is up and the bottom is down -- the opposite of the way it needs to be. We need to perform a Caesarian."

"Is baby being okay?" Rajiv cleared his throat.

"Yes. But we need to perform a Caesarian. Is that okay with you and your wife?"

He said what he knew. "Please. I no understand. You are being doctor. You are knowing what is best. You making baby okay."

Within the hour, Arun inhaled his first breath of life. Rajiv looked upon the baby with a sense of satisfaction, like a man who had dutifully fulfilled an obligation. The Gandharnis had an American citizen in the family now.

Rajiv maintained that expression when Arjun arrived. Although brothers, Arjun and Rajiv had very few similarities in terms of physical appearance; they were almost diametrically opposed. Arjun was tall, five foot ten inches, and well built. It was as if he had cornered the supply of milk and food in the house while growing up. While Rajiv was indifferent about food, Arjun relished it. Arjun had been a chubby baby, while Rajiv had not. Over time, Arjun shed the weight. He was more vain than Rajiv - passionate about what he ate, but disciplined about his physique.

"The first American in the family," quipped Arjun.

"No. He is being the first Indian in the family being born in America," clarified Rajiv. He cleared his throat.

● ● ●

Rajiv returned to his work after Arun's birth with earnest. He arrived early to work his first day back, as was his habit. He met Sam Harding, his boss and the founder of the company he was working for, for the first time when he returned. Sam had been on extended leave when Rajiv first joined four months ago. Sam had been one of Arjun's contacts. As a venture capitalist, Arjun had many entrepreneurs as friends. It was Arjun who had raised the job possibility for Rajiv to their father and uncle, both of whom agreed that Rajiv should take the job and migrate to America. It was also Arjun who pointed out that the baby that Meena was carrying at the time would be born an American citizen.

Rajiv shared with Sam about the birth of Arun. Sam talked about how his wife was expecting, due in the next month, and how his family had been in the area for decades, managing a farm.

"Oh you are also having a farm, is it?" Rajiv asked of Sam with great excitement. Rajiv smiled widely upon hearing the confirmation.

The next day, Rajiv brought to the office a photo of his family's farm in India and a canister he had kept with him since leaving India. He waited outside Sam's office door. When Sam looked up, Rajiv smiled at him.

"May I coming in, sir?"

"Hey, Rajiv. Yeah, sure, buddy, come on in."

Rajiv slowly walked in, his head down.

"There's no need to wait at the door. You can just waltz in and get my attention."

"Ok, sir," Rajiv replied wagging his head, and after clearing his throat he continued, "Thank you, sir. It is being very nice of you, sir. I wanting I showing you, sir…my home, sir."

"Well look at that," responded Sam. "It's very nice. It looks different than the ones out here. Different than the one I grew up on."

Rajiv began moving his index finger towards the picture to point out the mango trees growing in front of the house that he himself had planted. He was interrupted by someone entering the room. "Sam, did you review those numbers?" asked the person. Rajiv stepped back and stood straight.

Sam looked up from the photo. "Yeah, but the fourth quarter is missing."

"No, it's in there," contested the person.

"Let me see," said Sam as he put the photo aside listlessly and shuffled through some papers. "Yeah, okay, I see it now," responded Sam.

Rajiv suddenly felt conscious about the canister he was holding. He decided not to show its contents to Sam.

"Where were we?" asked Sam, turning to face Rajiv. He seemed to have forgotten about the photo.

A PERMANENT EXILE

"It is being nothing," concluded Rajiv as he leaned forward to take the photo back from Sam's desk. Rajiv quietly exited without saying another word.

● ● ●

The months after Arun's birth were completely occupied for Rajiv and Meena on the baby and focusing on his needs. Rajiv felt so overwhelmed with all of the things that he had to do. He had been in the US only six months. He had to learn to drive. Arjun, who had his license, helped Rajiv and Meena get around for those things that were not within walking distance of their apartment. Rajiv had grown accustomed to being driven when he was in India. Luckily Rajiv had found a place to live that was near a grocery store and within two miles of his office. It made the walk to work easy for him. It was actually the same distance he would walk daily when he traversed the family farm in India. There was comfort in that walk he did to the office. The path was lined with homes that had diverse trees, shrubs and flowers. He enjoyed thinking of the names of the various vegetation. Even after receiving his license, Rajiv preferred to walk to work.

When Rajiv and Meena had first arrived to the Bay Area, they stayed with Arjun. Rajiv had been surprised when Arjun suggested they live separately. Rajiv knew his family back home would never approve, so he kept it from them. Arjun would visit with them in the evenings. Rajiv liked to sit with his brother during those times. There was comfort with the presence of family, Rajiv had decided. But with each passing day, Rajiv and Meena saw less and less of Arjun. He was always busy doing this or another thing. Those nights that he wasn't there, Rajiv would sit with his photo and canister. Time passed without much notice.

Rajiv found his job very different than the jobs he had worked in India, which had also taken him some getting used to.

Nothing made as much sense to him as the plantation back home. But he eventually developed an understanding for the work here – *I provide these services and I get this salary.* He didn't think it was a bad trade-off, but it didn't speak to him the way working the earth did. He never felt that the money he received was as holy as the fruit that the Earth would bear. At the apartment complex where they lived, he didn't have any space where he could plant or grow anything. The only land he had access to was at work. He planted a few items there in a small patch, no bigger than a sandbox, at the back corner of the building. It was an isolated location and few people walked there. He chose it specifically because it wasn't noticeable from the front of the building, but there was ample sunlight. Rajiv would nurture his plants and flowers daily.

One day he saw that there was someone walking the grounds. At one point he was standing near the area that Rajiv had cultivated. "Hello," Rajiv exclaimed as he came running towards the man.

"I don't think that you can have these here," the man said.

"Please, it is being okay. I keeping this here. It is being little space," Rajiv pleaded with the man.

The man replied, "No, it won't be possible."

"You giving me one day, please?" Rajiv asked. He cleared his throat.

"Okay," said the man, "but you have these out by the morning."

Rajiv went back in the building. He walked frantically to Sam's office. The door was closed and the light was off inside. He turned to Sam's secretary. "Please, where is being Sam?"

She gave him a dumbfounded look. "Huh?"

"I am needing to speaking to Sam," Rajiv pleaded.

"Honey, I don't understand a word ya are sayin'," said the secretary, chuckling snidely to herself.

"I speaking to Sam," Rajiv said, growing flustered, his face turning red, feeling more self-conscious. He cleared his throat.

"Well ya can't be speaking to Sam, silly man, he ain't here," said the secretary.

At that instant her phone rang. She picked it up.

"Oh hi!" She started to talk.

Rajiv stood there for a few minutes. She showed no signs of ceasing her conversation or of turning back to him.

"And then ya know what he did? He took the sweater I gave 'em for his birthday and he…"

Rajiv walked away slowly. When he arrived home later that night, he was elated to see Arjun there. "Arjun, you please helping. I am needing some vessels for holding my plants," Rajiv asked. Rajiv didn't know where to find such things in the US.

"Oh, you mean pots? Well, tonight's a bad night. I've got plans. I'll help you over the weekend," Arjun said as he stood up to leave. Rajiv nodded his head reluctantly as Arjun went out the door. Rajiv found the photo and canister and held them both for awhile before going to sleep.

Sam was not in again the next day. Rajiv stood silently by as he watched the man pluck out all of his plants and flowers and replace them with grass and fertilizer. Rajiv thought about a Western-style funeral he had seen on television.

● ● ●

Rajiv always thought that he would go back to visit India within a few months, and maybe even convince his family that he was better off being at home and tending to the farm. He thought that perhaps after awhile he, Meena and Arjun could all go back to India together. Arjun, who had preceded Rajiv's arrival to the US, had different plans.

"Arjun, how much being cost of ticket to home?" asked Rajiv.

"Home? Why do you need a ticket to go home? You don't take a bus or train. You drive or walk there."

"It is being meaning our India. I am wanting a plane ticket."

"I'm not sure you should be thinking of going back so quickly," commented Arjun.

Rajiv called the airline. "Yes, how much costing ticket to India? One thousand three hundred? Okay. Thank you." He cleared his throat after hanging up.

Rajiv calculated that within ten months he would have enough money. Rajiv began setting money aside for a potential trip. He portioned his salary three ways now: living expenses, airfare and money he was sending home. Rajiv had been sending a monthly amount to his family in India, via his uncle, R.K. After three months of Rajiv saving, R.K. called and requested an increase in the amount Rajiv was sending. His uncle began doing this periodically, sometimes every two weeks, sometimes every three weeks. Soon, whatever reserve Rajiv had saved to finance a trip disappeared.

The family seemed to really need the money that Rajiv was sending back. This is what Rajiv was told in every conversation. In some cases they would request large sums of money at one time, a bulk payment, beyond the fixed monthly amount. Based on the exchange rate, it seemed like a significant amount. The farm in India was struggling, Uncle R.K. would complain during each call. Rajiv's own father rarely came to the phone. Rajiv had the plantation on his mind constantly, but felt powerless to do anything about it. He presented idea after idea about what could and should be done, based on his experience of working the land. His uncle would hear his advice. Much to Rajiv's dismay, the farm continued to deteriorate. As the farm continued to produce less and less, Rajiv grew more concerned. As Rajiv's salary increased, he would automatically increase the amount he sent back and he adopted the habit of sending instructions and thoughts on where and how it should be spent. He never thought to question whether it was being done. He felt implicitly that it was in everyone's interest to maintain the land.

Rajiv resigned himself to the idea of staying in the US awhile and continuing his life there, at least for the time being. He tabled thoughts of going back for several months. "I think it is being better for the farm if I staying here a little while so that I can being sending the money to saving it," Rajiv muttered to himself. He held the photo and the canister in his hands as he spoke.

After six months, Meena became pregnant again.

"Don't you want to enjoy life a little bit?" asked Arjun of Rajiv.

"Why you no understand? You still being very young. I fulfilling my duty. No better enjoyment is being there," Rajiv responded, betraying his embarrassment as he spoke.

Rajiv and Meena had their second child, Sanjay. Rajiv's family back home was again very proud of the fact that there was another boy in the family. They seemed most proud, Rajiv noted, that there was another American citizen in the family. Rajiv was secretly pleased that a new baby was a good reason to move to a larger apartment, preferably one where there might be some space for him to plant something, even if the land wouldn't belong to him.

"Another American!" cheered Arjun as he held Sanjay.

"Why you no understand?" asked Rajiv, to which Arjun did not provide a response. Rajiv cleared his throat.

● ● ●

Rajiv pulled out a piece of paper from his wallet. He had jotted down the name of a travel agent the last time he and Meena had visited the Indian grocery store. He dialed the number.

"How much being ticket to India?"

Rajiv did some calculations.   He thought that after a few months it might be possible for him to go.   He didn't think that he could manage having both him and Meena go together with the two boys.   It would be too expensive.   But perhaps with Arjun providing Meena some assistance it could be possible for him to go.

Rajiv next thought about work.   He approached Sam's office.

"You are interested in going back?   So soon?" Sam asked.

Rajiv shifted his feet.   He looked down.   He didn't know how to express his desire to go.

"Well, you have one week of vacation," indicated Sam.

Rajiv was hoping for the flexibility that he had experienced at his job in India.

"To have more time, you'll probably have to wait the five years required before your vacation time can accrue from one year to the next," Sam pointed out matter-of-factly.

Rajiv was quiet as he attempted to absorb what Sam was telling him.   He cleared his throat.   He looked at Sam to see if there might be a hint of generosity in terms of stretching the rules. Rajiv saw none.

In an acknowledgment of the quiet time between them, Sam offered, "I'm sorry, Rajiv.   I like you, I like your brother, but I gotta keep the rules consistent here, otherwise others are gonna expect the same treatment."

"Thank you, sir," said Rajiv feebly as he walked out of the office.   Rajiv called Arjun.

"He's a principled man," explained Arjun.   "He won't back down from his position, just because you don't like it."

"Maybe you asking him, yourself.   You seeing what he saying.   Maybe for you is being different answer.   You sounding like him when you talking.   I sounding different.   Maybe is being funny for him, the way I sounding," Rajiv encouraged Arjun.

"It's not worth it, Rajiv, I don't want to piss the guy off!" Arjun objected.

"What is this piss off? What it does meaning?" Rajiv asked.

"I don't want to upset him," Arjun clarified.

"Why you no understand?" Rajiv pleaded with his brother.

CHAPTER THREE

March 2007

The incident happened on a day when Arun had come back from a business trip.   He didn't even make it home from the airport.   He went straight to the office.   He hadn't heard from work all day, which was unusual.   Typically his team would call him six or seven times a day.   Andy Casper, who had worked with him, but had moved to the Business Development Department, had called three times.   Nowadays Andy just called to chat about how much he hated his job.   There shouldn't have been anything urgent there.   The number of times he called should have been a clue for Arun, however.   He chided himself for not being more alert.

When Arun arrived at the office, he was called into the glass conference room by Chet Masterson.   Chet was usually very quiet and aloof so it struck Arun as odd.   But Chet was the president and Arun deferred to him.   Arun did not recognize the other man in the room, though he knew Joseph Summers, of course, the head of Human Resources.   Arun shook Chet's hand when he entered.   Chet was distant and cold.

"Have a seat," Chet said.

"Sure," replied Arun.   His heart hadn't started to beat fast yet, which he would find odd when he re-played the scene in his mind multiple times.   Arun shook Joseph's hand.   There was a perfunctory exchange of greetings.   It was mostly initiated by Arun.   Arun had a tendency to look down on those people he considered administration. Arun extended his hand out to the man he didn't recognize. "Hello, I'm Arun."

"Oh, hello"

"You are?"

"I'm Ernest Faird."

"Did you just join the company, Ernest?" inquired Arun, betraying only casual interest as he took his seat.

"Not exactly."

Tension suddenly entered the room as if one of the walls had been the side of an aquarium and it had just shattered. A tidal wave of strain gushed in. Or perhaps the anxiety had been there all along, and Arun was only now catching a sense of it. As if the fog had suddenly thickened and its presence couldn't be ignored.

Ernest looked at Joseph.

Joseph looked at Arun.

"Ernest is with Smith and Janssen," responded Joseph.

"The law firm?" Arun attempted to confirm. He was actually well aware of the firm. He had worked with them extensively. He asked the question more to solicit an explanation for why he was being asked to sit down with the firm's outside legal counsel. There was a brief silence. It appeared Joseph, Ernest and Chet paused intentionally to let the impact of Joseph's statement sink in. Arun knew better than to expect an actual response to the question.

"Why don't you tell us about that check on your desk?" prompted Joseph after another few seconds had passed.

"Which check?" asked Arun with genuine confusion.

Ernest let out a heavy sigh and muttered, "jeez" under his breath.

"What is going on?" asked Arun while looking at Joseph. His tone was still calm.

"We want you to tell us about the check," commanded Joseph.

"You want me to tell you about the check?" repeated Arun, a slight bit of mockery to his tone.

"Yes," came Joseph's serious reply.

"It has numbers on it. Those numbers are also spelled out. There is likely a date at the top and in the lower right hand corner there may even be a signature," countered Arun. He folded his arms across his chest as he spoke. He was alarmed himself with how fierce he was becoming.

This time Joseph sighed.

"I can see that you are going to be difficult," commented Ernest while looking down.

"Oh, I'm being difficult? How about you guys stop being difficult," Arun demanded while making quotation mark motions with his fingers as he said difficult, "and tell me what the hell is going on."

There was silence. Ernest and Joseph walked out of the room.

"Don't go anywhere," Ernest directed Arun gruffly as Ernest stepped through the door.

"Don't worry, Rod Serling, I won't leave *The Twilight Zone*," responded Arun, sardonically.

"The name's Ernest," Ernest said back.

Arun couldn't help but laugh. When they had left, Arun turned to face Chet. "Who is this guy?"

Chet stayed quiet. He sat there with his sandy-brown round-rimmed glasses, an attempt to match the color of his hair which he parted on the side and didn't so much comb over as he did toss it over with his hand. It always seemed to fall forward, Arun would note. It made sense to Arun. He didn't see Chet expending much time in grooming. Chet would rather be seated in front of a computer. Arun reasoned that his sedentary predilections had contributed to his round face, which matched his round stomach. He was often dressed in plaid or in jeans and would sport his ubiquitous Nike sneakers.

Sunlight drowned the conference room. The late afternoon timing placed the sun on the downward trajectory of its arc. As Arun sat in the conference room he would have normally held his hand up or brought the curtains down to block the sunlight from agitating him. Today, that didn't matter. The sun bore down on him, blinding his sight, but he was immune to it. He was too focused on this sense of fear that was erupting inside of him and would soon be gushing through all corners of his body. He thought about the last time he had this sensation. It was with his parents, just before they began the three year period of silence. He considered his parents, his Uncle Arjun and his brothers again. Arun's shoulders involuntarily tensed, his head fell to looking down, and he bunched up the skin of his forehead so that it looked like blinds covering a window as he wondered whether he could turn to them or not. He had no idea how they would react to this. He wished he could lift open the blinds and be done with all these thoughts. There were trees and a flower-lined trail of serenity that were beckoning him. He wanted to get to that place; however, his thinking became dominated by another matter. How would he cover this up from his parents, uncle and brothers, if he had to?

Why is it so sunny? Arun glanced outside the conference room window. *Is it meant to taunt me?* There was Los Angeles sprawled out in front of him. Hills to the right, ocean to the left. He remembered fondly looking out upon this view and finding it beautiful. It had been a treat arguing with customers' and suppliers' lawyers when surrounded by this landscape. He didn't find it appealing now. On such a disastrous day, how could there be beauty? Beauty was gone. Like a mouse it had scurried down some alleyway, abandoning the lane in pursuit of a hiding place. There was no trace of it. Hope seemed difficult to come by as well; he couldn't find that street as he drove around in his mind. All that was left were the dark gulleys of depravity and the ugliness that comes when humans forget that other people have emotions, desires, or needs. *It must be spiting me*, he thought. *Both inside and outside of this building, I am being spited.*

His thoughts came back to the matter at hand as the glass door opened and people stepped in. Although he had been sharing the room with Chet, it felt like he had the space all to himself. Arun's thoughts changed slightly. *How do I figure out what the right thing to do is? If I get a lawyer does that make me look guilty? Why should I have to pay a lawyer? Inevitably, in the whirlwind of thoughts that was causing his head to spin, like a tornado, Arun would always come back to the same point – what to do with his parents?*

Joseph and Ernest re-entered the room. "We have caught you committing fraud," Joseph said. As if the silence were an invitation to add further clarification, he added, abruptly, "There are two million dollars missing, and the trail leads to you."

Arun felt like an explosion had just occurred. Maybe it was a bomb blast, maybe it was a fire that combusted with a large bang, maybe it was an earthquake causing buildings to come stampeding to the ground. His hands were shaking, he was short of breath and he was gripped by fear. The fear was almost paralyzing in its intensity. All he could do was observe his surroundings. Attempting to react to them was just a dream. His muscles were concrete – except for the involuntary, and at times violent, convulsing that he was experiencing. Moving was not possible.

"We have caught you committing fraud." He heard the words again, re-enacting the exact manner in which each syllable was enunciated, which words were emphasized and the pace with which they were delivered.

He surveyed the four walls of the conference room where he sat. The words seemed to bounce around those walls. How many contracts for the firm he had negotiated in this one room. He felt suffocated in that space suddenly. It was as it had always been, light brown table capable of seating sixteen, gray carpet, black leather reclining chairs. The room always smelled like cleaning fluid.

He remembered having these feelings in the aftermath of a car accident. He wondered what it would be like to be a firefighter or an emergency medical technician in an ambulance. When disaster strikes they were in firm command of the situation. They knew exactly what to do. No thinking was involved. They just acted. They acted on instinct, they acted on nerves, they acted on impulse; whatever it was, their bodies were propelled forward with clarity of purpose and intent. There was no faltering, no second-guessing, no fear. They were in control. *How does that feel?* He envied them. He was at ground zero. And he had no idea what to do. It never smelled like cleaning fluid after a car accident.

To whom do you turn in a time like this? Whom can you rely on? Who would be the emergency response team for his catastrophe?

"Excuse me one moment," Arun asked the men in the room. He stood to get up.

"You stay here," said Ernest. "We'll step out."

Arun stayed quiet. Once they left, Arun reached for his wallet. He pulled out a photo he had in there. He looked at his wife, son and daughter. He thought about the baby that his wife was now carrying.

He realized that they could help him. But only from within. They could support him emotionally, give him something tangible to fight for, champion his cause when his spirit was low. But they were also vulnerable as the potential victims.

Who would look after his family if he had to be away? Who would provide financial support if he couldn't? Who would re-assure him that everything would be okay?

Shouldn't there be someone else to turn to? There should be, Arun knew the answer. He had parents, an uncle and two brothers. There should have been plenty of people to turn to. But he knew he couldn't. They were the ones who had initiated a three-year period of silence – *how could I rely on them?* he wondered.

"No," he re-affirmed aloud, "family can't be relied upon in a crisis."

● ● ●

Radha picked up the phone. She had just entered the kitchen of her home. She heard the sound of air blowing into the mouthpiece of the caller. She thought for a split second, either the person was sighing, short of breath or they were in a windy place. "Hello?"

"Radha, it's me."

Arun usually wasn't that breathy on the phone. Nor did he start his conversations that way. It was usually some witty comment about events they were grappling with at the time. Recently, their son's teacher had complained that Zubin was leaving the classroom to water plants in the hallway. He felt the custodian was neglecting them, he had said in his defense, when questioned about his behavior. Arun and Radha had to go in for a parent-teacher conference on the matter. When Arun had called Radha later that day, he had quipped, "Yes, hello, this is the school psychologist calling. Your son is too caring. We don't like that around here." "Oh, well," Radha had retorted, "I'll have him bring a gun to school tomorrow." "We also accept drugs and alcohol," added Arun. They laughed together. Somehow, she could tell that wasn't going to happen today.

Radha's heart began to beat faster.   She put down the glass that she was holding onto the kitchen island-countertop and stood still.   She stayed in one position, not moving at all, hoping that it would allow her to concentrate.   She lowered her head also, as if straining to hear a whisper.   She put her hand on her round belly. "Are you all right?" she asked.

"No."

I suppose I should appreciate his honesty and forthrightness, thought Radha.   *Oh how I wish he would make a joke right now.* She felt sympathy for her husband.   Most people deliberated and paused repeatedly when telling bad news, leaning on such trite phrases as "I don't know how to tell you this", because it made it easier on them, the deliverer of the news.   Arun tackled the hard part for him head-on; he blurted out the difficult message.   He then immediately began trying to manage the impact on the recipient, ensuring a smooth aftermath, attempting to make it easier for the person who heard the bad news.   It was a thoughtful approach, Radha had decided.   *Her husband was a thoughtful man.*   A person was lucky if they had to hear bad news from Arun.   A faint smile almost appeared on her face as Radha had a realization.   *Maybe he just does this with me.*

Radha really couldn't recall what Arun said next.   Sound bytes were coming through.   "Work", "trouble" and "that bastard Derek" were what she remembered hearing.   He had a firm command of his voice, but she could sense something different in it.   His erratic intonations from time to time suggested he was attempting to suppress some emotion.   It was probably fear she reasoned.

"Some money is missing.   They are asking me questions."

Radha felt her body shudder.   It felt as if something was leaving her.   Instinctively, she moved her hand to the lower part of her belly.   She found the action silly, afterwards.   *How could the baby fall out?*   She tried to make sense of what she had just heard. Her eyes began darting around the kitchen, as if impersonating her thoughts as they bounced around in her mind. She was having trouble comprehending what her husband was saying. She had so many questions. She couldn't bring herself to ask them. It was as if the pinball had finally settled on a groove where all she wanted to ask was *are we going to be okay?* She thought to ask that, but something made her stop. She felt that sympathy again. Or perhaps it was pity now. *Even when things are bad, Arun tried his best to mask his fear* Radha thought. *How I love him.* She felt her body shiver again. She felt cold underneath her skin, on her back and on her hands. She didn't want Arun to learn of her feelings, so she spoke as calmly as she could, seeking a topic of practical importance, attempting to convince herself that life would go on. She could feel the moisture forming in her eyes.

"Are you coming for the appointment?" Her voice, a tree branch with the weight of heavy snow or ice bending it down to the ground.

"I'll meet you there," responded Arun.

And then the tree branch broke. Radha didn't have her voice anymore. The solitary tear in her eye had grown so large that it blurred her vision. By the time it dropped and she could see again, the dam of her willpower to remain composed had broken and several more tears followed the first. She put the phone down absentmindedly. She thought she heard Arun calling out for her through the receiver, but she couldn't be sure. Rather than picking up the phone to find out, she felt the urge to look for her kids. She felt this desperate need to be with them. *I must be a bad mother if they are not within my eyesight*, Radha began to think.

When she found the kids, she embraced them. Radha's maternal instinct had kicked in; she was able to cease crying, for the time being. Her son Zubin put his arms around his mother's neck purposefully and with a tight grip, after he looked at her face. Nandini, her daughter, didn't want to be distracted, but when she saw how long her mother was holding Zubin, she thought she was missing out. Nandini touched Radha's face. *Children can always sense when something is off*, thought Radha.

Radha went back to the kitchen. She put the phone back on the charger. She suddenly worried whether Arun would be calling her or not. She tried to imagine him in his current situation, fighting this battle by himself. Her friends would whisper confirmation to her of what she always knew since the day she met him - he was pleasant to look at. She smiled to herself as she thought about how he always complained about his rounded nose, even contemplating having it surgically adjusted to be more pointed. She liked how he maintained a thin frame. His medium build allowed him to fill a suit well.

Radha felt this urge to be with her mother and sister, Anjali. She thought of her mother. She wished her mother could be nearby to comfort her. Radha remembered how well all of them had pulled together when they had learned about the tragedy of her other sister, Pooja. Radha suddenly felt relieved that Anjali would be coming by soon. She felt a rush of warmth thinking about how Anjali had just organized a wonderful baby shower for her.

"Family," she found herself saying out loud, "they are so important in a crisis."

• • •

Arun was startled by the sound of Ernest entering the room.

"You need to get off the phone," Ernest instructed.

Arun calmly moved the phone away from his ear. He didn't say a word. He hadn't heard Radha respond to his repeated calling out of her name anyway. He pressed the red button to end the call.

"Who were you talking to?" demanded Ernest.

"It's 'with whom were you talking'," corrected Arun, looking at Ernest coldly, "not, 'who were you talking to'." Arun threw the phone down on the table in Ernest's direction.

Arun watched as Ernest grabbed for it. Arun could see Ernest press the green button on the phone, which he seemed to know would automatically re-dial the last number. He pressed the red button and put the phone back on the table when he saw the word "Home" flash on the screen.

I wish Radha had taken it better, thought Arun, as he turned his back towards Ernest and looked out the window. He wanted to, needed to believe that she was going to be okay with what was going on. But he knew what her reaction meant. He knew she gave it her valiant best to be strong, strong for him. He couldn't, and more importantly, wouldn't fault her for not being able to handle the news better. Arun became sullen for a moment. Yes, on a day like today it would be too hard for her to live up to the lofty ambition of her being calm and take everything in stride without flinching or faltering. Arun realized that sometimes, even for a woman who had taught him as much as Radha had, strength was a parkway out of reach when your capacities were consumed traversing the cul-de-sac of coping.

I wish this wasn't real, thought Arun. He repeated the statement again in his mind: "we have caught you committing fraud." The words fell on Arun as if a cannonball were landing on his head.

"Why don't you sign this statement?" suggested Ernest. Joseph and Chet had both re-entered the room and Joseph handed Ernest a document.

Another cannonball. The velocity with which they seemed to be coming at Arun made his head spin. He suddenly felt light-headed, faint and dizzy. As he began to feel the sensation of light fading and darkness looming, he lifted his hands to his face.   His wedding band caught his eye.   He felt a resuscitative jerk throughout his body.

While his eyes were bulging from his head, Arun began to review the document in front of him.   He had to put the paper on the table because his hands wouldn't stop shaking violently:

"I, Arun Gandharni, admit that I knowingly defrauded GoWire Systems through an elaborate money laundering scheme…"

The names they had chosen for the alleged crimes. Money laundering.   Is that even a proper legal term?   *I don't think it appears in the US Code.*   It was something clever journalists and broadcasters had drummed up.   Similar to terms like 'yuppie' or 'arms race'.   Who was running the show here?   It seemed so amateur.   Was this Ernest guy for real?

Arun knew he was guilty of many things: he had lied on occasion about where he was, he said an idea that Chet had suggested had merit, although he knew in his heart that he was placating Chet, he padded the occasional expense to make up for the receipts he lost or things he purchased for work that he never took a receipt for – that hot dog in the airport that was lunch, that luggage trolley at baggage claim or that newspaper while he waited for a delayed flight.

Maybe I should have been more political or diplomatic, Arun thought to himself.   *Maybe I antagonized them too much.   Why do I say some of the things I do?* Arun bemoaned.

That's when Derek Barber entered the room.   He was short, less than five and a half feet tall, thin and wiry.   He had curly brown hair, bushy eyebrows and an elongated face.   When he talked, he would animate those eyebrows.   Arun always thought he did that in a bid to feign intensity.   It rarely worked. He looked mostly sloppy.   Today, Derek couldn't look Arun in the eye.   *This must be his victory lap,* thought Arun.

That damn sun is penetrating a hole in my forehead, Arun thought.   As if the window were a magnifying glass and his head would spontaneously combust any moment. Arun's cell phone kept ringing. He saw his mother's number flash on the screen repeatedly. Arun had to roll his eyes. She always got agitated when he didn't answer the phone. She would accuse him of ignoring her. *How can I answer the phone now?* thought Arun. His mother would have to wait. He cringed as he thought about the wrath that he would have to face from her later. *If they knew what I was going through, maybe she wouldn't be so difficult,* he thought. No. Or yes? Was there a way he could tell them? It wouldn't have mattered anyway; they probably still would have been difficult, Arun realized.

Arun stopped reading. He looked down at his hands. They were still trembling. He observed his wedding ring. He touched it. He looked up. He saw his reflection in the glass of the conference room. It wasn't a crisp reflection, but that fit the atmosphere. He couldn't make himself out completely; it appeared as foreign to him as the situation that he currently found himself in. He reached for his wallet again.

"Either arrest me or I am leaving," he threatened after a few seconds. He stood up as he said it. Seeing the look of astonishment on their faces, and their inactivity, Arun methodically closed his brief case, took his jacket and walked out the door. His body had shaken violently as he spoke. He frowned and wondered where his strength came from and why it would betray him, leave him, abandon him when it came to his parents, uncle and brothers.

● ● ●

Anjali arrived at Arun and Radha's house. Anjali had been spending many days there since the end of her relationship with her husband, Matthew. Anjali knew that her sister cared for her a great deal. It wasn't that her mother didn't; Anjali just knew that if she went to her mother, unfortunately, she would have had to deal with her father. Anjali had always been attune to her surroundings and the impact they would have on her. She knew she needed a nurturing environment.

Anjali had followed her husband to Los Angeles and had been living there for many years. She had secured a new job doing research for a think tank group, after leaving Matthew. She had hope in her heart that she would find someone new; she knew at that time she would be at her sister's place less frequently, but it was nice in the interim to have those surroundings as a crutch to rely upon. Although everyone who knew her acknowledged her as a pillar of strength, she didn't mind admitting that she needed a little support and the love surrounding her sister's family was great for her.

As soon as she arrived, she grabbed Nandini and held her in her arms. She could hear that Radha was in the kitchen.

"Hello *Ma-si*," yelled Nandini.

"Well hello, my little munchkin."

"*Ma-si*, today, I told my friend Jessica that I was going to play with you," said Nandini.

Anjali smiled broadly and her voice grew more excited. "You tell your friends about me?"

"Yeah, but she said…she said, I was calling you a funny name," Nandini complained.

"Ah yes," said Anjali, "that's because she doesn't understand what the word *Ma-si* means. Next time you tell her that I am your aunt."

"How come she doesn't know what *Ma-si* means?"

"Because her family is not from India like ours is. In India, *Ma-si* means mother's sister. You call your mommy, 'Ma', and *Ma-si*, means 'just like your mother'. In fact it only means mother's sister and not father's sister the way aunt can also mean. In our culture, we can tell what the relationship is," Anjali explained.

Anjali was quiet for a few seconds while observing Nandini. Nandini looked up briefly.

"In fact, next time you talk to Jessica, you explain to her what I just explained to you," Anjali suggested.

"Okay," said Nandini. There was a lengthy pause. "Can I call you Aunt?" she asked, looking up at Anjali lovingly.

Anjali looked at her niece. "You can. But *Ma-si* sounds sweeter. I like hearing it. It reminds me of who we are." Anjali hugged Nandini as she spoke.

"Okay, *Ma-si*."

● ● ●

Radha came out from the kitchen to see her sister and daughter talking. She had stalled intentionally to come to grips with the news Arun had shared and to try to compose herself. Anjali's presence was a wonderful comfort. She was so eager to tell her what had happened. She knew Arun would not be happy about it.

She approached Anjali and hugged her. Radha could tell that she was surprised by it. But she responded accordingly, as Radha knew she would, her arms going from limp to actively holding Radha, maneuvering around Radha's enlarged mid-section. When Radha showed no signs of disengaging, Anjali remained in the embrace. Radha knew she was collecting clues; Anjali was clever enough to sense something had transpired. Radha caught Nandini's gaze. She raised her arm behind Anjali's back and put a finger to her lips. Nandini nodded. Radha didn't want the kids telling Anjali about her emotionally-charged hugging episode with the kids from earlier.

Radha marveled at how she and Anjali looked very much alike. Anjali was half-an inch shorter than Radha. Anjali's face was a little more rounded and her eyes were not as big, but they shared the same pronounced forehead, high cheekbones and pointed nose. Anjali's eyelids were also a bit heavier than

Radha's, giving the appearance of more weight above her eyes, instigating a more mystical, smoky aura. Anjali had mastered well the art of how to maneuver her eye movements to evoke sensations of being suggestive, mysterious, attentive or alluring. Radha managed a faint smile as she recalled how Anjali had declared that contact lenses were a gift specifically to her when they were invented and she had shunned the wearing of glasses. She hated having any obstruction to her prowess. Anjali also never kept her hair longer than her shoulders.

Radha broke the embrace. Anjali made quick eye contact with her and smiled, a fleeting acknowledgment that she sensed something was wrong. Her diving into her next activity and not dwelling on it was an indication of her recognition that the matter would not be discussed now; comfort was her primary objective. Anjali proceeded to sit down on the sofa and began going through the gifts that Radha had received during her baby shower. She happened to sift through the ones from Arun's family. His parents had provided a single outfit, again. Arun's uncle Arjun had provided a gift certificate, again.

"Ah yes, the antipodes of expectation and disappointment," remarked Anjali to Radha. "Could any two emotions be more diametrically opposed?"

Radha could only nod her head in agreement. Radha had been disappointed as well. She had higher hopes from them. Her own mother had sent so many clothes already.

When Arun had asked about what his family members had provided, Radha told him in an even tone. He didn't say a word, but Radha noticed that he scrunched his forehead in concentration, like he tended to do when he thought about his family. Radha had become so familiar with the expression that she could anticipate it forming as she reached down to pick up the gifts to display to him. She imagined that the thoughts were a gust of wind creating a ripple in an otherwise calm pool or instigating ridges, mounds or dunes in the sands of the desert. At other times she felt like the serenity of her husband's face was like the ground after a heavy snowfall. The thoughts of his family were like the footprints of someone trampling through the snow – the original grace and composition lost, only to be attained again at the next snowfall.

She remembered that during Zubin's and Nandini's birthdays, Arun would always buy three or four gifts and say they were from his parents. He would keep them hidden from Radha until the kids were opening their presents in front of the other children. In the beginning, he tried to do it without her knowing about it, but eventually she found out. She let him continue with the practice.

A photo from their wedding on a bookshelf caught Radha's eye. *If Arun were here now, I would touch his face and give him a hug*, she decided resolutely. She winced in sympathy for him.

"Poor Arun," said Anjali as she sorted through another pile of gifts, "So much for family being important. This goes to show, sometimes it isn't better to think of the family first, individual -second as they do in the East. Maybe these Westerners have it right. Individual first, family second."

● ● ●

Traveling down the elevator, Arun wanted nothing more than to seek solitude. He needed time to take stock, digest what had happened, and formulate a game plan. He had so many questions on his mind. *How do I get through this* topped the list. After that, with near equal importance: *How will I explain this to my family?* Not his immediate family; Radha and the kids would understand and be there for him. It was the rest of his family: his parents, his uncle, his brothers. What would the consequences be—potential jail, fines, giving GoWire money? How badly would his family react? He caught himself off guard—he found it odd that he would prioritize his family's reaction on par with *survival*. It was true though—he found himself worrying more about devising stories he could tell them to cover up than how to get himself out of his predicament. There was a battle for his neurons, and the excuses to the family were winning. But he couldn't make time to resolve those questions or conundrums now. He had too many other responsibilities.

His first reaction was to hide the incident from his parents. He justified this to himself as being considerate of his father's health. He had already suffered a heart attack. How could he burden his father with this news? No, he realized. There's more…it was the potential alienation that would sting the most. They would either judge him harshly, wouldn't help him or they wouldn't speak to him. He might have to face another three years of silence. Wasn't this similar to hiding from his parents being caught by the principal when he skipped class in high school?

He saw Andy in the parking garage on his way out. His six-foot-five lanky figure was hard to miss. He had a square face with brown, curly hair, an outgrowth of which would cover his forehead above his right eye and bounce, in time with his steps, as he walked. Arun thought to call out to him, but he decided against it. Andy got into his car without noticing Arun. Then it occurred to Arun why Andy had been calling earlier in the day.

He thought about calling Radha again. He started to dial. He quickly said, "I am on my way." Then he hung up. He didn't wait for her to respond. It seemed ridiculous to him that he would be resuming his normal habits, but it was for Radha's benefit. He wanted to show her that everything would be okay.

He started walking towards his car again. He thought back to how his mother called so many times earlier. He then pulled out his phone and began dialing. He closed the phone before he finished entering the numbers. He continued his walk. He stopped again. He dialed the same numbers again. This time he let the phone ring. He was quiet for several minutes after he said his initial, "Hello, Mom". He shut his eyes tightly and said his greeting through clenched teeth. His eyes began to swell with tears.

"Hello, Arun."

There was the typical silence that always ensued after initial greetings were exchanged.

"How's Dad?" Arun didn't know what else to ask. Rajiv rarely called his son. Nor did he come to the phone often when Arun's mother phoned him or when Arun called his parent's house. Arun imagined telling her everything about what he was suffering through. "I had a disaster today" or "I am in deep trouble" or "people are after me". He couldn't get any of that out. He stalled for more time. *Damn it*, he thought, *can't she tell that something is wrong? Why won't she ask me!* He thought about the three years of silence. His mind worked quickly. He clenched his jaw again, pursed his lips and stated, "I resigned my job today."

"What?" Meena, his mother, proclaimed.

Arun had expected her shock. "I found something better," he replied quickly. "And yes, there will be more money," Arun remarked in anticipation of her next question. He rolled his eyes as he said it. Her silence indicated that she was satisfied with the response.

"Your Uncle Arjun say is good job?" his mother asked. Arun hated how his uncle had a God-like status in the eyes of his parents. Everything his uncle did was right. Arun wondered when, if ever, he might enjoy a time when he wasn't questioned on everything he did. It must be the fact that his uncle had so much money, thought Arun. It was a typical immigrant pitfall, Arun realized, as he saw it in some other Indian families, if you have money, you must be right. He had been referring to it for years as "the immigrant manifesto".

● ● ●

Arun arrived at the gynecologist's office. He was thrilled to see his two kids there. He had recalled that Radha had arranged for Anjali to be with the children while they came to the appointment. He was glad she had changed her mind. He held them tight, first Nandini and then Zubin.

"Everything is fine with the baby," said the doctor.

Arun was relieved. Nothing was fine anywhere else, but there was peace in knowing that inside his wife's belly there was a tiny life that belonged to him and to her and all was okay in that little world.

Arun looked at Zubin and Nandini. *Now how do I ensure that for these two?* Zubin was eight years old. He had short hair that followed the round contours of his head. He had an elongated face, developing into a look that would be similar to his father's. Nandini was five years old. She had the round face and big eyes of her mother.

"Daddy, I'm going to be a big sister," said Nandini.

Arun held her. As he fought back tears, he said to her, "Yes, darling. You are going to be a big sister."

Arun thought back to Derek's words from earlier that day.

"I'm sorry, but we are going to have to prosecute," he had said.

CHAPTER FOUR

1970s

As a child, life was straightforward and without problems or painful memories for Arun until after he started kindergarten and elementary school. Perhaps it was that nobody really remembered that earliest part of their lives. Or maybe the issue was that conflicts really did not come into focus until Arun was thrust into society, forced to interact with other children where his differences became magnified.

This was also the age when Arun became more aware of his surroundings. His family lived in an apartment building that was a drab grey color. It wasn't so bad when it was bright and sunny, Arun determined, but when it rained, it seemed particularly sad. They lived on the second floor. There was a broad staircase that he would take to get home. There were two bedrooms, one for his parents and another that he shared with his brother. They had a balcony off the edge of the living room, where his mother kept a plastic cabinet full of dry foods bought from the Indian grocery store. The kitchen had one wall of cabinets and enough room to fit a small table that seated four. The walls were all white, and lacking in adornments, and there was hard-surface carpeting throughout the apartment, except for the linoleum tiled kitchen and bathrooms. He always noticed the smell of Indian food when he walked into his apartment, whether or not his mother had been cooking.

Initially, he would speak Hindi from time to time with his parents while at home. Once he became more engaged with television however, it became his habit to respond to his parents in English when they spoke to him in Hindi.

At the time he started kindergarten, he realized the differences between him and other children. He wanted the benefit of birthday parties. He wanted to participate in soccer and baseball.

When he tried describing this to his parents, they were a bit lost. Birthdays had always been just a nice meal, with a birthday cake and Uncle Arjun visiting. Sports were not something to focus time on. It was not a commercially meaningful pursuit. When he was seven Arun went out on his own to pursue Little League, initially unbeknownst to his parents. He showed up to a practice without a baseball glove. The coaches had insisted that Arun come to practice with one the next day or he would not be able to participate. Arun tried convincing his father that he needed to buy a glove to join the team. That night Rajiv did not want to go out to buy one. Arun had to borrow another kid's glove the following day, and every day after that. Every night Arun would plead with his father, "Dad, I am so embarrassed." Arun could tell his father did not see the point of it, but after Arun made numerous pleas, he was able to convince his father to go along with it. Arun had to ask his friends which was the best equipment to get, something which they gathered from their own parents. Arun's sense of feeling out of place at those practices and games persisted, even after the purchase of the glove. It was as if he was missing out on something because while all the other little boys had their fathers or mothers cheering them on, Arun was on his own. He had been the only brown kid on the team. There was always a silence when he approached home plate to bat. He felt the weight of all of those gazes, at times feeling like a sideshow freak, people in awe that as a foreigner he might participate in this greatest of American pastimes.

One day when Arun noticed a neighborhood kid from his apartment complex and the child's father playing catch, Arun asked his father to join. "Hey, Dad, can we practice?"

Rajiv came out wearing slacks and his work shoes, black leather lace-ups. He initially tried catching the ball without a glove. "I have being seeing cricket," replied Rajiv, when Arun asked him to use a glove.

Arun stepped up to bat. He hit a ball pitched from his friend. It hit the building where the Gandharni's had their apartment and it landed in a patch of flowers that Rajiv had planted immediately in front of the building. Arun's friend trampled through the flowers to get the ball.

Rajiv carried an expression on his face that Arun decided was one of more hurt and resentment than it was anger. Rajiv walked inside the apartment building without saying a word to Arun or anyone. Arun didn't know what to do. He felt silly doing it, but he asked his friend, and his friend's father, to carry-on without him. Arun couldn't express why, but he just felt like it would be inappropriate for him to continue. Arun felt ashamed when he caught the quizzical expression on his friend's father's face as he looked around to try to say bye to Rajiv.

Arun attempted to play a musical instrument. He had chosen a violin. He managed to convince his parents to pay for the annual rental of the instrument. In addition, however, all of the other children were receiving private lessons. Arun tried every possible method of persuasion he could muster, but he was never able to induce his parents to pay for them.

When Arun was eight, his parents had their last child, a boy named Raj. Arun remembered overhearing his father bemoaning to his mother the cost of an additional child. "Every year, my uncle asking more. How can there being money for more child?

This university fees business, I hearing Sam stressing about this only. I saying to him 'Isn't so early? There being many years before children going university', he say 'No, never too early'." Sanjay kept his nose buried in a book during their father's tirade. Arun felt physically worried for his father. "Maybe we getting home before their university starting," Arun's father concluded, "they studying in India. They will all being doing sciences. I no wanting my sons getting useless degrees. Sciences I will making sure about. Sciences is being top in India." Arun watched as his father waggled his head and left the room. That was Arun's first memory of being scared.

When Arun was ten, his father lectured him weekly about the importance of studying and challenged him about why he was allowing himself to be distracted by sports and musical activities. Arun assumed his father feared that if he got side-tracked he may not be able to be successful here in the US. His father always emphasized the need to be successful, the need to pursue wealth and security, the need to be like his Uncle Arjun.

Arun's father seemed to not want to make the same mistake with his brother. With Sanjay, his father insisted on a focus on his studies and did not encourage Sanjay to follow what Arun did. In fact, Rajiv would do his best to quash Sanjay's natural curiosity for his brother's activities. Arun would cringe at observing how delighted his father was that Sanjay, after some nudging, showed no proclivity towards what Arun found enjoyable.

Much to Arun's chagrin, Rajiv would praise Sanjay in front of Arun. "Vhery good. Being better than your brother" was the worst comment that Arun had to hear. When Uncle Arjun would come by, it was a double dose of poison.

Sanjay never seemed to be moved by any of this. He only seemed comfortable with his books. Arun had the image imbedded in his mind of his scrawny brother, looking wafer-thin, hair cut in the shape of a bowl, wearing round-rimmed glasses, sitting cross-legged, a book on his lap and elbows on his knees, with palms supporting his chin. Sanjay read everything. Whatever he could get his hands on he would devour. At a young age he had not only been through the whole Hardy Boy series, but embarrassingly for Arun, he was also reading Nancy Drew. Sanjay comfortably graduated to the more challenging C.S. Lewis and J.R.R. Tolkien.

Later, when Raj would read only Nancy Drew, Arun would become really frustrated. For the most part however, reading was never really Raj's interest. Raj had the nicest physical features of all three brothers, Arun decided with envy. He had a round face, sharp nose, eyes framed by curly lashes which drew a lot of attention and a smile that made whomever was experiencing it instantaneously happy. He was largely left to his own devices, mostly exploring what was interesting to him and grew in this fashion, largely unfettered. Raj never got the focus or pressure on academics that Rajiv had expected of Arun and pro-actively got out of Sanjay. At times, Arun felt, that was to his detriment. Arun always sensed that his youngest brother actually craved and could have benefited from more attention. As a boy, he would naturally cling to his mother, holding onto her skirt when they went to the grocery store – seldom running about when, ironically, his doing so would have been okay.

Arun read some of the Hardy Boys, but he never felt engrossed by the books. He was interested in playing with other kids, trying to be as much like them as possible. He was ashamed to admit it to himself, but he secretly admired those friends of his who had American parents. He felt like they had it artificially easy. They would always seem to have the latest video games, branded clothes and toys and be going on exotic vacations that Arun could only dream about.

"Sanjay, why don't you help me out on this? If you ask for stuff as well, we could get more things together," Arun pleaded with his brother.

Sanjay never listened.

• • •

When Arjun came to the house that year for Arun's twelfth birthday, Rajiv had to listen to Arjun aggressively convince him to buy a house.

"Follow my advice," said Arjun, "buy a house, settle down a little more."

"I wishing for us to being getting back to India," Rajiv commented, "there is being no needing buying a house. Anyway, I am having little the money."

At this last comment, Arjun's head snapped up. "Well, I can give you the money," he said. "Also, think of the increase in the property value you will have in a few years. It will be more cash that you could take back, if you go."

For the first time in the conversation, Rajiv actually smiled. He followed his brother's advice and within a few months, using Arjun's money as a down payment, purchased a home.

Rajiv found a modest home roughly forty-five miles away from the Bay Area that he had to commute to. It was a two-storey home with four bedrooms, although he noted that two of them barely had space for more than a twin-size bed. He hated how little land he had. He also found it awkward that he could see into his neighbor's home from the house. The outside was yellow in color. It was the best he could do given his financial situation – he had three kids here, and he was sending money back home. He thought that Arjun might help with the monthly mortgage payments – he recalled how in India, it was a matter of pooling the family's collective resources together, but Arjun never offered. Rajiv found that odd but said nothing about it, choosing to internalize his emotion. He was hopeful that

Arjun might live with them, as at least he thought they were buying the house together, but quoting long hours at work, he said that he needed to stay close to the city. Rajiv's enthusiasm for the home diminished a bit after hearing this.

After receiving the keys to his new house, Rajiv went to the backyard. He brought out from his car a canister. With his hands, he removed a bit of grass at the edge of the lawn. He dug the earth with his fingers. He placed the contents of the tin – a light brown, dry, fragmented, almost dust-like, powder into the earth. He closed the hole he had made. He kept the canister in a safe place.

The following day, Rajiv called the travel agency.

"One thousand three hundred is the best we can offer you," the agent told him in response to his question.

Rajiv hung up the phone. He thought about the house he had just bought. The financial obligations that it brought with it. He threw out the paper that he had written the ticket price on.

●   ●   ●

"Mom, why are we doing this?" Arun asked his mother.

"Keep quiet. The priest is talking. Don't be disrespectful," his mother responded.

Meena was insistent that there be a *puja* – a religious ceremony with a performing of traditional Hindu rites. None of the three boys who had been required to sit in front of the fire with a priest chanting away understood the significance of what they were doing or why it was being done.

"Dad, why are we doing this?" Arun asked his father.

"Shh…" Arun was instructed.

So he kept quiet. He was getting confirmation that it was more respectful to remain ignorant than to seek enlightenment. He tried to make sense of his parent's diffidence. He was really uncomfortable not knowing about what was happening. *How can I be expected to be Indian when I don't know much about India?*

•   •   •

After the prayers, Rajiv and Meena hosted a housewarming party.   There were mostly guests of Indian origin present.   Sam from Rajiv's work also came.   He had his son Thomas with him, who was Arun's age.   Arjun had initially indicated that he wouldn't be able to come, but after he heard that Sam would be attending, somehow his schedule became free.   Meena also had her friend Dipti Singh in attendance.   Dipti had been in the U.S. for a number of years, well over a decade prior to Rajiv and Meena's arrival.   Dipti's husband owned a series of gas station pumps.   She was determined that her two sons would become doctors, although they were only in high school.   Raj called her the gossip queen.

When Arjun arrived, he had a woman with him.   Arjun approached Rajiv with her.   She was almost as tall as Arjun and looked exceptionally thin.   Rajiv noticed some orange colored freckles on her pale, white arms.   Her face looked like a painter had just finished a canvas – Rajiv noticed so many bright colors. Her eyes seemed a bit sunken.   Her face was oblong.

"Rajiv, I want you to meet someone," said Arjun.

The woman extended her hand out.   "Hi," she said, smiling broadly, "My name is Saraswati."

Rajiv involuntarily jerked his head back.   He was so lost in his thinking that he never extended his hand out to meet hers.

She laughed nervously and put her hand to her side.

Arjun stood there quietly.

Rajiv, feeling suddenly very shy, but with a strong desire to end his confusion, blurted out, "How being you having name Saraswati?"

"Oh," she chuckled, waving her hand listlessly in the air. "I was born Susan Waterford, but I changed it after Arjun and I got married. I figured the last name was Indian, so why not the first one? But you know, none of my friends can get their tongues around it, so they end up calling me Sara."

Rajiv had ceased listening after a few seconds. He was stuck on the word 'married'. He looked at Arjun. Rajiv could feel his own face falling. It met up with his heart, which had already made the journey to his feet.

Arjun shifted his body.

Rajiv stood quietly. He looked down.

"It's a shame you couldn't make it to the wedding," offered Sara, sheepishly.

Rajiv didn't respond.

"Why don't we get a drink inside?" suggested Arjun. He walked away with Sara.

"I'll speak with you later," she called out to Rajiv. Rajiv continued to look down.

● ● ●

Inside the house, Arun and Sanjay were helping their mother. Meena was tending to the food which had been spread, buffet-style, across the dining table.

"The food is good, Meena," commented Dipti. Arun laughed to himself. Dipti's size indicated that she was neither fond of missing meals nor had she, in fact, missed many.

"But I think you made the *saag paneer* too salty," she added.

Meena tasted it. "Is true," she was forced to agree.

"You feeling hungry, isn't it? Please have food," Meena suggested to Sara, after seeing her lingering about. Arun didn't know much about her, except she was the woman who came in with Uncle Arjun. Arun found her exceptionally thin. It was a strange contrast to his mother, he thought, who was looking more and more plump every year.

"Oh, I just love this dish, how is it made?"

"Well, is simple. It is having spinach and…also…it is like…we call *paneer*," responded Meena with a hopeful expression that she could escape further explanation.

"Oh, *paneer*, I have heard of this – what is it exactly?" asked Sara, brimming over with excitement. She seemed to be intentionally pushing her eyeballs out of their sockets, Arun observed.

"It's like a cheese for us," Dipti chimed in, laughing a bit to herself. Dipti made a comment in Hindi to Meena. *How is she going to understand paneer?* Meena responded back in Hindi. *I know. White people can be so funny!*

Arun understood enough Hindi to know what they were saying. He then suddenly found it strange that they would alienate Sara. He struggled so hard to ingratiate himself with people like Sara.

"Where did you get that sari?"

Arun overheard Sara asking his mother.

"Oh…I thinks in Berkeley." Arun noted his mother's tone. It was soft, without much life. He knew she responded that way because she was suddenly shy; as he observed Sara's reaction, however, he saw how it could have been misconstrued the way Sara seemed to take it – as indifference. Arun suddenly worried about how many such instances had occurred in the past with his parents or all the other people that came from India. *There can be so many obstacles for people from two cultures to communicate well* Arun reasoned.

● ● ●

Rajiv had been spending a large portion of the afternoon away from his family and guests, milling about the flowers he had planted in the front part of the house. Most people were in the backyard. He had an urge to put on his gloves and do some work, but he knew it would not be appropriate.

As he stood about, he suddenly heard voices approaching. As he turned to look, he noticed Arjun and Sara coming towards him. They didn't seem to notice Rajiv just yet. Sara's voice seemed elevated. "They hate me, all of them!" she was saying in a forced whisper. Her back was turned to Rajiv. Rajiv caught Arjun's eyes first.

"Rajiv," he called out.

Rajiv noticed Sara make a motion with both of her hands towards her eyes. She was wearing a rather large brimmed hat that obscured Rajiv's view. When she turned around, her eyes matched the white with red polka dots of her dress. She managed to feign a smile and a laugh.

"Wonderful home you have here, Rajiv!" Sara beamed. "It's so lovely outside!"

Arjun looked down and let out a tiny sigh.

Rajiv stayed quiet.

"Those window dressings are so pretty. Wherever did you get them?" asked Sara.

"We bringing them from home," Rajiv answered in a gentle tone.

"Oh, you mean India? Next time I go I will have to get some," she said. She was speaking at a fast clip.

"Oh, you having being to India?" asked Rajiv in a surprised tone.

"Oh brother," said Arjun and he walked away.

"Yes, several times," she commented. She was smiling broadly. "How often do you go back?" she asked Rajiv.

Rajiv suddenly looked sad. He waggled his head from side to side. "No," he said meekly. He cleared his throat.

"Not often?" enquired Sara, leaning forward, straining to hear him.

"There is being no chance to going," Rajiv said as quietly as he had spoken earlier. The sound of him clearing his throat again was significantly louder than his voice.

"All of these years, you have not gone back?" Sara asked in disbelief.

It was now Rajiv's turn for his eyes to turn red.

"Oh, I'm so sorry," indicated Sara. She touched Rajiv's arm with her hand.

The move startled Rajiv. Meena never touched him like that publicly. He wasn't expecting it. He moved his arm away with a sudden, swift motion.

Sara put her hand down, slightly more sullen than the previous few seconds. After another few moments had passed, she turned to Rajiv. "It's just that Arjun goes so often. I just assumed that everyone from there goes often."

Rajiv was startled for a second time. "Arjun going *off-ten*?" he asked in disbelief.

"Why, yes. At least once every three months or so." Sara had folded her arms after Rajiv moved his arm away. She had been using her right hand to play with her pearls. As she spoke, she made a gesture toward Arjun.

Almost instinctively, Arjun looked back. He wore an expression that made it seem as if he knew what had just transpired. Rajiv locked eyes with his brother. Arjun turned back to his conversation, ignoring Rajiv and Sara.

Rajiv walked away from Sara without saying a word. He approached Arjun. He cut off another person talking with Arjun. "Why you never saying you going India *off-ten*?" Rajiv questioned him.

"Well I guess it never came up," Arjun said in a standoffish manner.

"You being going to the house?" Rajiv asked. His tone was non-threatening. It had softened. There was a tenderness that came through, almost a longing.

It had an impact on Arjun. He didn't respond right away. "No," Arjun said without looking at his brother.

"Why never going?" Rajiv asked. Now he was becoming agitated.

"Because there is no time when I am there. I am very busy," Arjun said emphatically.

There was silence.

"Why do you want to stay tied down to that place anyway? You are here now. Focus on making a life here!" insisted Arjun.

"Why you no understand?" asked Rajiv.

● ● ●

Rajiv heard the beep again. It had been two months since the party. "Please be calling your brother," Rajiv said to the machine. It was the fifth message Rajiv had left for Arjun on his answering machine. He had so many things to ask him. About his getting married, about his going to India. If he goes so often, maybe he can visit the house, see how the farm is doing, reasoned Rajiv. Perhaps he could even let Rajiv know about the progress that was being achieved with the money Rajiv was sending. He looked at Meena. "My brother must be being a very important, busy man."

● ● ●

When Arun was fourteen, Rajiv and Meena threw another party. It was around the time of Arun's birthday, but nobody mentioned a word about that. Arun and Sanjay had been enlisted to help their parents with the set-up.

Meena had been interacting more frequently with her friend Dipti, who would be a regular guest at the house.

"My Vijay just loves girls. Can't get enough of them. But Pratabh is such a bookworm," highlighted Dipti.

52

Arun hated how she would bring her two sons up in just about every conversation. He made himself busy in the dining room, where they couldn't see him.

Arun overheard Meena whispering. He hid behind the wall to the kitchen so he could hear well. "You see, Arun never close with us. Neglecting. It is as if we have losing the boy to *Amrica*. Sanjay is so good. He stay close to us. He not betraying. And little Raj, he very good boy. Very cute," Meena described as she gave out a lengthy sigh of relief.

Arun wondered what he had done to make his mother feel that way. He certainly didn't feel lost to America. He just felt lost.

"Ah yes," said Dipti. It seemed to Arun that she was satisfied by hearing some negative news and was losing interest.

"Have you been cooking all day?" she asked Meena with minimal interest.

Arun continued his work.

"Today morning, all morning, I pray. Today *aw-speech-us* day. Priest tell us this. Anything we ask, the God will be listening. He give to us."

"You shouldn't be spending so much time in front of a temple, sitting cross-legged and hunching your back over praying. You will lose your posture," Dipti insisted.

"Where is Raj?" demanded Arun after entering the kitchen. "You know he could be helpful here too, running and grabbing things."

Sanjay kept working and Meena ignored his question. Dipti looked down her nose at him. They all kept doing what they were doing. Rajiv eventually broke the silence to ask Arun to help him get something from the car.

After another hour had passed, Meena began panicking. "So long I no seeing Raj. What if is trouble?" she asked.

"Sanjay, go find him," instructed Arun.

"I am busy filling the ice," protested Sanjay.

"Oh, all right," said Arun, "I will go and find the little runt."

Arun searched in all of the downstairs rooms and then proceeded to go upstairs. He began scanning the bedrooms. After looking in Sanjay and Raj's room, he went to his parent's room. His mouth opened wide with what he saw there. He tiptoed backwards and went to his mother. "Mom, you have to come see this," said Arun.

Standing in their mother's closet was six-year old Raj, wearing his mother's necklace, lipstick, sari blouse, sari and shoes. He was singing in front of the mirror.

Meena shrieked. Arun felt pity for the boy. The look on Raj's face indicated he was feeling shocked. Sanjay took one look and left the room to get back to his work.

"Remove these clothing!" Meena yelled, attempting to pull the clothes off.

She then began using her hands to smear off the lipstick that he had put on. Arun watched her as she frantically tried to transform Raj. It occurred to Arun that she didn't really seem all that upset with the fact that he was using her things. She seemed to be more concerned that he liked it enough to do it.

She immediately tracked down Rajiv and told him what had happened.

"You explain your son, he cannot wear women's clothing, he cannot." She was speaking so fast she could barely get the words out.

Rajiv was silent.

"You making your son to understand. You must do." Meena was furious.

Rajiv finally conceded, "Okay, okay."

CHAPTER FIVE

March 2007

As they drove home from the gynecologist's visit, Arun kept reflecting on Derek's parting comment. "I'm sorry, but we are going to have to prosecute." *Why do people say things they don't mean?* Derek wasn't sorry at all. He did it so that he could ease himself into the delivery. His point was also baseless; Derek and GoWire weren't required to do anything, it was what they *chose to do*.

Derek's voice had cracked as he spoke. He emphasized the last word as if he were relieved to get it out, as if it took some effort or strain. Was that excitement or nervousness causing him to fluctuate in his speech pattern? Arun had watched the expression on his face. He didn't seem sincere at all, but that was hardly significant; he was never sincere. Was that restrained joy? Arun thought to the last time he had interacted with Derek.

"Come on Derek, that will never fly," Arun had said with a dismissive tone.

"How can you be so sure?" Derek demanded. With each word he increased the intensity with which he spoke, leaning further and further forward as he finished his question.

He hated when Derek got that way. "Why would Starbucks agree to carry our product without getting a percentage of the sales? They always get a cut," explained Arun.

"Hey it could work. Our product is hot - it will get more people in the door," replied Derek.

"Starbucks doesn't have any problems getting people through the door. If anything, we need them because of the traffic they have. Forget it. I am not drafting the contracts that way. Go negotiate the terms and come to me with something that has a chance of being reasonable," instructed Arun.

Derek mumbled something under his breath. It sounded to Arun like he'd said, "We'll see about that". *How trite can Derek be?* thought Arun. He decided to press him on it.

"What did you say, Derek? I'm sorry I couldn't hear you. You were mumbling," enquired Arun.

"Lawyers shouldn't concern themselves with business matters," responded Derek. His voice was very deliberate. His eyes even seemed a little bloodshot. It was as if he were threatening Arun.

"I'll concern myself with common sense. Is that okay with you?" Arun asked.

Either Derek understood that it was asked rhetorically or his indignation held his tongue back.

If he wasn't also a vice president, had thought Arun, *I would really let him have it.*

● ● ●

Arun's first step inside the house after coming home at the end of a typical day had always been taken with his head held high and his chest protruding forward as if he were a runner about to triumphantly break through the finish line tape of a race. He was a man who was proud of his accomplishments and achievements and felt he had earned the right to bask in them.

On this day, after the doctor's office visit, he felt no such emotions. He felt like a grandfather clock, his emotions vacillating between being strong for his family and coping with the terror that was gripping him. He was required to undulate between normalcy and aftershock. His head felt like embedded rock with someone attempting to drill a hole in it.

As the family became busy about the house, Arun quietly went to the bedroom. He draped his suit jacket over the shoulders of the arm chair, dropped his tie on the floor a few feet away from that, and his shirt and pants by the entrance to the bathroom. He stood in front of the mirror in his underwear. He hated what he saw.

"You have just given your parents, uncle and brothers proof of what they have always thought. You are a worthless piece of shit," he said to himself. That felt good, he thought. *Very authentic.* Just the way he would imagine his parents doing it.

"You are useless. Meaningless. Nothing." *Oh, these words were soothing.* Tears began to stream down his face. "Your parents are right." He was mumbling now. His tone was softer. "Why did they come to this country? Just to give birth to a screw-up like me?" He was barely whispering. "Why should they talk to you? Three years of silence wasn't enough. You deserve a lifetime of it." The words were struggling to get out amidst the tears. And there it was. The next words were caught in his throat; he couldn't voice them. He had to think the words. He couldn't say them. *I am so damn scared.* Arun was face to face with his fear. He began sobbing more intensely.

He heard movement from outside the bathroom. He immediately turned on the water. As the door opened he began splashing water on his face. It was Radha.

"I'll be right down," Arun said.

"For the kids' sake…" Radha began.

"Of course, of course," said Arun. All the while he was in awe that Radha was grasping what he was going through.

"Well…," Radha added with hesitation in her voice.

Arun looked at her.

"Maybe we could call Anjali back so that she can be with the kids and you and I can talk about this."

"No, there is no need to disturb her. Plus, she will wonder what is such an emergency for her to come back so soon." Arun knew that Anjali liked to work late or meet with friends for dinner in the evening. He knew she did it so that Arun and Radha could have a bulk of the evening with the kids without being disturbed. Otherwise, she liked to be around the house. Arun reflected how this notion would only work in the West; in India, it would be blasphemy to think that a sister of the wife would need to allow privacy.

"I was thinking of telling her," said Radha.

Arun could detect how meek her voice had become. "And what good would that do?" challenged Arun. He felt a little guilty in being so firm. He glanced down at her stomach.

"Arun, I know how you feel about this, but remember how well we all supported each other when we found out about Pooja's death," Radha contested.

Arun thought about how rational his wife was being. He looked at her. She had remained standing in the same position. "I don't have any answers right now," Arun said, softening the sound of his voice, "I don't know what or if I am going to tell my parents, uncle and brothers. Once your family knows, they should know too. Let me figure this out."

Radha nodded her head. Arun could tell that the slow manner in which she did it was a reluctant acquiescence. He could see the sadness in her eyes. He kept that mental image with him as he put on a pair of sweatpants and a T-shirt and followed Radha downstairs.

As they congregated with their children in the kitchen, Radha, with a seeming lump in her throat, began to talk. "Zubin's team won the science competition."

Arun looked at his wife. *I recognize that hesitation*, he thought. *It is more than just the strain of managing her emotions from the incident. She is easing into something more difficult.*

Remembering what he acknowledged a few minutes ago upstairs, Arun turned to his son, "That's great Zubie, well-done my son."

Arun moved closer to Zubin. Arun recalled an earlier time, years and years ago, when another father said to another son in cold, awkward, learned English - the words were English, but the intonation and emphasis as foreign as the person delivering the sentence. "Dhat iz good". Arun had received a quick glance from his father and Rajiv went about his business. There wasn't even a smile and it was over before Arun could react. In response to this memory flash, Arun decided to gratuitously add a hug to his high-five and backslap with Zubin. Arun himself felt elated at the joy it evoked from his son. Arun thought about how he never had a chance to express that happiness himself with his own father. He suddenly felt glad for his son.

"I did it on plants, Daddy," said Zubin excitedly.

That's odd, thought Arun. *I don't know where he gets his fascination for plants, but he seems to not be able to live without them.*

"Let's be sure to tell Mom and Dad," said Arun, directing his comment to Radha.

Arun watched as Radha managed a smile. He then noticed as her expression grew grave. He could see that she was struggling a bit. *My goodness, how I love this woman,* he thought to himself. Suddenly the self-inflicted name-calling that transpired in the bathroom seemed silly, as if he found some sense of self-worth for himself in his wife's eyes. *Regardless of what my parents, uncle and brothers think of me, if she saw enough to say yes to me,* he thought to himself, *maybe I am not so useless.* And then he thought about their lives together. He knew then. His fighter instinct was beginning to come back to him, thanks to his wife.

"Go ahead," said Arun to Radha, softly.

She looked up at him with a slight jerk. She let out a whisper of a sigh, looked down and ever so gently grimaced, tightening the muscles of her forehead delicately. "He also got into a fight," she added.

"Let's be sure not to mention that to Mom and Dad," added Arun.

The two chuckled and shared a glance. Arun gave her a smile. He tried, the best he could, to reassure her without words that everything was going to be okay. She fluttered her eyelashes slowly in acknowledgment. Arun loved how he could communicate with his wife this way.

Arun saw Zubin's expression fall when he looked at his son. The boy had a look of dejection, displaying a sense of dread on his face. It was clear that he wanted to continue to bask in his father's glow. Now, delight had been replaced with fear. Arun took a step back from his son and he could feel his own brow wrinkle in concern – his son's expression was all too familiar to him. *Hadn't Arun just seen this expression in the mirror upstairs?* At first he felt sympathy for his son. This quickly turned to empathy as he recalled being his son's age. Arun started to feel miserable, for himself and his son. He thought for a few seconds about what his father had done in a similar circumstance.

"I'm sure it was for a good reason," said Arun. "I know my son."

Zubin gave out a sigh of relief. A smile returned to his face. He seemed to be glowing with confidence thought Arun. His eyes took on a steely determination. In a glance, Arun beamed with pride as his son seemed invincible.

Nostalgia crept back into Arun's mind. *Would it have been so hard for my father to say something like that once in my life?* he thought. *A simple defense. A simple acknowledgment that I understand my son and his character and I know what he is capable of and what he isn't. How come all fathers don't have similar perceptions? Why do some fathers assume their kids are guilty until they prove themselves innocent - if they are even afforded the opportunity to prove themselves innocent? Why couldn't*

Arun have the confidence that what he just did with his son would be done with him?

"All of my friends like me, Daddy," said Nandini to break the few seconds of silence, looking up at her father.

"That's my good girl, Nandini," said Arun, almost with a sense of relief that less parenting was required by her for the time being. Radha was distracted by the phone ringing.

It wasn't that Arun didn't like parenting. It was just that right now, too many streets were intersecting in his mind. He needed a chance to re-align the grid of pathways, trying to get back to his normal self. There was such a process involved in parenting, because he was so keen on getting it right. Arun had to weigh every decision. Think about its impact. Think about what others might think. Think back to what his parents did with him and how he resented so many of their actions. Arun didn't want Zubin and Nandini to resent him. *How do I avoid those potholes, those uncovered manholes, those road blocks?*

● ● ●

Radha watched her husband. She noticed his scrunched forehead. His running his hands through his short, black, hair. His looking about listlessly. She thought about an open field with disturbed snow.

"That was Anjali. She's on her way home," indicated Radha.

Arun responded with a smile. Like her son earlier, Radha felt emboldened, "You know, when Anjali gets here, we will have someone safe to talk to."

"What are you talking about? Didn't we discuss this?" asked Arun, his tone harsh, his stance defensive.

Radha remained calm. She thought maybe his position had been eased a bit. "She's not my parents, Arun. I can understand if you want to wait to tell them. You can air out your feelings with her. She can provide us with a lot of support," pleaded Radha. She felt frustrated that she had started her sentence with a reassuring tone, which changed to reveal a slight quiver in her voice.

"No such thing will happen," Arun stated firmly. "We can't tell any family about this yet."

Radha looked at her husband. She began to speak slowly.

"Arun, it will help take a load off your chest. We need to get it out so that we can begin to cope with this," Radha said.

"Family is not always of help, Radha. I don't think I should allow it," Arun pledged with conviction.

Radha decided to stay quiet. Arun's expression went from scowl to frown. As if he was making a U-turn back to the blind alley of his thoughts.

After a lull in the conversation, Radha took the opportunity to let Arun know that his mother had phoned. Arun's eyes grew wide, suddenly, as if he was waking up from a coma – like a thousand emotions in the form of bricks came crashing down on his head. Radha watched as Arun looked at Nandini. His face became less tense. Perhaps our daughter's smile allowed him to defend himself against that avalanche.

"I called her back already, actually," Arun reported.

Arun was about to walk out of the kitchen. His forehead had more ripples than a wading pool full of children. Radha stepped in front of him. "I know why you are hesitating with your parents," she told him.

"Do you?" he challenged.

"We can work this out together. I can help you cope with your parents. We can figure out a way to deal with them," Radha insisted. "Even if they refuse to speak with you again."

Arun looked at her. His eyes became small. His forehead grew more concentrated, as if those children in the pool were splashing about furiously. Radha knew what he was going to do. His knee-jerk reaction was always to question her apparent audacity and presumption. She remembered his comments from the last time they discussed this, "How could you possibly understand?" and "How could you know what I have suffered through with my parents?"

Arun's eyes went back to their normal size. His shoulders eased a bit. She knew he wouldn't say another word, but she could tell that he understood what she was saying. She recalled the first time she had seen him do that. It was shortly after they had first met.

• • •

Arun lay in bed that night, his eyes transfixed on the ceiling. It was as if his own body mass in the area surrounding his heart had suddenly collapsed in on itself – an implosion to balance the explosion of that day. In its place was inserted lead, mercury, iron or some other heavy metal whose density made it feel as if he were carrying an unbearable weight around. His chest felt like it was dragging on the floor. He understood how prisoners with shackles on their hands and feet felt. He was living through life's greatest punishment – fear. Fear was the shackle that was imprisoning him, torturing him, tormenting him.

Fear was a diaphanous beast, an apparition, a shadow. Escaping it was not possible; it was like a cloak enshrouding him that he could not grasp to pull away. A fog, a spirit, a haze. He couldn't rid himself of the fear. Nights were the worst, when all other distractions were gone. It was like the morning dew that crept up on you, the skin rash that suddenly appeared or the wound you didn't know about until you saw that you were bleeding. Suddenly it's there. Attempts to be rid of it seemed futile. There was no lane or passageway where he could hide.

"What angel will rescue me from this fear?" Arun muttered in the darkness.

He began running the very next morning. He hadn't run in over seven years. Somehow, it just felt like the thing to do.

There must be some conduit to outrun his fear. First an hour passed and then another. While the passageway to safety eluded him, another phenomenon was occurring that he welcomed. He began feeling pain in his legs. It was a strangely inviting, seductive sensation. It was the sexy, scantily clad woman at the bar flirting with him incessantly, making him feel like he was all that mattered in the world. He knew he shouldn't, but he couldn't help himself. Once the pain set in, he ran harder, he ran faster. The more pain he experienced the better he felt. He kept pushing himself. Faster. Faster. Faster. His legs gave way. They were Jell-O. He fell forward. Tumbling over himself several times. Pavement. Sky. Pavement. Sky. Pavement. He had scratches on his face, he had cut his nose, and blood was flowing onto his neck. He clenched his jaw. He got up. He walked home.

The next morning when he decided to get out of bed - he never really woke-up that day because he never really fell asleep - his thighs felt like two concrete pillars. It was wonderfully satisfying. He put on his shoes. He began his running again.

A man coming towards him in the opposite direction accidentally dropped a box in front of Arun that he didn't have time to avoid. Arun tripped over it, falling on the concrete. Arun turned around to face the man, awaiting an apology. The man grabbed his package and walked away without saying a word. Arun was shocked. And then he felt something. It was now okay for people to be rude to him – he didn't think he deserved better. Arun found that he could not hold his head up high anymore. He no longer felt like he needed respect or that he was worthy of good things happening to him. Such were the terms of his self-inflicted punishment. Such were the terms bestowed upon him by his fear.

He didn't abandon that avenue of thinking as he ran. He pushed himself so hard he fell again. The pain was wondrous.

It distracted him from the agony that he felt in his chest. *Could there be a better medicine?*

When he got home that day, his clothes had been ripped at the knees and at the elbows. His lower pants and arms were full of blood streaks.

"What are you doing to yourself?" demanded Radha.

"I'm running," was Arun's callous response. His tone was distant. He didn't offer Radha any further explanation. There was no banter.

He looked in the hall mirror. He could see how his eyes carried the weight of his sadness. He looked lost. He could tell the image of him was bringing Radha down also. *She can see the lack of direction in my eyes.* Arun turned away – from the mirror and from his wife.

As he showered, the pain in his chest came back with resurgence. *I can't outrun this*, he thought to himself. His limbs felt like they had detached themselves from the rest of his body. Walking felt like he was trying to move a truck.

That night, he rummaged through his alcohol cabinet. *Perhaps this was the alleyway.* The deleterious effect that he was seeking was there, temporarily. After two empty bottles, he had ensured that he could not feel anything. It was bliss. He thought he might pass out. No such luck. *I can't even force myself to sleep*, he thought to himself.

When he sobered, he felt the onset of fatigue. But he denied himself. Somehow it felt better. When the sun rose, the ensuing headache he felt was met with joy. He finally had something to overpower the sensations in his chest. As the day wore on, his headache subsided.

Radha offered him food. "You must eat something."

"No, no, I'm okay," he insisted.

"It's been thirty-six hours since you ate something." He had lost track, but Radha was keeping count.

After another full day of the same behavior had passed, Radha confronted him. "You have to eat something," she demanded.

"I'm okay, really," he attempted to say. To himself he thought, *The pain in my stomach is easier to swallow*.

Radha brought Nandini to her father.

Arun sensed what was going on. "Don't pull that shit with me," he insisted to Radha. There was a desperate exasperation in his voice. His eyes turned red, and moisture began forming in them. He clenched his jaw and tightened his lips to hold back the tears. He was trying to resist what he knew he couldn't. His dear wife had bested him. She knew what it would take to turn him.

"Why aren't you eating, Daddy?" asked Nandini.

With bloodshot eyes, but no tears, Arun picked up his daughter. He looked at his wife with a cruel resentment. "I'll eat darling, don't worry," he said to Nandini to try to re-assure her.

"Eat now, Daddy, eat now," Nandini insisted. She put her tiny hands on Arun's face.

Arun looked at his daughter for several seconds. He let out a weak chuckle. Arun walked to the kitchen while holding Nandini. He opened the refrigerator door. In the vegetable bin he found what he was looking for. He pulled them out. One by one, he began eating Thai chili peppers.

"Daddy, can I have one?" asked Nandini.

"No darling, this is not for you," responded Arun. His voice was even. It never wavered.

Tears were rolling down his face when he caught sight of Radha entering the kitchen. He was on pepper number seven.

Radha didn't say a word. She threw out the rest of the peppers. Arun could see she was fighting back tears.

Arun was disappointed, but he hadn't expected anything different from her. He missed the sensation of the excruciatingly spicy chili peppers. The burning of his mouth, tongue and throat were welcome compared to what he had over his heart. There was a battle for control of his body. The harsh physical beating he was putting himself through should conquer and defeat this veil of fear and its wretched shackles that Arun was so desperate to be free of.

Was there a worse torture than fear? At that moment, he knew of none other.

Radha was leaning over the sink. The water was on, but she was not using it. The flowing water masked her own water works. The shaking of her shoulders, however, was a telltale sign. Arun had a hard time coping with this sight. Especially with her being pregnant. He turned her around.

He realized then that there was another phenomenon out of his control. He had a responsibility that he couldn't back away from. He had to be strong; it was what others expected of him and he realized, needed from him. If Radha and the kids were to witness him break down, they would see the extent to which there was a problem and they might begin to believe that it was beyond the scope of Arun's ability to handle it. And he desperately needed for them to believe he could pull through.

She beseeched him, "Why are you being so self-destructive? You need to be at your best in order to fight this. Soldiers do not go into battle after inflicting torture upon themselves."

Radha could not have been more right, but he felt a perverse sense of resentment towards her and the kids. He pondered death frequently, but he knew he couldn't take his own life, now. He was aware it would not absolve him, but he could escape the fear. But that was not an option for him, now. He knew he had to live for his family.

Ironically, contemplating death gave him strength; he decided that if he were going to plead "game over" anyway, he may as well keep fighting to see if anything improved. His rationality had never completely left him.

He put Nandini down and moved towards Radha. He held his wife in his arms and ran his fingers through her hair. She rested her head on his chest. Somehow, the pain in his chest felt less excruciating. Like holy water to a vampire, an army in retreat or the sun causing the rain drops to evaporate, the shroud seemed to dissipate. His wife had set him on the right course.

● ● ●

Several days after the incident had passed, the phone at home rang. Radha wondered if it was Arun; he had gone out for awhile. She looked at the caller identification. It was her mother-in-law. Radha was inclined to pretend that all of them were not home. Unfortunately, Radha overheard Nandini answering the phone.

"Hello?" said Nandini.

"Yes, Grandma," replied Nandini.

"Fine…No...Yes…MOMMY!"

Radha picked up the phone. "Hello?"

"Hello," replied Meena. Her voice seemed distant.

"Hi, Mom."

"Where is Arun?"

"He went out to the store to pick up something."

"I try his cell phone. Three times I try him. I don't know why that boy never answer his cell phone when I call him," complained Meena.

"Maybe he isn't getting reception," offered Radha. She couldn't help but find it a little amusing, although she knew it wasn't appropriate, that Arun would not answer her calls. She recalled the real reason why however, and it made her sad once again.

"Hmm. Tell him he call me," instructed Meena.

"Is there any message?" Radha probed.

"I am wanting to know what my friends give for baby shower."

Radha thought to herself, *You mean the one that you didn't bother to attend yourself?* "Oh, I can tell you, Mom. They didn't bring anything."

"Nothing? How can? Not even Dipti send something?"

You caught me, my dear mother-in-law, I am lying to you. Radha hated Dipti. Radha found her overly opinionated and she would always insist on providing Meena with unsolicited guidance. Radha sensed that her mother-in-law's caustic side had its origins in her friendship with Dipti.

"Well, we went through all of the gifts and every one is accounted for. Nothing from Dipti," Radha explained.

"Hmph. Tell my son he call me," snapped Meena.

"Okay, Mom." Radha heard a dial-tone.

● ● ●

Arun called his parents later that day.

"Hello?"

"Hi, Mom."

"Yes Arun. I waiting so long you call me. Never think of your mother, isn't it?"

Arun hated how calling one another was a competition. The one who got there first had a "holier than thou" attitude. Of course, this only seemed to work when Arun's mother would call him. He couldn't quite get that same benefit when he was calling her. It also troubled Arun how his mother mostly did this to him and less so to his brothers.

Time had not been kind to Meena's appearance. She had become excessively round with fleshy arms that would jiggle as she emphasized points. The roundness extended to all parts of her body, with a concentration in her mid-section, making her appear like a walking pear. Arun made himself chuckle thinking that Halloween would be a breeze for his mother – just wear a lime green sheet. She still retained some of the features of her youth – her round eyes and sharp nose. He thought about how his father, in contrast, had always looked the same, save for a few additional wrinkles and the black of his hair yielding to the color white.

Arun imagined his mother sitting at the kitchen table and throwing darts at a target with a photo of him in the bull's eye. Unfortunately, her aim was impeccable. "How are you?" he enquired, desperate to change the subject.

"Fine."

There was silence.

"How is Dad feeling?" Arun asked.

"How you think he feeling? He have heart attack in the life already, isn't it?" Meena retorted.

Arun let out a sigh.

There was additional silence.

"When you starting new job?" Meena asked.

"I started already," said Arun, clenching his jaw.

"Your father say you no speak to your uncle. He know how to do things, isn't it? You must asking him."

Arun didn't feel like he could contain his emotions much longer. He felt scared, but he was being compelled by his exasperation. "Why do you find him so infallible? Why do you think he is always right? Don't you think I am capable of making smart choices like him?"

"Arun, you no yell at me. I no understanding all you talk. He very rich, isn't it? He make much money, isn't it? You no making money like him. He know. You learning."

And there it was, thought Arun. The "immigrant manifesto" cited once again – he who acquires gold acquires invincibility.

"Have you spoken with Sanjay or Raj lately?" Arun asked.

"Yes."

"How is Auntie Dipti doing?"

"Fine."

"Okay, Mom. I'll talk to you later," said Arun. The conversation was beginning to irk him. Why didn't his mom enquire about how Radha was doing? She was due in a few months. His face began feeling warmer.

"So how much more money you are having now?"

"It's more," said Arun without flinching. His mother also never bothered to ask how Zubin or Nandini were. This realization made Arun angry.

"Oh. You no want tell me?" snapped Meena.

"No," came Arun's response. He wondered where his fear had gone. He thought about Radha and the kids. There were a few additional moments of silence. "I really have to go."

His mother didn't say anything. She did what she always did to protest, she hung up the phone.

Arun recalled all of those times that he hid things from his parents. Bad grades, girlfriends, detention. He had been burned many times before when he had told his parents the truth. Was it worthwhile going through that again? Had he learned nothing from his previous forty years of life? It was as if he was being goaded into punishment. Into silence. Into exile.

"What a relationship," remarked Arun sarcastically under his breath.

CHAPTER SIX

September 1981 — June 1985

      Arun's first day of high school was meant to be a day of significance in his thinking. It should not have been as trivial as every other in his schooling. He had heard so much about what an exciting time this should be for him. Numerous television shows and movies had glorified this period – but all their main actors and actresses were not children of immigrants. Arun wondered where that magic would be. And whether it would be something he experienced. He thought he might actually enjoy his life during high school.

      His first order of business was to get people to say his name correctly. It was a fresh start; he wanted them to get it right. He walked into his homeroom class. He noticed several girls whom he found pretty seated there. *Amazing how girls develop at different rates*, he thought, as he glanced at chests and back-sides, excitement rising up in his veins. He recognized some of the faces of the other students, but some were new. *Oh, how I wish I could be cool. I would love it if they were to like me.* He let his thoughts wonder. *Maybe I could even be kissing them, fondling their breasts.* Then he passed by the room mirror. He became crestfallen. *Why would they like me?* The color of his skin was a handicap, he felt. *Would they see my color first or would they notice me as a person? All they see when they see me is some dark, goofy kid who wears funny clothes.* Arun never found himself handsome at that age. *Oh I wish I was cool.*

As the teacher started to read off the names of each student, his heart started to beat faster. *Oh god*, he thought, *how I wish I had a name like Edward, Ben or John.* Just then the teacher called out the name Steven.

"Here."

And then she came to him. He could always tell when it was his turn. The pause gave it away. In a sea of white kids, he was the only foreigner. He looked up to see the teacher hesitating. He knew she would struggle with the name. *If I had more guts*, thought Arun, *I would just say my name to her first.*

"*A-Run?*"

The kids in the class laughed.

"Uh, its pronounced *Uh-roon*," corrected Arun.

"*A-roon?*" asked the teacher attempting to reconcile the phonetics he was employing with the actual westernized spelling of his name.

"Uh...sure," said Arun, thinking to himself that Indians are so different they can't even get the westernized spelling of their names to conform. He just wanted to die. *None of these girls are going to find me cool now.*

"My, what an unusual name," said the teacher.

Thanks for pointing that out thought Arun. *I hadn't realized that.*

She looked up when she said it, expecting a response. As if somehow Arun needed to be apologetic for having this complicated name that she had to work at to be able to say. As if he was causing some difficulty for her because she couldn't just run down the list. As if it wasn't acceptable for him to be different that way. He felt like he had done something wrong.

"Yeah," said Arun, looking at her and then looking down.

The next morning, the teacher stumbled over it again. And then the next day. And then the next. He had suffered through this all through elementary and middle school. He had made a promise to himself that he would get them to say it correctly now. Arun couldn't bring himself to correct her each time. He just didn't have it in him. He simply settled for "*A-Run*".

In the beginning he would cringe when he would hear it. And then he got used to it. He had suffered through it for years.

"Read aloud on page twenty-one, *A-Run*."

"Come to the board and solve this problem, *A-Run*."

"Did you complete your homework, *A-Run*?"

The boy named Steven, whose name was called before his in homeroom, turned to him, "I don't know why they have such a hard time with your name."

Steven was roughly the same height as Arun and had sandy brown hair that was wavy. He combed it back, parting it on the side. He appeared to be using hair gel, because it didn't move around too much. He had small blue eyes and his lips looked oversized for his face, as if they were constantly swollen, stung by a bee each morning.

Arun didn't know how to react. "Yeah, I guess 'coz it's so different," Arun suggested.

"My Dad told me he had an Indian friend in college," said Steven.

Arun's face lit up. Is it possible – an olive branch? Someone who might take pity on him and talk to him? Someone who might be a friend?

Steven continued, "My Dad told me that they butchered his name so badly, he just went by David."

Arun looked at Steven. Both laughed together.

● ● ●

Arun had a history teacher, Mrs. Adams, who smiled broadly when he entered her classroom. *She seems like she will be a nice teacher*, Arun thought to himself. Before the class started she came to the desk he had chosen to sit at. Arun was alarmed; he didn't know what to do. He wondered what he had done wrong.

"Gandhi is one of my favorite historical figures," she said to him in a hushed tone.

Arun immediately smiled.

She had a large format computer printout in her hands, with alternating green and white stripes running down the page. She showed the paper to him with her pencil pointed at a precise location. "How do I pronounce that, dear?" she asked Arun.

"*Uh-roon.*"

Arun was elated. She said it back to him perfectly.

"What a nice, distinctive name."

Arun couldn't have been happier. Somebody knew his background. Somebody knew a little about him. Knew what he was about. Took time to understand him. *Was there anything more wonderful than being understood?*

Arun found a nice niche for himself in high school as an intellectual. That is how he differentiated himself. He tried to do things that excited him, that made him feel good about himself. Excelling in academics and the praise that came with it, somehow made him feel more comfortable about how different he was.

It turned out that Mrs. Adams was also the coach for the debate team.

"Hmmm," muttered Arun. "Maybe I could try that." Arun tried out and was accepted onto the team. Initially he would give prepared speeches. He liked the security of having what he was going to say right in front of him. Over time, as he became more confident, he became a rebutallist. At that point, he had to create a portion of his speech during the debate, in direct response to what his opponents were saying. Arun began to really enjoy people recognizing him as a debater and not as the awkward foreigner, so different than the rest of them.

Initially, people were surprised with his interest in debate. He had always been focused on science. He had won the Academy of Science awards several times in a row. Admittedly, this was a bit forced for Arun. He wasn't as enamored by the sciences, but his father was a big champion and it was a chance for him to interact with his father. He could ask his father questions and seek advice. It seemed to be the only way that he and Rajiv would spend any time together.

There was a girl who had tried out for the debate team, but didn't make it. On occasion she would come to the competitions. She smiled at Arun before one debate began. Arun stopped in his tracks. His heart started to beat fast. He had no idea what to do. He was out of his element. When he gave his speech that day, he stumbled in a few places.

That night at home, he couldn't stop thinking about that smile. He had always been attracting to girls, but he never anticipated that anything would come of it. He didn't think he could get over the racial divide. In his mind it was an insurmountable hurdle.

He couldn't help looking out for her in the hall in between classes from then on. When he would look for her, he would stare, he couldn't help himself. And then he began routing his walks so that he could maximize his views of her.

One day, as he was gawking, she came to him. "I'm Christina," she said. She had blonde hair that came to her shoulders. It had loose curls in them. She had large blue eyes, a broad smile, and she wore glasses. She was slightly shorter than Arun.

Arun was shocked. He felt really awkward. He didn't know what to say. "I'm Arun," he finally blurted out.

"I know," came her response. She giggled as she said it.

Arun looked at her and then looked down.

She did the same. She shifted her weight. "Would you like to walk me to class?" she eventually asked.

"Oh, yeah, that'd be great," said Arun. Arun walked with her to her next class. There was silence for a long time. Arun turned to her and awkwardly asked, "Would you like me to carry your books for you?"

"No," said Christina, laughing.

"Oh, okay," said Arun. His face turned red. He thought he had made an error. They arrived at the classroom. Arun knew he needed to go. He had no idea what to say. He didn't want to go, so he just lingered.

Finally, Christina asked, "I was wondering…"

"Yeah?" asked Arun.

"That history project for Mrs. Adams…" she began.

"Oh…right," said Arun.

"Wanna work on that together?" she asked him.

"Oh…yeah…that'd be great," said Arun. He was astounded himself with how great that sounded.

Christina ripped out a piece of paper from her notebook, scribbled her number on it and gave it to him.

Arun couldn't concentrate in his next class. He kept looking down at the sheet of paper. He liked how feminine she made the loops of her letters. The "c" and "h" of her first name and the "w" of her last name, Warren, were so exaggeratingly and dramatically round they felt like an open, flirtatious invitation. He found Steven after school.

"That's great!" Steven exclaimed, high-fiving Arun.

"Oh…I don't know…" said Arun. "What do I say when I call her?"

• • •

Rajiv saw the signs pointing towards a detour. He was agitated that he could not go straight home. He happened to drive past a nursery that he had never seen before. He couldn't believe what he saw. It appeared to be a baby mango tree. He pulled into the parking lot.

When he walked in, all of the people behind the counter were busy with others. He stood in front of the register. Someone within an office came out.

"Can I help you?"

"Yes, is that being a mango tree you are having?" asked Rajiv as he made a motion with his arm to the front of the store.

"Oh, no, *señor*," said the man, "No mango here." When he spoke he smiled broadly. He was short in height, about eye level with Rajiv. He had a very large belly. The strain of his weight could be detected in his voice and the manner in which he aspirated his *S*'s. He wore glasses and a cowboy hat. He wore a shirt with stripes and a name patch that said Pablo.

"Oh," said Rajiv, clearly disappointed.

As Rajiv turned to walk away, he heard Pablo ask, "You like mangos?"

Rajiv turned back. "Yes."

Pablo smiled broadly. "Follow me, *señor*," said Pablo.

Rajiv's curiosity was piqued, so he followed Pablo. Pablo led him past a cramped walkway to the back door of the store. The path was lined with potted plants. Rajiv enjoyed walking and naming in his mind each of the plants that he passed by. Pablo took him outside. The door closed behind Rajiv with a thud. For the first time, Rajiv was a little nervous. He began hesitating slightly and widening the gap between him and Pablo.

Pablo turned around. "Don't be afraid, *señor*, I have something for you."

Rajiv smiled politely, thrown off because what he was feeling had been detected. His lackadaisical effort continued to punctuate the fact that he was not at ease.

Pablo went to his pickup truck and opened the back. Inside were several boxes of fruit. Pablo balanced a box of mangos between his arm and his stomach as he closed the door. He handed the box to Rajiv.   The weight was a surprise to Rajiv. His slight frame fell forward slightly as he took the box from Pablo.

"Oh," said Rajiv, finally allowing himself a broad smile. "What is being the cost?" asked Rajiv.

"Oh no, *señor*, you keep it," said Pablo, nodding his head in a jovial fashion and waving his hand as if to sweep away the suggestion that he would accept money for it.

"It is being very kind of you," said Rajiv.   Looking pensive, Rajiv added, "It is really not being possible for me to being taking and no money.   Please, you letting me to pay."

"Oh no," said Pablo definitively.   This time both of his hands were up.

"Thank you so much," said Rajiv.   He smiled at the man. Rajiv walked to his car.   He placed the mangos in the back seat and sat down behind the steering wheel.   Before he turned on the car, he smiled to himself.   He turned around.   He saw Pablo there.   When Pablo saw him turn, Pablo waved emphatically to him.   Rajiv let out a laugh.   He waved back.

• • •

Arun looked up as Sanjay walked into his room.

A year after teachers had Arun in their classes, Sanjay would be their student. Although he looked nothing like his older brother, teachers would often look at Sanjay and call him Arun. Arun would overhear this from time to time in the hall.   A part of him felt a little badly for Sanjay.

"For biology last year, did you have to do a project where you diagrammed a cell?" asked Sanjay.

Arun knew that Sanjay had found a way to exact his revenge.   Arun kept all the papers, reports and tests that he had taken.   Arun's school files were often fished through by Sanjay.

They were a wonderful reference for Sanjay to have at his disposal, especially, Arun would note, the tests he had taken.

"Yeah," said Arun turning back to his textbook. "It should be in the file," he added.

"No, it's not there," Sanjay said.

"Oh, I don't know what happened to it."

"Do you remember what you did?"

"Not really. I'm kind of busy. I have a test on this chemistry stuff in two days," Arun mentioned, hoping to encourage his brother to leave.

"Did you get an A?"

"I don't remember, I think I did."

"Do you think Mr. Trichet will like it if I did a 3-D one?"

"Probably, he likes extra effort. But why waste the time? He'll probably give you an A for a good hand-drawn diagram." Arun tried to offer his brother some advice that would help him minimize his effort.

"Okay, good." Sanjay proceeded to make the 3-D version.

● ● ●

"I took five dollars from your wallet," Raj informed Arun one day.

Arun was never approached by Raj for academic advice. The gap in age was partially to blame. He always wanted money instead.

"What do you need it for?" Arun asked.

"Stuff."

"How come you never take it from Dad?" Arun questioned, finding the situation irksome.

"Oh, I could never take it without asking from Dad."

"Don't you think it would be nice if you asked me too?"

"I dunno." And then Raj started walking away.

"I know you are spending it at that gourmet food store. It'd be nice if you shared some of your creations," Arun shouted out after him.   As Arun was speaking, Raj placed the earphones of his walkman over his ears.

● ● ●

Rajiv took the lychee he had found at the Indian store. He asked the store owner for a box of it.   Meena, Arun, Sanjay and Raj were surprised.   Rajiv never ordered a whole box of anything.   In fact, he would just push the cart while everyone else loaded it up.   He would place something in there only if Meena asked him to go get something.

Raj was the one who asked the question, "Why so many, Dad?"

"Oh," said Rajiv.   He paused a few seconds.   He hadn't thought of a response.   "It is being for my working place.   Some peoples may being enjoying this."

Raj rolled his eyes.   "Whatever."

Sanjay helped his father carry the box.   Arun stood by, observing, a look of surprise on his face.

Rajiv drove to the nursery again.   He asked the counter person for Pablo.   She led him into the office behind the register. There were three desks in that office, a table in one corner.   She led him through an open door to an even larger room with an even larger desk in the center of it.   Seated behind the desk was Pablo.

"Oh, hello, *mi amigo*," said Pablo, his face opening into an exuberant smile.

"Hello," said Rajiv with a smile and nod of the head.   "I thought you might being enjoying this fruit.   We are having it in India."

Rajiv handed the box to Pablo.

"Oh, you are too kind, *señor*," said Pablo.   "Did you like the mangoes?"

"Oh very much," said Rajiv. "They were being very sweet."

"*Muy bien*," said Pablo. "Those are very typical mangoes from our Mexico."

"They are being very nice," said Rajiv.

There was a slight lull in the conversation.

"I have some more," said Pablo, pointing in the direction of the back of the store.

"Oh no," said Rajiv, waving his hand and swaying his head in resistance, "you have being too nice." Rajiv looked up to see Pablo smiling at him broadly.

"Okay, I going," said Rajiv, smiling at Pablo and waggling his head.

"Thank you for these. You are most kind *señor*," said Pablo.

Rajiv turned to walk away. He came back to Pablo's office. "How you saying thank you in your language?"

"*Gracias.*"

"*Gracias,*" Rajiv repeated, emphasizing the 's' sound of the 'c' to be sure he got it right.

"How do you say thank you in your language?" asked Pablo.

"*Dhanyibad.*"

● ● ●

His parents didn't allow him to date, so Arun had to resort to speaking with Christina on the phone; they also wrote notes to each other throughout the school day. He felt a certain validation by her interest in him. He would ask her about it frequently. In the beginning she was always very sprightly about offering her thoughts on him. Over time, she would resort to a rehearsed response. He could tell she was getting agitated. He attempted to not ask as frequently.

Arun relied heavily on Christina's support during his debates. If he was feeling under siege, he would seek out her smile in the crowd. It was like a gust of wind at his sail. His parents had yet to come to a debate match, which would leave Arun downtrodden at times, particularly when he saw all of the other students' parents there. Christina was an important friendly face for him.

He and his team had won a series of debates. He was now emerging as a leader amongst the other team members. He provided some pointers to Christina and helped her land a spot on the team. He was becoming overjoyed that now his classmates would applaud his achievements in the hallway, in the classroom and even when he would bump into them at the mall. He abandoned playing the violin. He had only been average at that. His successes in debate made him a bit courageous; Arun decided to try to deploy his new found boldness to other areas of his life.

• • •

The door bell rang at the Gandharni household. Arun felt a tingling sensation of joy that rippled through him. *She's early,* he thought to himself. He had been planning to wait outside for her. They were going to spend some time together to work on their debate speeches and their preparation. He wasn't ready yet however, and didn't have a chance to make it to the door. He waited to finish ironing his shirt, carefully making sure that his quick motions didn't burn him, and he swiftly combed his hair.

His mother got to the door first. He imagined her only opening the door wide enough to let her head through like she always did. He couldn't hear her say a word.

"You must be Arun's mom." He could hear the sound of Christina's voice clearly. He tried moving faster.

"Yes," came Meena's response. Arun could visualize his mother's mouth open, in almost an "O-like" shape of bewilderment. She said nothing else.

Arun looked over the railing as he put on his shirt.

"I'm Christina," his girlfriend said and Arun could see her extend her hand to shake it with his mother. Meena opened the door wider and offered her right hand, but Meena's grip was so loose that Christina's hand fell out partially and they ended up having a flimsy, fingers-to-palm handshake.

Christina laughed at the clumsiness.

Meena was serious.

"Is Arun home?" Christina asked, slanting her head to one side, with a slight bobbing motion.

"Uh…sure," said Meena. Meena turned around, "Arun! *Idher ao!*" Come here, she commanded in Hindi.

Arun's heart took a leap and his legs felt like an electric charge was going through them. He didn't so much descend the stairs from the top floor, as he made two leaps from landing to landing, bounding over the steps in between.

When he came to the front door, he caught the expression on his mom's face. It was a stern, questioning look. He immediately felt guilty, like he had done something terribly wrong.

"For you," said Meena. She jerked her head in Christina's direction in a fast motion.

"Hi," said Christina.

"HI!" said Arun.

They had become accustomed to some form of intimate greeting as of late, a hug or holding of their hands. But now, they just stood there with an awkward distance between them.

"I'm sorry I'm early, my mother couldn't drop me off later. She has a friend she is meeting."

"Oh, that's okay," said Arun.

Meena was still standing there.

"Come in," said Arun.

Guests at the Gandharni home typically sat in the living room. But whenever Arun's male friends came over, they would always go up to Arun's bedroom and close the door. Meena waited by the living room, but Arun went upstairs with Christina. They passed by Arun's father as they went up. Rajiv stopped in his tracks.

"Uh, Dad, this is my friend, Christina," said Arun.

Rajiv was silent. He just looked at her.

"Hi, Mr. Gandharni," said Christina hesitatingly.

Rajiv reacted with a terse, "Hello".

"We are just going to work on our debate stuff," said Arun, pointing to his room. As Arun and Christina went to the room, Arun turned around to close the door. He saw his father still standing there. Arun lost his will to close the door.

By then Sanjay came out of his room. He looked as stunned as Rajiv.

Raj also came running up the stairs with some video game toys. He peeked into the room and saw Christina. She waved at him.

"A girl!" shouted out Raj. "A girl! A girl!"

"Shut up, Raj!" yelled Arun.

"A girl! A girl!"

Arun found the strength to close the door then. He didn't even look at his father or brother as he did it. After he closed it, he thought to himself, *That little squirt actually helped me out.*

Arun went to Christina and gave her a quick kiss on the lips. He felt a sense of relief to be with her alone now. It was a safety zone. He knew while she was there, he'd be okay. After she left, he sensed there would be punishment.

"Your family hates me," Christina said to him, sullenly.

"No," said Arun. "They really just don't know what to do with you."

After an hour, Arun had to go downstairs to get a different notebook. When he came back, he saw Raj in his room. "What are you doing?   Get out!"   Raj scurried away.

"What did he say to you?" asked Arun.

"Well, first he asked if I was going to marry you and then he said 'Dad's mad and stuff'," responded Christina.

Arun was outraged.   He could feel the anger rising within him.

Christina looked pensive for a few minutes.   "Are you gonna be in trouble for having me here with the door closed and everything?"

"Oh no," said Arun, hoping he could mask the reality with his confidence, "It's cool, don't worry about it."   He didn't want to seem like he wasn't normal enough to be doing this.

"Because I'm getting this, like, really bad vibe from your family," she said.

Oh man, thought Arun. *This girl is too perceptive.   How uncool would that be though, not even being able to have a girl over? That's such a loser situation.   No, I can't have her thinking that.*

"No, don't worry, everything is fine."

Nothing was fine.   No matter what, Rajiv and Meena kept ignoring Arun after Christina left.   They wouldn't speak to him.   *What time is dinner?   So how about this weekend at Auntie Dipti's place?   Is Uncle Arjun coming any time soon?*   There was silence.   They were quietly angry.   Arun wondered what he did wrong.   He had no idea why they were so angry, but he knew that he felt terribly guilty.   He had done something wrong.   *Was it because I did something I wanted*, he thought to himself, *outside of the prescribed order of things in their mind?*   Part of him was also embarrassed for the situation.   The silent treatment was what he had seen girls do to each other in middle school.

● ● ●

"Dad, I'd like to get my license," Arun pleaded with his father.

"Why are you needing this license?"

Over time Arun had developed a hatred of taking the bus, it was not what the cool kids did. They all drove to school. Arun devised a three-step approach: first, get his parents to agree to a license, second, convince them of purchasing a car for him and third, cajole them into paying the insurance.

"Dad, come on, everyone has one. I'll be the only one," Arun pleaded.

"Your mother and I taking you everywhere. If I getting you license, I must paying insurance. I am having no money for senseless things," Rajiv stated. There was finality in his tone. Arun didn't think he would get anywhere with his father. He never bothered mentioning it again.

● ● ●

Later that month, Arun had to stop off at home before his debate practice, because he had left a speech he was working on. Steven, who had a license and a car, and had become a member of the debate team, drove him there. When Arun walked in, he didn't announce his presence. He overheard his mother on the phone.

"I not knowing what to do. I no want this white girl playing the tricks and trapping my son," said Meena.

It must have been her friend Dipti. His mother was always going on and on with her.

"That is being the best idea. We go to one of these 'D-beht', isn't it? We see what is it. Maybe the whole thing is trick by her. Maybe there is no such thing. She teach my son to lie, isn't it? He spend time with her only."

Arun had heard enough. He went to his bedroom, took his speech, and came back downstairs. He quietly exited the house.

"Looks like my parents may come to one of our debates," Arun told Steven when he got into the car.

"Hey, that's great," exclaimed Steven. After a few second pause, he asked, "How come you don't seem so happy?"

"Never mind."

• • •

Arun was asked by his mother that night at dinner about the next debate. He feebly informed her. When his parents arrived one week later at the high school auditorium, Arun had a strange sense that he was imposing upon them to show up. Arun couldn't help but feel responsible for them. They weren't interacting with anyone. They were just standing about.

"Mrs. Adams, can I introduce you to my parents?" Arun asked his debate team coach.

"Why certainly," she responded with a beaming smile.

"Mom, Dad, this is Mrs. Adams," Arun offered.

"Hello," they said in unison. Arun noticed his father bow his head slightly and look down.

"You must be very proud of both of your sons," Mrs. Adams said.

Arun watched as his father looked up.

"I had Arun for my history class two years ago and I taught your younger son Sanjay last year. Both are very bright and accomplished young men," she said.

Arun watched as his father shifted his feet and looked away. A guttural sound came from his neck, as he cleared his throat.

"Did I say something wrong?" enquired Mrs. Adams a little concerned, looking at each of their faces.

"No, no," interrupted Arun. He was eager to end the exchange which he now found cumbersome. "I'll see you on stage."

Mrs. Adams walked away, a bit perplexed.

Arun turned to his father, "What's wrong?"

Arun could see his father getting angry, "She saying you like Sanjay?   He at the home studying now.   Having discipline. Not wasting the time doing this nonsense and chasing after the girl.   Even your uncle not being so foolish.   You seeing how rich he is."

Arun could feel the warmth rising in his face and his cheeks getting flushed.   He looked down.   He turned around and walked away, his best effort at attempting to stop what he knew was impending.   He didn't say a word as he left.   He hoped in his heart that his parents would just go home.   *Sure, his brother was more studious.   But why was Arun's 94th percentile so much worse than Sanjay's 99th percentile?   And his uncle.   Getting married without telling his family was okay, because he's rich.   But what I am doing is wrong.*

He saw Mrs. Adams as he walked to the stage from behind the curtain.   She smiled at him.   Arun feigned one back.   He nodded his head to Steven, who was sitting at the table already. He sat down himself and touched Christina's hand.   He didn't say anything.

When the curtains opened, Arun saw that his parents were still there.   As a rebutallist, Arun was the last one to speak. When he took the podium and began speaking, he noticed the entire audience snap their heads toward him, as if in obedience. He could even see the surprised gaze of Christina from the right corner of his eye.   He then realized that the volume of his voice was significantly higher than usual, yes, maybe even screaming. As he worked his way through his speech, he got snide chuckles and jeers from the crowd at certain points, "Our opponents are wildly quixotic, that's hopelessly idealistic and naïve, in case our counterparts are not so well read."   Or looks of shock from Christina, "Their argument is so puerile.   I don't know what education system is being utilized for them, but high school for us starts at the ninth grade, not the second."   Even Mrs. Adams had a look of mortification when Arun dramatically turned to the opposing team with both arms in the air, palms up and shouted "Why did you even bother to show up?"

The crowd clapped for him when he finished. But he had disappointed himself. He knew they were applauding the performance and not the content of what he had to say. When he sat down, Christina leaned in to him, "That was not a part of your usual speech."

He immediately thought of his parents and how they would witness this intimate exchange with Christina. When he looked at them, he saw they were not clapping. The tension that had built up in his shoulders was now suddenly more intense. He turned to Christina. "I think I got carried away a little."

"A little?" she asked. She then turned to face him directly. "Why are you frowning?"

"What?"

"Your forehead has a million creases. Why are you frowning?"

"I don't know," Arun said, brushing her inquiry aside.

The judges announced Arun's team as the winner.

When Arun walked off the stage, he approached Mrs. Adams. "I'm sorry."

"It's okay," she said. Her smile a little more taxing on her to deliver than usual. "Why don't you tend to your parents?"

While other parents were talking about how proud they were of their kids, Rajiv and Meena began pushing Arun towards the car to go home. It bothered Arun that his parents were not mingling with the other parents. As they were walking, Arun caught sight of Steven's parents.

"Mom, Dad, these are Steven's parents," Arun said, anticipation in his heart.

"Hi, I'm Don," said Steven's father.

"Hello," said Rajiv.

"I'm Carol. It's so nice to meet you," said Steven's mom with a chipper smile.

Meena was silent, but smiled, in a clearly perfunctory manner, towards her.

Arun shared a pleading look with Steven.

"Boy, these kids were great weren't they? I don't remember being that clever when I was their age. And being able to speak and argue well in front of a crowd of people? I tell you what, they deserved to win." Don's gaze remained fixed on Rajiv and Meena, in anticipation of some kind of response. Arun observed the blank expressions on his parent's faces.

Hearing no response, Don turned to Steven, "All of that hard work paying off, hey champ?" Don play-punched his son on the arm. He then looked back towards Rajiv and Meena.

Rajiv shifted his feet a little bit, smiled, and said, "Yes."

Carol laughed a little towards Meena.

"We go?" asked Rajiv, wagging his head. He directed the question to Meena.

I hate when he does that, thought Arun. *He knows she won't ever say no.* Arun grimaced. He slumped his shoulders a little and could feel his face turning red. He had a hard-time looking Steven's parents in the eye. He wished he could change the behavior of his own parents.

"Mr. and Mrs. Braun, I'll see you later." He tried his best to sound as adult-like as possible. He felt silly, puberty was making his voice crack. He also felt ridiculous. Like he was overcompensating for his parent's lack of social grace and failing miserably.

"Hey you bet, Arun. We'll see you later," Don said to Arun. The way he pursed his lips, Arun could tell, he was confused by the exchange, but instead of feeling slighted he seemed to feel a little badly for Arun.

On the ride back, Arun couldn't help but feel resentment for his parents.

"How come you didn't talk to my friend's parents more?" enquired Arun.

There was silence.

• • •

"What, you buying a vineyard?" asked Rajiv. "What is that thing?" he questioned.

"It's where they grow and harvest grapes and make wine," explained Arjun.

"Is it a farm?" asked Rajiv. He tried hard to contain the excitement in his voice.

"Well, yes, I suppose, it's like a kind of farm," said Arjun.

"You must being taking me to seeing it," said Rajiv. It was rare for Rajiv to ask his younger brother for anything.

Rajiv took a day off from work to see the vineyard. He surveyed the land. He walked through the planted rows. He took joy in the clouds of dust that he created about his feet. The tiny specks of residue that it left on his shoes, pants, shirt and glasses were like confetti evidencing a grand celebration. He had a smile about him. His shoulders were at ease, and his face seemed relaxed, the typical twin wrinkles of concentration and anxiety smoothed out like a fitted bed sheet.

"Oh, you are using metal stakes to being holding up the plants," said Rajiv, jovially.

"Yeah, the vines, actually," clarified Arjun. "It's used to hold up the vines."

"The what?" asked Rajiv.

"The plants are called vines. That is where the grapes grow," explained Arjun, exasperated.

"That is why they call it wine?" asked Rajiv.

"Forget it," said Arjun, making a throw down motion with his hands.

Rajiv was undeterred. "These plants are called wines. And they make wine," he mouthed to himself, as if repeating a lesson he had just learned in a classroom.

That weekend, Rajiv took the kids and Meena to the vineyard.

"Dad, I think it's the first time that you have actually wanted to go somewhere," commented Arun. Rajiv wondered if that was true. It might be the case, he decided. Usually, other than to go shopping, Rajiv just drove to wherever Meena told him to. She was the one who kept in touch with all of their friends and arranged the social calendar.

Rajiv nearly leapt out of the car when they arrived. He took a deep breath of the air through his nostrils. He felt like a kid again.

"And now you looking over there," he told his three boys, excitedly, "those metal stakes. You are seeing them? Is where they hanging the wines."

"They hang wines from there?" asked Arun.

"Yes," said Rajiv, feeling proud about his knowledge.

"Uh, as in wine in the bottle?" asked Arun.

"No, wines. That is where the plants are being, where the fruit is being growing," explained Rajiv.

Raj was the first to laugh. Sanjay told him to stay quiet.

"Oh, Dad, those are called vines, with a 'v'," explained Arun. "The plants are called vines and then when it is all done, wine is what is in the bottle."

"Oh, I see, there is difference," said Rajiv. He was pensive for a brief second, but the smile quickly returned, like a boomerang thrown a short distance.

"Dad, I can't remember you ever drinking wine. I didn't know you liked it," Arun said.

"No, never I drinking. I never touch the meat, I never touch the alcohol," explained Rajiv.

"But now you are going to start to drink?"

"No, is no possible."

"Dad, how can you be involved with a vineyard and not drink wine?" pressed Arun.

"Why you no understand?" demanded Rajiv.

• • •

The following day, Rajiv called the travel agent again.

"Maybe I can get something for one thousand one hundred twenty-nine," the agent indicated.

He did some calculations.   For the whole family it would be close to six thousand dollars.

He tore up the paper that he had written on and threw it away.

• • •

Rajiv called on his friend Pablo.

"We are having a vineyard," indicated Rajiv.

"That is wonderful, *señor*, wonderful," said Pablo.   "What types of grapes are you growing there?"

"Oh…I am not knowing," revealed Rajiv.   He was intrigued with Pablo's question.   It created a sense of wonder in him and a feeling of admiration.

"I see," responded Pablo.

"Maybe you would liking to be visiting the vineyard.   You are knowing very much more than me.   You can having a see," invited Rajiv.

"Oh, it would be a great pleasure for me, *señor*.   *Un gran placer para mi*," replied Pablo.

"Please, you teaching me this phrase," requested Rajiv.

• • •

Arjun received his citizenship before Arun's last year of high school.   Arun thought that it was a bit odd to be celebrating such an occasion.   *I suppose that's what happens when you really have to work towards something.   I got my citizenship just by being born.   I suppose my Uncle Arjun really wanted it.*

They even had a cake, which was even more to Arun's surprise.   It was in the shape of an American flag.

"Are you going to have candles?" Raj asked Uncle Arjun.

Uncle Arjun wasn't amused.   He made a speech before the cake was ceremoniously cut.   "While for most people to whom this is granted they need not work for it," he started, and as he talked he shot a glance at Arun, Sanjay and Raj, "I had to strive for this."

Arun suddenly felt self-conscious and of course, guilty, for quite frankly, being alive.   *What had he done wrong?*   He was born.   That's it.

Arjun went on.   "I set a goal for myself and I worked very hard in that direction to achieve it.   There wasn't much help along the way.   I had to do it mostly on my own."

Arun wasn't sure that he agreed with his uncle's revisionist history.   He thought that there was more to it – that his father had helped him out.   He wasn't quite sure.   Nobody really talked about that time period much.

"I don't remember Uncle Arjun being that arrogant," said Arun to Sanjay.

Sanjay just shrugged his shoulders.

Sara, Arjun's wife, came over to where Rajiv was standing.

"When will you get your citizenship?   How is the paperwork coming along?" she asked.

Rajiv gave her a blank stare.   He walked away.

Sara looked around to see who else was in earshot or watching her.   She threw her hands up in the air when she felt nobody was looking.   Her eyes became as red as Rajiv's had just become.

● ● ●

Later that night, Rajiv called a travel agent.

"How many will be traveling?"

"Maybe it is only being one," Rajiv responded.

"One thousand two hundred twenty eight," said the agent.

Rajiv took note of it and hung up the phone.

Meena immediately picked up the phone to talk to Dipti. Rajiv stood by her.

"What is it?" Meena asked after awhile.

"I…I think I go visiting to India.   I…I going myself," Rajiv stated with some difficulty.

"We discussing later?" Meena asked him.

Rajiv looked at her for a few seconds and walked away.

● ● ●

Later that week, Arun overheard his mother talking with Dipti. She had visited and both were in the kitchen. Arun entered the kitchen to take something from the refrigerator.

"Maybe Rajiv going to India. He say he go himself," Meena mentioned.

"Don't ever let him do that, darling!" Dipti insisted. "If you let him do that he will give even more money to his family! You'd better go and keep an eye on him. All of these husbands are the same."

Meena looked at Arun and their eyes locked. Arun quickly looked away.   At dinner that evening, Arun listened as his mother told his father that he should wait to go to India until at least the two of them could go together.

● ● ●

By the time the prom came around, Arun had already had to do so much sneaking around that he didn't even bother telling his parents about the event.   They had made a point early on of not allowing him to attend any school dances when he had asked. It hadn't affected Arun as much then, because he wasn't involved with Christina at the time.   Hence, for the prom, he was simply, "spending the night at Steven's place." He had to go with Christina's mother to rent his tuxedo.

Arun, Christina, Steven and Rachel returned to Steven's house a little after one in the morning. All the house lights were on. The four were still in a festive mood when they entered.

"Dad, what are you doing up so late?" asked Steven.

Don didn't even greet his son. "Arun? Your father is here."

Arun was shocked. He went into the kitchen. "Dad?"

Rajiv didn't say a word to his son. He passed him while walking and went to the door. He turned around as an afterthought and said to Don, "I am being sorry to disturbing you."

"It's okay. My condolences again."

"What?" asked Arun. "Who died?"

Rajiv exited the door, holding it open for his son to follow.

"Who died?" Arun looked at Don.

"You'd better speak to your father," Don said.

"Dad, Christina needs to be taken home," Arun said.

Don piped up before Rajiv could say anything, "We'll take care of that."

Arun looked at Christina. He mouthed the words 'I'm sorry'. He wanted to embrace her, touch her in some way. But she was too far away and the situation was too difficult for him to do anything. He left the house.

On the car ride home, Rajiv said nothing to his son. Arun asked him again who had died, but when he was met with silence, he kept quiet himself the rest of the way home.

When they finally arrived, Arun asked his mother what was going on. She remained quiet.

Sanjay was still awake. Raj had fallen asleep on the couch.

Arun went to Sanjay. "What happened?"

"*Dadaji* passed away," said Sanjay.   He used the Hindi word for paternal grandfather.   His tone was one of disgust, almost revulsion, towards Arun.

He felt silly standing there in his tuxedo, amongst all of his family members, feeling so distant from all of them.

Arun thought about his grandfather.   He had never met him.   He had seen an old photo of him.   He had no idea what he was like, what the sound of his voice was, how he smelled.   It then dawned on him.   He didn't even know his name.

CHAPTER SEVEN

———

April 2007

Anjali made her way back to her sister's place. When she entered the house, she immediately caught sight of Nandini. Both of their eyes grew big when they saw each other. There was a pure joy that each felt relishing the other's company. Zubin was busy playing a handheld video game.

At the time, Radha was busy finalizing dinner in the kitchen. They greeted each other through the walls, Anjali not wanting to be distracted from playing with the kids.

As Anjali sat down on the couch next to Zubin, Nandini stood up and began dancing like a ballerina to the music she heard from the television. Anjali showed how moved she was by placing her hands over her mouth in awe.

"Radha, you have to see this!" Anjali shouted.

Nandini continued.

"Radha!" Anjali tried again. Anjali heard a thump from the kitchen accompanied with the sound of shattering glass. She went in. There she saw Radha bent over the floor cleaning up a broken jar of tomato sauce.

"Didn't you hear me?" challenged Anjali, as she bent down to assist her sister.

"Wh…What?" asked Radha, her voice betraying tremendous strain. She never looked up at Anjali.

Anjali caught a glimpse of her face streaked with tears, her bloodshot eyes, and puffy eyelids. "What's wrong?" asked Anjali, her tone softening a bit.

Anjali held Radha's wrist when Radha didn't stop moving about. "What's wrong?" she asked again in an even softer tone. This time she sounded as if she was pleading with her sister.

Arun entered the room. He noticed the scene on the floor. "Hello Angel," he said.

Anjali kept her gaze on Radha who remained quiet while standing up. "Hi Arun," offered Anjali. She was gravely concerned.

Later that night, Anjali accosted Arun, "Did Radha catch you cheating? I thought you weren't going to do that."

"No, Angel. It's not like that."

Anjali wasn't convinced. She remembered that woman Meenakshi. She was troubled for her sister. She wanted to know what was going on.

● ● ●

Radha was really eager to share her woes with Anjali. It was hard for her to suffer through it alone. Radha thought about how Arun had used Anjali's nickname while they were in the kitchen. She wondered why he had done that, it had been ages since he had. It had been a long time since Radha had used it as well. Before she had started school, Anjali had come to be affectionately regularly known as Angel. It was a moniker that was used frequently when she was young by everyone with whom she interacted. As she matured, she liked it less and less when non-family members called her that. When she entered secondary school, Anjali had announced to the family that no one in school could call her anything but Anjali. It took her two years to put her friends through detox, as their natural inclination was to refer to her with her customary nickname.

A PERMANENT EXILE

Radha knew how the name came about; it was from their mother. Parvati had grown up with a fairly typical life for a prominent politician's daughter – she was privileged and sheltered. Parvati had been well educated, spoke well and had been trained in all social graces. She was most famously known for her love of literature. She had developed an early fascination with it and devoured as many books as she could find. In university she studied English Literature and, to Radha's grandfather's surprise, completed a Master's Degree in the same three years it took her to get her Bachelor's Degree. Unfortunately, Parvati had to demurely decline her professors' encouragement that she pursue a Ph.D. and teach at the university. It just wasn't appropriate for a young lady of her upbringing.

Radha reflected on how beautiful her mother was now and how stunning she must have looked while younger. She thought about her mother's lean figure compared to most women her age, her firm command of English, and how sweet her mother's voice was. It always seemed to bubble over with an enthusiasm and caring. Radha began to miss the softness of her mother's eyes. For Radha, her mother seemed to impart an equal amount of caring from her voice and her eyes.

Parvati's favorite author was E.M. Forster. "One of the first popular multi-cultural novels was *A Passage to India*," she always commented. Radha suspected that her mother gave Anjali the nickname "Angel" because of Forster's first novel, *Where Angels Fear to Tread*. Radha later commented that her mother knew Anjali's fearless nature, so the title was ironic. Perhaps she even sensed that Anjali would fall in love with and marry someone not of her background, a non-Indian. Radha would later come to know that Forster's title was derived from Alexander Pope's "An Essay on Criticism", source of the oft-quoted "For fools rush in where angels fear to tread." *Mum knew Anjali would be wise.*

As the eldest daughter, Radha showed a great deal of maturity at a young age. She was always the one to reconcile her parents when they fought. She developed a keen understanding of how relationships worked based on that. This also contributed to her fostering, nurturing nature. She could tell that when her father got angry, he would begin to speak less rationally. The seeming cause of his anger would not fit the degree to which he would get angry. When her mother further tried to rationalize away his anger, he would get even more agitated. To Radha, her father always seemed upset about something else and not what he actually said he was upset about.

Growing up, Radha kept herself busy with reading, dancing and music lessons and helping her mother with the younger girls, Pooja and Anjali. She became steeped in literature and the arts. In fact, literature was the common bond among the three girls. When they were all of the appropriate age, Parvati would do a "book club" with the girls. They would all read the same book and discuss it around the table. At the time, B.P. would mumble, "Thank god they have something to keep them busy." The girls grew up largely detached from their father. During dance and music recitals they would always ask – *Where is Papa?*

The Bhardpuri kids were surrounded by a large Indian and English community. Radha became well versed in Hindi, speaking it at home and with her family's social circle. It was easy for them to hold onto their Indian traditions – in a modified English setting. India was also only about eight hours away by flight. This afforded the Bhardpuri family frequent visits to India during the summer, although it was mostly Radha, her sisters and mother. Parvati was also a strong advocate of the trips. This empowered the Bhardpuri girls in their ability to learn and comfortably converse in Hindi.

Radha drew a wealth of experience while growing up from those visits to India.   She, like her mother, was only ever exposed to a privileged life in the UK.   Her opportunity to witness some diversity came while she was in India, but only in particular arenas. Radha found that her mother was more overbearing in certain regards when they were in India; in the blistering heat, Radha wanted to wear her shorts, but her mother wouldn't let her. Anjali had been the worst at adjusting.   She would cry vociferously and fight voraciously with Parvati over restrictions on clothing.   The only one who felt comfortable in those more constricted surroundings was Pooja.

However, Parvati couldn't control the poverty that Radha witnessed at her grandmother's orphanage or the stories of hardship that she heard.   Radha wondered if this was by design as Parvati would encourage all three daughters to spend time at the facility.   While Radha enjoyed going to the orphanage, Pooja relished it, and over time Anjali resented it.   Their grandmother seemed to always take a keener interest in Pooja over Radha and Anjali.   Although her grandmother had chosen Radha as the one to whom she divulged stories about Radha's father, Radha had to admit that she did get jealous with the doting that Pooja would receive.   While Radha learned to tolerate it, Anjali became indignant.   This unfortunately fueled backlash from their grandmother.   Anjali refused to go to the orphanage after age fourteen, when her grandmother said she was spoiled and ungrateful.   Pooja did nothing to defend Anjali; it was Radha who consoled her and brought her home to Parvati.

Radha kept her resentment in check largely because her grandmother was the key to Radha understanding her father. Radha's father had always been a portly man.   He had short hair, mostly grey and maintained a moustache.   He wore round wire-rimmed glasses.   His eyes were small and set back a little. He seemed to carry most of his body weight in his large chipmunk-like cheeks; they protruded in a way that made his eyes seem even more sunken. Radha remembered when Anjali had asked him if he had any food tucked away in there; Radha remembered thinking at the time that he could easily have accommodated a mandarin orange on each side.

Radha had been keyed in to her father's aloofness at an early age. Through her grandmother, Radha learned that it was merely a product of his upbringing. She had heard all the stories: how generations of her father's family had become lawyers and then politicians in India, about her father's time at Cambridge, his competitiveness with his five older brothers, his desire to stay on in the UK because he had declared that there wasn't enough room for him to flourish in India.

"He was always so jealous of the attention going to his older brothers," Radha's grandmother told her. "He tried to be better than them. When told to play, he would fight back 'I don't want to bloody play. I'm going to go read Dickens. Did you hear that? *Sharless Dickens* I'm going to go read! My two-bit brothers can't read Dickens and they are at least four bloody years older than me.'" Radha's grandmother would lift her upper body in a haughty manner as she imitated her son. Radha liked how her grandmother would laugh in re-counting these stories.

"He was glorious to be with when he won and got his way, but a retch when he lost. He would become depressive and gloomy. He started to kick things and sulk. When anyone asked him anything he would snap, "I don't know." He would maintain this very maudlin mood for hours. So when he announced his decision to stay on in the UK in order to start a legal practice there, I was the only one who was sad. I think the others were happy to be rid of him." Radha's grandmother looked off in the distance and her voice trailed a bit as she finished this last sentence.

"He had no one to talk to about his plans, so he chose the house servant's son. He didn't know it, but I overheard him. I have forgotten exactly what he said, but it was something like this, 'You see, ol' boy, things are too crowded at home, and I want to make a name for myself on my own. I'm smarter than this bloody lot, I am. I'm smarter than my father and my brothers, so it is my divine right to pursue a more glamorous path. You see, I can become a proper bloody Englishman. Not these chaps! You see that, don't you? Don't you?'" By now, Radha's grandmother was laughing heartily. She attempted to continue, "In all his years there, he never noticed that the boy didn't speak English!" Radha laughed until her stomach hurt when she heard this. She could imagine her father doing that.

"At Cambridge they called him BP, because Kishan Bhardpuri was too much for those English boys. Thanks to his rival S.K., he married your mother."

"Oh," Radha had said at the time she heard it.

"S.K., Shiva Krishnamurthy, I believe, was supposed to marry your mother. In order to spite his nemesis, your father came back to India and demanded to marry your mother. The wedding was very grand. There were eighty-four vegetarian dishes served."

Radha didn't clearly hear the last two sentences. She had begun to feel a little sad to hear about how it transpired. She was hoping it would have been more romantic. And then she remembered how her father had become an MP. She was a young girl at the time her parents had thrown a cocktail party and she saw her father get into a debate on politics with his colleagues. Her father began a row about how Indian politicians were better than British politicians because Indian politicians could be more conniving. What helped his point the most was the fact that he was in an audience of English people who had grown up in Britain and were too young to have been affiliated with the British Raj, let alone Indian politicians.

B.P.'s partner, yet long-time rival, Edgar Moore, concocted the only retort he could come up with at the time. "Your comment is useless B.P.; while we ruled over India effectively, no Asian would ever be effective in governing here in Britain," declared Edgar, plainly.

After that incident, B.P. decided to accept his partner's affront as a challenge. When he had become an MP, Radha was sad to think that her father had to be motivated by others in this fashion and didn't do it because he wanted it for himself.

Radha also learned in those conversations with her grandmother that her father was always disappointed that he never had a boy. Radha had always sensed that from him. His distance finally made sense to her.

● ● ●

Anjali carried her strong sense of independence through to her selection of university. Naturally, the girls were educated at the best schools and each passed their A-levels with comfortable ease. Neither Parvati nor B.P. were keen on sending their daughters to a dormitory, so Radha, as the oldest, was limited to her choice of University. She had to stay in the London area. She gained admission at King's College at the University of London. She would take a train and tube combo to class everyday.

To Anjali's benefit, B.P. and Parvati became more lenient with each progressive daughter. Pooja was allowed to study in a different city at the University of Edinburgh and allowed to stay in the dorm there. When it came to Anjali, rather than stay in the UK for her studies, she headed for the US. She applied to all of the top schools and was admitted into Princeton. She had to go through the rigors of the US application system, including taking SATs and Achievement Tests. While Radha and Pooja had followed in their mother's footsteps and opted for English Literature, Anjali decided to major in Philosophy. She had to do some campaigning with her father for him to accept her going to Princeton. It wasn't lost on her that she needed to grovel for her tuition expense.

Anjali was an aggressive student who took her studies very seriously. She worked towards being a lawyer like the leading males of her family. Her father gave her grief for wanting to come to the US to study rather than stay in the UK, but she knew that she needed to come out from under her father's shadow and make a mark of her own. She knew it would take her more years to achieve the same result.

"You left India when it became too crowded," she insisted with her father.

"Where is it crowded here? I'm not interested in sending you abroad for your studies. And of all places, America. You can get a first rate education right here," B.P. proclaimed.

"I am going, Father. Whether you agree with it or not," Anjali said with determination.

"Oh bother," responded B.P.

At Princeton she made many friends and had a very active social life. She was involved in various clubs and activities. She also debated regularly with her classmates and professors. In one of her political philosophy classes she engaged in a debate in support of David Hume over John Stuart Mill. Her adversary in the discussion was a fellow named Matthew Ashton. "I can't agree with what you are saying," she protested in class.

He smiled back at her.

It had disarmed her a bit. At the end of the class, she went to him. It helped that he was very handsome to look at. "You do, however, have a sound basis for what you are saying."

"Would you like to have a coffee?" asked Matthew.

"Sure," said Anjali with a smile on her face.

Matthew was an English major with a keen love of movies. Anjali had always been interested as a casual consumer of film, but had never seen movies from an analytical point of view the way she did with Matthew. She felt her first romantic inclination towards him when he rented the movie *Where Angels Fear to Tread* and asked her if that was her namesake. During the next several months, they were in each other's company frequently. Unbeknownst to Anjali's parents, they were practically living together. After they both graduated, they had to decide whether or not to stay as a couple. They chose to get married.

Anjali moved to LA to be with Matthew, who wanted to become a screenwriter. Anjali knew she was attracted to him because of his creative talent. Anjali decided that practicing law wouldn't be engaging enough for her. She joined a management consulting firm instead. Radha expressed her understanding for Anjali's choice in marrying Matthew. Parvati was a little hesitant in her reaction, more so than Anjali wanted her to be, but she eventually came to terms with it and Anjali could tell her mother was happy for her. Her father never commented on it, much to Anjali's disappointment.

● ● ●

Anjali had gotten married while Radha was expecting Nandini. As a result, because of their proximity distance-wise, Anjali was able to experience Nandini growing up and the early years of Nandini's life intimately.

After her divorce, Anjali moved in to live with Arun and Radha for awhile. Nandini was excited to have someone who gave her so much attention. She found her own place after a month, but had grown accustomed to spending a lot of time at their house.

"How come Mommy married Daddy and you married someone white?" asked Nandini.

Anjali was surprised. She hadn't been expecting the question.

"Well, Nandini, when you are older I can explain it better. When Mommy chose Daddy, she found someone who was similar to her and had the same ideas about the future and having a life together. I did the same thing. Where they are from originally doesn't matter. What is important is the understanding. You see, your Daddy's Uncle Arjun also married someone white," Anjali explained.

Nandini leaned in closer to her aunt.

"I don't think you like her," Nandini whispered, directing her comment towards Anjali's ear.

"You are too keen," Anjali laughed as she held Nandini.

• • •

Arun watched his daughter and his sister-in-law interact. Arun was happy for Nandini, that she had someone of Anjali's intellect and perception around to learn from. Arun found himself thinking that he would be really pleased if Nandini turned out like Anjali.

"So how come you are home all the time?" asked Anjali. Arun's focus had been on Nandini. He turned to look at Anjali. *She must have noticed me standing here for awhile*, thought Arun. It first registered for him that she was speaking to him and then he thought about what she had asked. Her question woke him from his dream state. Arun felt like he had been caught. His attempts to keep the incident from Anjali were proving challenging.

"I'm just on extended leave," Arun offered. His eyes found Radha's as she entered the room.

"Oh," said Anjali.

Arun was certain that she was not convinced. Arun approached Radha later. "Do you think she knows?" he asked Radha.

"I didn't tell her, but I don't see the sense in hiding it from her." Radha attempted to plead her case.

"No, no, no. I don't feel like we should tell anyone, Radha," Arun persisted.

"Don't you think she could be helpful? At least I would have someone to talk to," Radha continued. She placed her arm over her round stomach.

"It hasn't been my experience that family is helpful. You have me to talk to," Arun declared as he looked at her coldly. His gaze went down momentarily and he was cognizant of the message his wife was attempting to send him. It wouldn't change his mind.

"What about the time that Pooja…"

"I don't want to talk about her." Arun hated how he seemed insensitive. He had felt horrible for his wife at the time of the tragedy. He remembered crying a lot at the time.

"So we will just try to keep this a secret forever?" Radha asked him.

Arun sensed that Radha was growing exasperated. He took her comment the wrong way, as if it were a challenge for him. "Yes," said Arun sternly. He instantly regretted it.

Radha sighed and walked away.

● ● ●

Radha was really longing for the comfort of her family and was feeling increasingly more frustrated with her inability to convince Arun. Radha thought back to the time that Anjali showed up at their house a few months ago. Radha greeted her at the door. "Wow, what a surprise," said Radha cheerfully. Seeing her sister's bloodshot eyes, Radha's expression changed to one of concern. "What's wrong?"

"Matthew and I are no longer together."

"Oh my God," Radha said as she hugged Anjali. She deliberately held her embrace for several moments. Radha brought Anjali into the family room.

Arun entered. "You don't look so good, Angel," he said to Anjali.

"No, I'm not." Tears began to roll down her face.

"I am leaving Matthew," Anjali said. Her voice was suddenly more firm. "We are growing apart. It is no longer healthy for us to be together. We can't support each other the way that we used to be able to do. I just feel that he is so focused on himself. He is always writing and never makes any time for me."

"You are leaving him?" Radha asked.

"Yes. Why do you ask it that way?" Anjali began getting defensive.

"Oh, it's not that. It's just that you are crying, so I thought maybe he was leaving you," explained Radha.

"No," Anjali said, "I'm crying because I don't know how to tell Dad."

Radha reflected on this. Their father had boycotted the wedding. It was a Christian wedding. Anjali was to be given away by him but instead chose to walk down the aisle alone. It seemed odd to Radha that for as advanced as her sister was in her thinking, both emotionally and mentally, some basic fears from childhood still troubled her. It seemed that the earlier one starts walking down a street of trauma, the harder it is to veer away from it as one gets older.

"You know Mum will help you with that," said Radha.

Suddenly Anjali's face brightened slightly. "You are right. I was so worried about how disappointed Dad will be and I forgot about how wonderful Mum is."

Radha awoke from her thoughts and wondered if she continued to put effort towards it, whether she could convince

Arun of the virtues of sharing with family. Radha knew she would benefit tremendously from the support of Anjali and her mother right now. Radha lamented that she couldn't do anything more to help her sister Pooja. She understood all too keenly the dangers of keeping problems locked inside.

Not only had the way Radha's parents had come together been unromantic, it was detrimental to her sister Pooja. Three years prior to Anjali getting married, Pooja had her wedding and got settled in India. Her husband, Sandeep Chawla, had provided her with a comfortable life there. Never really asking for much, Pooja fell into the existence gracefully. She enjoyed her style of living and the things she was doing. "My life is complete," she would chirp in the phone to Radha.

After Pooja had been in India for months, Parvati called Radha, a bit frantic. "I haven't heard from Pooja in days," she cried. Radha was able to get a hold of Sandeep while he was on a business trip. He went rushing home, only to find Pooja hanging from a ceiling fan with a rope about her neck, the life gone from her.

The autopsy reports revealed the news that she was carrying a baby. Sandeep did the math; he had been traveling extensively, often for two months at a time.

"Your sister was a whore!" he yelled at Anjali when the family arrived.

"You don't know our sister. Look at the bruises on her body. She was raped," declared Anjali. Anjali stood in between Radha and Parvati. BP stood at the far end. The three women embraced. They stayed in close proximity to each other for the entire time of the funeral and after leaving India together. They knew, they understood, they lived the fact that each would be a part of the other's wellspring of hope and support to pull through this time.

In the days and weeks following Pooja's suicide, Radha learned several disturbing facts. Pooja had not been Parvati's daughter. She was the result of an affair that B.P. had had with his secretary. The reasons why she didn't look like Radha or Anjali became clear. Radha appreciated her mother so much more from that day forward. Her strength and composure were awe-inspiring. Radha heard about how Pooja's biological mother, Indra, came to their house while expecting, and how her father had demanded of her mother, "What are your plans?" Radha's mother had gracefully agreed to pay for the birth of the baby and finance Indra's return home to India. Parvati also helped her in obtaining employment there. Radha felt pain in her heart the most when she learned that Indra's husband Vikram had been the one to violate Pooja.

For weeks the family couldn't understand how Vikram came to know about Pooja and her presence in India. Sandeep himself provided the final clues. Sandeep's boss at his law firm was B.P.'s former rival, S.K. S.K. had been the one to bring Pooja's presence in India to Vikram's attention, exacting revenge on B.P. for marrying Parvati. Radha felt that her mother must have been relieved to not end up with a man as brutish as S.K.; however, Radha wasn't sure that her father was a significant improvement. Radha wondered why her mother stayed with her father. Radha could then see why her mother was able to be more assertive with her father, but she couldn't comprehend her father's continued arrogance.

CHAPTER EIGHT

September 1985 – May 1989

As Arun began to think about a career choice, he grew perplexed. He was not sure what he should pursue. He found what his uncle did interesting but he could never get him to talk about it enough. His father was insistent on him pursuing the sciences and it felt at times that it was futile to argue with him about that. Arun also wanted something that would create a stir or would impress people – he liked the attention he got from people being excessively laudatory over his achievements. He liked the fame; he enjoyed it when people would speak highly of him. Debate had given him a great taste of that. He found that Indian families would be particularly vocal when praising academic success; he wondered if it was true for all immigrants. American families would celebrate athletic, musical and artistic talent, emotional development and social presence. For Indians, where he seemed to have his widest audience, it was all about academics. Arun liked that. He was a master in that domain. He wanted his string of successes, and the praise that came with it, to go on as long as possible – in many ways he found it addictive. The only hindrance to his efforts was when Sanjay would eventually outdo him. With every new endeavor, Arun felt that he had to achieve enough where his brother could not touch him. As he thought about all of these issues as it related to his future, feeling like he was stuck in a roundabout with a half dozen streets feeding into it, he realized what he had to do to maximize his fame – he needed to become a doctor.

Dipti would always stress the importance of being a doctor to Meena. She always claimed to Meena that medicine was the most respected profession. But he knew what their motivation was. It was the mantra born out of the immigrant manifesto: wealth and security.

Who could really blame them? realized Arun. Revolutions were mostly started by the middle-class – those not desiring to have a worse lot in life. Immigrants were the same; the wealthy didn't leave their well-to-do situations in life to embark out into the unknown. Immigrants did it so that they didn't slide backwards and lose their status. The safest path to wealth creation for immigrants was through education.

Rajiv exhibited pleasure at Arun's decision. Arun thought he would; it was in the sciences. Arun overheard Rajiv describing it for the family back home and others in the community. When his father experienced resounding support and enthusiasm for Arun's career choice, Arun noticed that Rajiv provided a more excited endorsement. "Medicine is being the most *press-tea-just* profession. It is being top of sciences. Most important is you going to best school," said Rajiv, complementing his comments with a head waggle.

"Thanks be to the God," said Meena when Arun informed her about the direction he had chosen. Arun overheard her later suggesting to Dipti that Arun had decided on this because it was his mother's wish. "Oh yes, everyone looking up to us...uh...you..., isn't it?" added Meena to Arun. She clapped her hands like a little child.

Arun learned that he had been accepted to the University of Pennsylvania and he was elated. He brought the news to his parents, expecting them to be overjoyed as well. Initially they seemed pleased. "It is being the same university as my the boss's son, Thomas," Rajiv had commented with seeming satisfaction. After Arun came home from school the next day, they seemed less so. Arun sensed that the lukewarm response was a result of Meena speaking with Dipti.

"Well, it's not like it's Harvard" he could imagine her saying, which is where both of her sons had gone. For Arun, it was like falling off a cliff. He felt remarkably dejected.

• • •

"Please, you telling me about your family," encouraged Rajiv. "I am wanting to know more about you."

Rajiv had invited Pablo to an Indian restaurant for lunch. He wanted to expose Pablo to traditional Indian food.

"Oh, *señor*, my family comes from Mexico. My father came here when I was a young boy. The two of us started a landscaping business. Then I saved enough money to buy a nursery. My father was real proud of me that day, you know."

Rajiv felt a sense of calm in hearing his friend speak. There was a rhythm to his talking, like being in a swing going back and forth gently, that Rajiv found pleasurable. "It is being so nice. Father and son working together. Such nice work. It making you being very happy."

"Well…times, they were tough, you know. We couldn't always make ends meet. My father wanted to bring my *abuela*, er, grandmother, to the US, but we couldn't save enough money. She died waiting to come here."

"I am seeing that family is being very important in your culture. It is being same for us. Family is being the center. For elders we are giving much respect."

Rajiv took the basket of *naan* from the table and presented it to Pablo. "Please, you having another piece."

"Thanks so much. These taste a lot like our *tortillas*, you know."

"What is that being? It is a kind of your food?" asked Rajiv.

Pablo smiled. "I will share with you my food next time we are together, *señor*."

Rajiv looked up from his meal. They both shared a smile together.

"What were we talking about? Oh, yes, *señor*, ain't nothin' more important than family, you know," proclaimed Pablo.

"Are you having any children?"

"Yes, I have myself one daughter. Aren't children the best thing in the world?"

Rajiv managed to smile. He became deep in thought.

● ● ●

During Arun's first year of college, he thrived in his new environment socially. The world that he had been exposed to prior to university was such a small microcosm. He entered this universe that had so many more people than he was accustomed to interacting with; he found it all very wonderful. Arun and Christina parted ways after they started their respective colleges. It was a gradual parting, but one which they both sensed was inevitable. They were attending different colleges and were aware that they would be meeting new groups of people. It didn't make sense for either of them to be left yearning for the other far away at this stage of their lives. Arun had wished he had come to that realization; he had to acquiesce to Christina's more mature thinking. Part of him was sad to be losing his intimate relationship with her.

After his courtship with Christina, Arun felt emboldened. He was more aggressive in his pursuit of women he found interesting. He liked the rush and giddiness that he felt when he was receiving positive reinforcement for his advances. He hated the opposite. He wanted to bury himself and never show his face again. He always came back to the notion of whether or not it was based on race.   He felt at times that his character was secondary and that troubled him a great deal.

For the first time, he was surrounded by several women of Indian origin.   He thought that it might be the solution, that there would be a natural kinship.   However, he had a string of negative experiences and chose to avoid them.   It turned out that there was just too much confusion, too many questions.   His head would often hurt, because neither would really know just how Indian or how Western they should be.   His own insecurities and uncertainties about identity would come into sharp focus.   He much preferred sprinting down that dark alleyway.   It wasn't much fun being one of two blindfolded castaways washed ashore, stranded on a dark beach, attempting to avoid drowning in the water.

Unfortunately, Arun struggled academically.   He was no longer one of the top few in his class.   All of the people around him were as capable, if not more capable, than he was.   He felt out of place; he had lost his identity.   Arun had taken for granted that he had excelled in every aspect of the sciences prior to college. Everything had come easy for him because his prior pursuits were largely superficial.   There was nothing in-depth or intense about them.   As he worked toward something with such an extreme level of detail, he realized that he didn't like the sciences as much as he thought.   He also realized that he couldn't fake it.   He was constantly unhappy; this was not what made him passionate.   He couldn't see himself doing this for the rest of his life.   This dilemma gave Arun a great deal of anxiety.   It would keep him up at night.   He had this sickening sense of fear.   It wasn't a street he wanted to go down.   However, he had reached a point where he couldn't avoid it.   He struggled to hold his life together.   His grades on exams went from mediocre to abysmal.

He was at the intersection of torment and crisis.   He didn't know what he was really interested in; he didn't know what he was moved by. His father could not understand it and simply yelled at him over the phone when Arun admitted that he was struggling. The most impactful comment he made was when Arun went home for fall break and in front of him, his father turned to Sanjay and said, "Don't being like your brother." Arun found it painful and humiliating. Sanjay just walked away.

Arun found it challenging to cope with his emotions. He tried to seek comfort. He became involved in a string of vacuous relationships with the most promiscuous women he could find on campus. It provided him with an alluring sense of validation, until he saw these women with other men.

Arun struggled to find some direction. He tried talking to professors. He tried observing friends to see what they were doing, see if they were enjoying themselves, in the hopes that it might trigger something in him. He felt like he was drowning. He had reached a dead end and there was nothing left but a precipice over water. The world was moving on without him, and he was not able to participate. The airplane had taken off and he didn't have a seat assigned. He had no idea how or where he fit in. *What am I supposed to do?*

As he was walking about campus, lost in his thoughts, he heard a voice from behind him.

"Hey, Arun, right?"

Arun swerved around to face Thomas, the son of Sam Harding, the owner of the company where his father worked. It was the first time Arun saw him on campus. They last saw each other the summer before they started college. "Yes," replied Arun. "How are you Thomas?"

"Things are going great. I just aced my finance mid-term."

Arun looked at Thomas. He wasn't gloating, but there was a sense of pride coming through in his voice and his posturing that seemed born from purpose, drive and initiative.

"Congrats.　That's great," Arun thought to say.

"How are things with you?"

"Fine," Arun responded.　He was desperate to tell him the truth, to learn about what secret Thomas seemed to possess to understand how to be happy himself.　However, he just stood there quietly, somewhat lost as he looked around.

"Okay, catch you later," Thomas said as he walked away.

"Bye," called out Arun.　He felt in need of a life jacket.

● ● ●

Arun knew that Sanjay would begin applying to colleges while Arun was in his first-year.　Arun had tucked away all of his application materials in the basement.　When he came home over Thanksgiving, he saw the box in his old room.　Sanjay had commandeered both the space and the documents for himself.

"You really scoured through all of my applications," Arun said to Sanjay as they were sitting down to dinner.

"Oh…yeah," said Sanjay in a desultory manner.　He went back to looking at and eating his food.

"How are your apps coming along?"

"Okay.　It's a lot of work."

"Yeah, I remember it being a pain in the butt.　Especially all of the essays," recalled Arun.　"Do you want some help with those?" asked Arun.

Sanjay looked up from his food and said, in a rare show of enthusiasm, "Yes."

Arun spent the rest of his weekend helping Sanjay on his college essays.　He felt proud to be able to help his younger brother out.　"I get to show you the ropes," Arun said to his brother.

Sanjay managed a slight smile which he held briefly.

Where else would he go for this? thought Arun.　*Dad never went through this here and Uncle Arjun went through it so many years ago that he probably doesn't even remember it.   I wish there had been someone to help me out.*

On Sunday night, the night before Arun went back to school, the family was all seated at the dinner table.   "Sanjay," said Arun, "let me know when you get to the Penn application.   I don't think they changed it much from last year."

Sanjay stayed silent.

"You should also let me know when you want to come and visit me," said Arun, "I can show you around."

"Oh…okay," said Sanjay, finally.

"I thought you said you weren't going to go to Arun's school," said Raj.

Arun looked at Sanjay, who was still looking down.   "Is that true?" asked Arun.

"Yeah…kind of," said Sanjay.

"Look, Sanjay, it either is or it isn't," said Arun, his tone becoming more aggressive.

Sanjay stayed quiet.

"How come you don't want to apply to my school?" asked Arun, "I'm a little hurt by that.   What's up?"

Sanjay remained quiet.

"Other than Harvard and Yale that we worked on this weekend, where else are you applying?"

"Princeton, Dartmouth, Brown, Columbia and Cornell."

"Every Ivy but mine."   Arun turned to his parents. "Don't you think Sanjay should apply to my school?" he asked.

Neither said a word.   After several minutes passed, Meena finally spoke up, "Sanjay?"

"Yes, Mom?"

Arun waited with interest to hear what his mother was going to say.

"Take plate into kitchen and cut more the turkey."

• • •

Rajiv went to see Pablo again.

"*Señor*, last time I tell you why I come to this country. I wanna hear why you came."

Rajiv was dipping another chip into the salsa. "You are liking spicy food. Is being the same for us," he mentioned.

Pablo was silent for awhile. It felt like a heavy burden for Rajiv. He started to talk, "My brother, he coming here before me. He telling family how nice is being here. My wife having baby then."

"Oh, so you came when Meena was pregnant?"

"Yes. My brother saying my child being American citizen. My uncle getting very excited this news."

"How about your father, *señor*, did he say anything?"

"No, my father being quiet. He only nodding his head."

"So you were living on the farm at the time?"

"No, before times, my uncle sending me to city to studying and working. I very sad. Before I enjoying very much being in fields. One time, I getting injury. I riding tractor, worker not there, I wanting finish soon. I liking go with my uncle to selling sugar cane at the trading market. I never riding tractor before. I hitting the rock in the field. The tractor flipping over and one blades coming down and cutting my arm. I no can seeing. Everything white, white. I not moving. My father's cousin, his name Lakshant, he and workers carrying me to house. There I waking up, can seeing again. Doctor sitting there. He say if blade cutting bone, I losing arm, if reach here," Rajiv pointed to his torso, "I finish."

"Wow, *señor*. *Que suerte*. You are lucky to be alive!"

"The next morning, I going back to the fields."

"*Increìble*. That's incredible."

Rajiv observed the mesmerized look in his friend's face. It made him smile.

"Why do you like farming so much, *señor*?"

"I being oldest of six childrens. My father also eldest. There being big family. I eldest, I must take care."

"But that doesn't mean you run back to the fields the next morning. No, *señor*, there is something else there. *Es tú pasión.* It must be your passion."

Rajiv found himself smiling. He liked the time he spent with his friend.

"You are being right. Some days I not going to the school. I staying in the fields with workers. Also, once I getting telegram after uncle sending me to working in the city. It saying 'come home immediately'. I so exciting, I quitting my job and bringing all of my things home. I coming home very happy. My uncle starting beating me. He say I coming home only for marrying. Hearing this, I get exciting again, I asking 'I staying with my wife and working farm?'"

Pablo complemented Rajiv's chuckling with laughter of his own.

"He getting more angry, beating me more and more." Rajiv became more animated as he spoke, beginning to use a sweeping motion of his hands to emphasize his point. "He seeing me smiling, he getting more angrier. He calling me *'insulin'* bastard. I thinking – why he talking about the diabetes? Later I understanding what 'insolent' is meaning. He tell me I going back to the city to earning money and sending home."

Rajiv saw his friend take a napkin from the table and dab his eyes as he continued to laugh. "My sides are hurting, *señor,*" exclaimed Pablo.

After a few minutes had passed, Pablo asked, "But you haven't explained to me why you love it so much."

Rajiv became thoughtful. "The Earth, it always being giving something back. I working the soil, providing food and water. The earth, it repaying me with its fruits. Is like being an equation. It always being the same, always giving me something.

It never betraying me." Rajiv stalled for a few seconds. He could feel his eyes becoming watery. He tried his best to prevent it from happening. "The Earth is being so different than family."

• • •

Rajiv continued to progress in his career. He enjoyed enough the job that he did. He had reached the highest levels of his capability by being the most senior mid-level manager. He didn't mind having people report to him; he was accustomed to his younger brothers or his children seeking advice and direction from him. But he also liked having someone to validate or prove out correct what he was doing. He would have headhunters call him about higher-level positions to be in senior management, but that always seemed too risky for him. He liked the idea of having more pay to send home, but he was nervous about things not going well and leaving for a firm that had not become established.

Contact with India was frequent for Rajiv, but interaction with people from there in person was minimal. One day he received a telegram from someone who claimed to be a cousin and said he'd be arriving the following week. Rajiv checked with his uncle, who confirmed that he had given the man Rajiv's details.

"What I doing when he coming?" asked Rajiv of his uncle.

"He family. You taking care him while he there."

• • •

Arun met the relative from India, Prem, during his summer in between his first and second years of college. Prem was a portly man and stood 5' 5" tall. He had a round face, dark skin and a moustache. He had an expression on his face where he seemed to always be smiling. He was in his mid-thirties. He had a wife and four kids, who of course did not travel with him. Somehow, Arjun managed to avoid having Prem stay with him. Arun had many awkward conversations with the visitor.

"You are beary lucky, isn't it?" asked Prem.

"Lucky about what?" Arun asked in polite earnest. Arun knew better than to be rude to an elder, especially family.

"Your fadher. Very much money. Big house. My fadher. No much money. No big house. You beary lucky." Prem said. He aspirated and emphasized this second-to-last word heavily. His eyes opened as he said it and his hand gyrated up and down as if he were pleading with Arun.

Arun wondered how lucky he was. He recalled how much of an outsider he felt like in this country. He remembered the kids hurling racial insults. He could picture them now, chanting away their racist slogans: "Dot!" "Indians Stink!" "Go back to your country!" Fighting back the tears while hearing this was hard for Arun. He intuitively knew that crying would give them the satisfaction they wanted – so he didn't do it. Why was it that people were so intent on breaking others? How did they learn that at such a young age? Steven would later explain to him that it was because they were so miserable with their own lot in life that they had to take it out on others. At one point when being tormented by a line of boys, Arun noticed Peter. His family was from China. Arun found it odd that one minority would hate another. And then he understood – you did anything to be a part of the majority – to be accepted by them. *How he wished he were standing where Peter was standing.* He noticed that Peter only repeated the slogans that the white boys chanted: he looked at them, seeking their approval as he chanted – pleading, ever seeking the re-affirmation, "See, I'm just like one of you! Right?"

The worst was when it wasn't a member of another minority, but a member of his own race. It had happened to him once. There were a group of white boys and an Indian who was trying his best to be just like them. He was hurling insults. Arun never understood why no one saw the irony in that situation. Or maybe it was too sad to comment on.

Arun had tended to be more comfortable around other minorities – he found that in the mix, people either became indifferent to the difference or they celebrated it – *let's all be different together* became the mantra. He would look the white Americans in the eyes and wonder – *are you going to hate me because of the way I look? Has someone from my race upset you? Did they not understand what you were saying? Did they have an incomprehensible accent? Did they smell bad? Did they not dress like you? Did they prance around in their traditional clothing in a way that was offensive to you? Did they not assimilate enough? Did they not let your kids play with theirs? Did they not greet you when they passed by? Did they pack too many in the house next door and not properly tend to the lawn? Did they decrease your property value? DID THEY MAKE YOU UNCOMFORTABLE?* I'm sorry. I'm really, really sorry. I'm not like them – honest. *I'm like you – really. I dress like you, I talk like you and I smell like you.* He would look for clues – *are you looking me in the eye, are you smiling, is your tone friendly? Defensive? Hostile?*

On the flip side, he could barely understand this guy talking to him from his own country. Listening to him in Hindi was even more painful. And when Arun himself attempted Hindi, without fail, by the second word, he could see the corners of the mouth go up, the formation of a jeer from the person listening to him. How he wished people wouldn't laugh at him when he spoke. He knew it was not that different when he had a sensation of laughter come over him to hear Prem emphasize the word "beary". *Why,* Arun would wonder, *can't these people get it right?* The difference for Arun was that he knew not to make Prem feel uncomfortable. It was offensive how he was never afforded the same courtesy.

Where do I fit in? He felt like he was becoming a member of a burgeoning sub-culture of the dispossessed. No place was home. He was a vagabond without any roots. He only had endless streets with no name. The prospect for him proved to be a bit scary.   He didn't know where, or if, he belonged.   *I suppose I am of many places,* he pronounced in order to give himself some comfort.

It wasn't that comfortable though.

Raj would ask Prem to say increasingly more complex words and would laugh uproariously when Prem attempted to say them.   Sanjay would always turn red with embarrassment and Arun would do his best to keep his laughter to a minimum by simply chuckling.

"Can you say 'difficult'?" Raj asked.

"Vhat you dhinks?   I am no educated?   I shtudy many years, English"

Raj kept giggling.

"How about sexual?"

"Fabulous?"

"Encyclopedia?"

"Asphyxiate?"

"You have beary bihg house," Prem repeated again the day he left.

The very next telegram that Rajiv received from his uncle requested double the amount of monthly remittance.

• • •

Arun's grades for his first year arrived at his parent's house. His father had gotten the letter.   When Arun arrived home, Rajiv was sitting in a lawn chair in the garden, just looking out into space.

"Come here, Arun," his father called out to him from the yard when he went to say hello.

Arun was surprised.   It was the first time that his father had actually called him like that to talk about such a matter. Arun had become so accustomed to his perfunctory platitudes, "Work hard", "Be like your uncle", "Study like your brother", etc.

"What being this?" his father asked.   He cleared his throat. His father's hand was trembling.   His voice cracked.   This sight and sound created so much fear in Arun that he could barely find his own voice or keep himself from shaking.   *It's always that first heartbeat after the initial sense of fear.   It comes so heavily*, he thought. As if in a sling, the heart seemed to bounce down dramatically, severely, with a lot of weight to it.   As if there were a sudden injection of adrenalin, a turbo-boost at that instant, a missile launcher that just projectiled its load.   It slinged back in place, and then would yo-yo for awhile, falling into a periodicity; the intensity of the amplitude decreasing with each back and forth motion.   And then you got scared again and the process started anew.   *What a roller coaster*, thought Arun, knowing that he was just stalling as he thought about such things because he didn't know how to face his father.   He hated this fear that would paralyze him.

"I don't know what to say, Dad," is what finally came out.

Why did he have to say anything?   Why couldn't he just stay quiet like Sanjay would have done or like his own father.   He wondered if his father or Uncle Arjun had ever screwed up and what their interaction with their family had been.   *No*, he realized. *The way they are strict with all of us, it made it seem as if they never did anything wrong.*

Arun was finally able to catch a glimpse of the grades.   He guessed his father assumed that Arun already knew what was on the paper, because he wasn't making any effort to show it to Arun. Arun noticed a few Cs and then his eyes got larger when he saw a D.   He strained to see what class that was in.   He never recalled it being that severe.   Arun kept trying to observe the paper.

As time passed, Arun wasn't answering his father's question and Rajiv looked like he was getting increasingly more agitated.   Arun didn't know what to do or say.   He kept shifting his body, trying to get another view of the report card.

When he saw the class, Arun blurted out, "That can't be right."   He knew he had not done well in Principles of Biochemistry, but he was shocked that it could have earned him a D.   "Dad, that can't be right," said Arun.

Rajiv didn't seem to be moved by the comment.

"Dad, I'll figure this out," pleaded Arun.   "Please give me some time."

They sat there in silence for several minutes.

Arun wished that sometimes his family would simply acknowledge what he was saying.   *What a thrill that would be*, he said to himself.

And then Rajiv broke the silence.   "Is this being reason I coming to this country?" Rajiv asked him.

Arun looked at his father.   He genuinely didn't know why his father had come to this country.   He never thought to ask. He was just here.   Arun had heard about his Uncle R.K. wanting Arun to be a citizen, but nothing else was ever discussed.   Arun had heard about and read about India.   He knew it was poor. He assumed like everybody else, his father was referring to the fact that he came here to do better, make more money.   *Was the question rhetorical?* Arun wondered.

And then the weight of his father's words hit him. During his solitary year of confusion, of trying to find his place, his groove, his rhythm, Arun had managed to call the whole undertaking into doubt.   Arun suddenly felt awesomely responsible for the whole endeavor of his parents migrating falling apart and being unsuccessful.   *It's all my fault*, he caught himself thinking.   *I screwed up.   I ruined it for everyone.*

As he was saying this in his mind, trying to grapple with his father's disappointment and the guilt it was engendering within him, he kept trying to rationalize the comments.   *Did that even make sense?*   How could he suddenly be responsible for everybody and everything?   How could all hopes of success rest on his shoulders solely? *Man, I thought my Catholic friends had it bad with guilt, but this is an extraordinary amount for me to be feeling.*

"Why you no understand?" interjected Rajiv. He didn't look at Arun as he spoke. His voice was weak, almost feeble.

Arun didn't know the answer to his father's questions. Maybe it was all his fault – he certainly was feeling responsible for everything. *Why is there no room for me to stumble a little bit, with a sense of feeling secure? Why is it that every time I do something for myself, explore, develop, it is not a safe haven for me to do so. I enter this hostile, unfamiliar territory with them, my family.*

He saw Sanjay come around the house to where he and his father were sitting. *Oh great*, thought Arun. *Just the person I wanted to see, golden boy.*

"Now you know why I don't want to go to your school?" said Sanjay under his breath.

"What the hell does that mean?" demanded Arun. Arun knew why Sanjay was even more pointed than before. He had gotten into Harvard. He imagined his parents must have been exceptionally happy. No post-conversing-with-Dipti revisionist sulking for Sanjay to experience.

Sanjay looked at his father. And then he stayed quiet.

Arun decided to do the same thing. They all only moved when Meena called out for dinner. They walked inside without saying a word to each other.

• • •

Towards the end of summer, Arun's parents had a gathering with friends and Uncle Arjun came over. It had been a few years since Arun had interacted with Uncle Arjun, since the time of the citizenship party. Rajiv of course gave Uncle Arjun the full download – the whole fiasco of Arun's lousy grades. Rajiv was laying out all of the facts for Uncle Arjun and waiting for a verdict, as if he were a litigator awaiting Uncle Arjun to pass judgment. Rajiv seemed like an animated version of what was going on inside of Arun.   Arun could sense active desperation in his father's voice.   Rajiv kept referring to the money that was being spent.   Arun felt like he experienced a bee sting when his father said, "This money could being saving the farm!"

Arun looked at this father.   He then looked at Raj.   He went back to his father.   *If you love your damn farm so much, why don't you just go back to it!* Arun was dying to say.   For a man who had not been back in twenty years, it amazed Arun how much his father still cared about the place.

Nobody in the room said a word.

Arun's parents fueled his seemingly permanent residence in his uncle's shadows.   It amused Arun to think about how his parents had given him an involuntary green card that cast him forever in that dungeon.   It was handed to him at birth.   He was required to present it, every time he discussed any aspect of his own life, any achievements, any ambitions, any goals.   But there wasn't a finite point in time where he could pinpoint it happening. Nor was there a definitive transition point.   It occurred over time. It transpired in all of the under-the-breath comments, the snide remarks after he did something they were not happy with, the brutal, spirit-shattering comparisons.   A mental image of a green card with the title "Uncle Arjun's Shadow" came to Arun's mind. It made him laugh.   He was glad to have the release of tension.

Uncle Arjun was quiet, looking reflective.   He seemed to be absorbing all of the details.   Arun had always felt a burden of needing to impress Uncle Arjun.   How good he would feel if his uncle had applauded his efforts.   Arun attempted to get his uncle's approval for years.   He had this nagging sensation that maybe he would never receive it.

Uncle Arjun approached Arun.   He asked him one question: "Why are you studying medicine?"

Arun was silent for several minutes. He attempted to come up with a clever response, but eventually abandoned it, knowing that he was inventing something. He eventually answered honestly. "Dad says it is a prestigious profession."

"Indeed it is," said Uncle Arjun, "but why are *you* studying it?"

Arun was on the verge of tears. His lower jaw was quivering as he attempted to say something. He was moving his right hand about, as if emphasizing a point, but it came across as a flailing arm.

Arjun seemed to rescue him by offering him the following advice, "My boy, it is important that you do what you love and what comes naturally."

"Yeah, I thought about that," admitted Arun as he collected himself, "but I don't think Dad would be happy with me leaving the sciences."

"If you stay on your current path, I can't see you doing much of anything," Uncle Arjun said, delivering his verdict. "And as the one financing your education, I insist you make something of yourself."

The news stunned Arun. He thought his father had been paying. He felt a mixture of emotions at that point. He suddenly felt uncomfortable, but with an odd new sense of appreciation, no, obligated gratitude, for his uncle.

Arun approached his father later that night, "How come Uncle Arjun is paying for my college?"

Rajiv remained silent.

Arun was going to let it go. As he was about to walk out, his father called out.

"I give money for Arjun studies. Now he have money, he give for you."

Arun suddenly felt better about the arrangement.

● ● ●

The advice Arun received from his Uncle Arjun weighed heavily on his mind. He wasn't sure he was convinced.

"Steven, this is a crisis," Arun had to admit to his friend later that night when Arun called him in desperation. It wasn't easy for Arun to come clean like that. While Steven was his best friend, there was always a little bit of competitiveness between the two of them. Steven was studying at Yale, where his grandfather had gone. Arun hated having to admit to his good friend that he was in a weakened position. No, worse than that, he was lost.

"Try to remember what you loved and what made you successful in high school," was Steven's advice.

"I can't come up with it," lamented a dismayed Arun. "All of the stuff I was great at is not working here. I was good at so many things, but everything was so shallow. It wasn't really challenging."

"You loved debate more than anything," said Steven.

"I know," said Arun nostalgically. "I was even really good at it. But how can that impact me here? I can't become a professional debater."

"But maybe you need to lay off the sciences," suggested Steven. "You were great at history and literature, don't forget."

The suggestion caught Arun off guard. It was almost revolutionary. He had never thought about that as a possibility. He thought he just needed to beat out a path in the jungle of the sciences. He had always been the ace science guy. Ever since he was a kid, he always thought his career would have something to do with the sciences. The suggestion was so novel. How could he be Arun without that? And then it dawned on Arun. How could he be his father's son without this career path? There was no way he could imagine telling his father that he had abandoned the sciences. "Indians are all about the sciences. It's in the blood or something," he told Steven.

"You are being stereotypical. The reality is you are afraid of your parents more than you are afraid of not having a career you are pursuing that you can do well in," responded Steven.

Arun was quiet. He was partially in awe with how his friend could be so quick to understand the crux of the issue. Arun had to accept what Steven was saying, but his inclination was to resist it on the surface. "Steven," said Arun with emphasis, "I love what you are saying, but there is no way that I can stop pursuing the sciences. My family would probably disown me." Arun wished he could tell Steven, 'I'm only kidding', but the reality of the statement was all too true.

"Well," said Steven, "You have a choice. But I know that the only way you are going to be happy is if you pursue something you are good at. If you're not good at it, you are going to be miserable. More than anything about high school, I remember how much you liked to win. You hated losing. You liked doing well in just about anything and everything."

Arun was silent as he absorbed what Steven was saying.

"Remember the time in metal shop, you were excited because you had the best cabinet of anybody?"

"Why do you remember that?" asked Arun, a smile creeping onto his face.

"Because you were so annoying with how you kept showing off," said Steven with a laugh. "I mean, nobody gave a damn, but you kept prancing around, all happy."

The reminder made Arun laugh. He did like to win. He did like to do well. Maybe that was why he had been feeling so frustrated as of late. He hadn't been that good at college thus far. It was hard for him to come to terms with that. More importantly, Arun knew he needed to get over his fear. It was beginning to stifle him, cripple him, prevent him from pursuing the lofty boulevards of his ambition. These revelations proved wonderful for Arun. He was feeling better about himself. He felt relieved. The pressure that he had placed on himself didn't feel quite so severe. He felt light, excited about life once again.

As if he had averted that landmine in the road or found a way to avoid the edge of the cliff.

A week before his second year began, Arun modified his classes to reflect areas that he found fascinating and interesting for him. He canceled several of the science classes. When the semester began, he tried hard to recover. It was challenging for him. He focused less on his direction, where he was going and whether or not he liked it, and turned his attention to the sole purpose of getting good grades. *Sometimes,* he thought to himself, *maybe we need to use the palpable cobblestones on a street to guide us and not the distant and elusive stars that shine over it.*

One month into the new semester, Rajiv called him. It was unusual for his father to initiate the call. Generally, his mother would start the conversation and Rajiv would eventually come to the phone. His father would mostly stay silent for a majority of the phone call.

"What is being the news you are having?" asked Rajiv. He cleared his throat.

Arun was confused. "News about what, Dad?" asked Arun.

His father paused for a few seconds. Arun could sense his unease and exasperation. It immediately struck fear within him.

"About your marks," said Rajiv.

"Dad, what do you mean?" asked Arun.

"You saying all of them being wrong," said Rajiv in as stern a voice as Arun had ever heard. He remembered this voice when he was younger and Arun and his brothers didn't want to leave a party with other children when their father wanted to go home.

Arun recalled the conversation. "No, Dad, I said one of them couldn't be right," Arun stated matter-of-factly, as a knee jerk reaction.

His father was quiet again. Arun suddenly felt like he had been caught in a lie. He could tell his father was thinking that.

Arun felt so small again and scared. *It was a miscommunication,* he thought to himself. *Yet, somehow, I lied to my father and it was all my fault.*

Arun's mother got on the phone. "Arun, what happening to you?" Meena asked him.

"Mom, what do you mean?"

"You lying to your father now. You are not doing good in the school. What is problem?"

"Mom, I didn't lie to Dad," Arun pleaded.

"Son, you must pray to the god. You needing his strength now."

Arun remembered this conversation many times. He knew how it went. This was where his mother would begin her preaching and he would not be able to say anything in response. He could be saying things like "My eyeball just fell out" or "My roommate just committed suicide" or "The building is on fire" and he would have been met with the same response.

"This is no good time for you. You must pray to the god."

"Okay, Mom," was all that Arun could say. He then thought that he wished his mother knew how to use definite articles. It occurred to him that this was a chronic problem among Indians.

● ● ●

When he went home for Christmas break of his second year, there was a lot of tension in the house. He and his father weren't speaking. Arun never felt comfortable making the first move because he had no idea what was going on in his father's mind. He didn't know what he could say to make him feel better. He looked like he was suffering. Somehow, Arun felt responsible for it. At least, they all made him feel as if he was responsible for it.

When Sanjay got home, Raj hugged him deeply. He held on until Meena and Rajiv walked into the room. And then Raj pulled away and winked at this brother.

"I've missed you," he said.

Sanjay's presence was all the more difficult to cope with for Arun. Arun was sure his brother's grades were fine.

At dinner that night, everyone was eating quietly.

"Can Sanjay and I share a room?" Raj asked aloud.

Meena and Rajiv looked up at him. When he saw that they were looking, he blew his brother a kiss.

Sanjay looked more scared than upset. Arun observed the episode. He could see that his parents were also reacting to Raj with concern. After dinner, Raj kept trying to sit next to Sanjay and hold his hand.

"What the hell are you doing?" Sanjay asked.

"I miss you, brother," said Raj, hugging Sanjay.

"Get the hell away from me," said Sanjay, pushing him away as he got up from the sofa where the two had been seated.

"Don't push me away, Sanjay," yelled out Raj. "It can be like it was before. Before you left me and went to school."

Arun laughed to himself. *What a clever brother I have.*

Raj then got up and started shouting out to Sanjay, "Don't tell me you found someone else! Is he white or Chinese? I know how much you like Chinese boys!"

Later that night, Arun found Raj alone in the family room watching a movie.

Arun turned to Raj. "Where is everyone else?"

"Mom is having a talk about God with Sanjay, and Dad is listening," said Raj.

Arun couldn't contain his uproarious laughter. He high-fived Raj. Raj had a knowing smirk on his face.

"You are a genius, kid brother," Arun said to Raj. "Did they talk to you, too?"

"Yes."

"Well, what did you say?"

"I told them that in Hinduism, an older brother is like a God, so I was just following what my older brother was asking me to do, even if I felt that it was wrong and it made me feel dirty." He emphasized the last word with a maiden-like innocence that impressed Arun.

"You are such a little punk," said Arun. "How come you don't ever live up to what you said – a brother being like a God? You never give me any respect," continued Arun.

"Come on, man. This is America. We can practice religion of convenience. Don't you see Mom and Dad doing that? When it is convenient for them, they talk about duty, responsibility, family, but when it comes to something more challenging – something for us that they have to give up, they don't remember the way it's supposed to be," Raj expounded.

When did my little brother get so smart? thought Arun.

"How come you don't harass me the way you harass Sanjay?"

"You don't walk around here with a superiority complex. Plus, he never gets yelled at. We've had our fair share."

My kid brother, the arbiter of justice. Arun marveled at him. He relayed the conversation to Steven. Arun also felt, admittedly, a little scared by him. He decided he was actually intimidated. *I wonder what else he'll surprise me with. We should have watched him more carefully while he was growing up.*

Arun got his grades back from school. He had mostly As with one B. He ran into the house from the mailbox to show his father. "Dad, check this out," Arun said, beaming with pride.

Rajiv reviewed it. "Is being better than before," he said plainly. He handed the sheet back to Arun and walked away. Arun felt dejected. *Do you know how hard I had to work to earn that?* Arun thought. He knew it was futile. He quietly walked away.

During the balance of his second year, Arun thought a lot about what he was good at, what excited him and what he eventually wanted to become. Arun recalled being fascinated with what his Uncle Arjun was doing. He also remembered enjoying reading *BusinessWeek* magazine at his uncle's house. Arun decided to explore it further. All of those articles that he pored over in *The Economist* were very exciting. He had to admit, he never understood what it all meant, but he enjoyed reading them nonetheless. Arun made a decision. He decided to enroll into the Wharton School of the university to pursue finance.

Arun's father responded with disinterest to the news of the switch. Arun could tell his father had lost some faith in him; he hoped it wasn't all gone. Arun's mother was more cautious in her approval. "So long as you having good the job can make money," she said to him.

Arun had not planned on mentioning it to Uncle Arjun. His parents, however, did it for him. His uncle called him. It was the first time in his life he had gotten a call from him. His advice was pithy. "Make sure you get better grades. People won't cut you much slack."

● ● ●

Rajiv went to visit Pablo again at his nursery. He was excited to see that his friend was expanding into the lot adjacent to his.

"You being growing," Rajiv said when he entered Pablo's office.

"Yeah, *señor*, thanks be to *Dios*, we are growing."

Rajiv watched as the expression on his friend's face began to show some concern.

"*Señor*, you don't look like you are doing too good."

Rajiv looked up at Pablo. His first inclination was to deny that anything was wrong. In an Indian setting, Rajiv always had to maintain appearances, you could never let anyone in society know that you were experiencing any problems. At times he wished Meena would do a better job of not revealing everything to Dipti.

"It is being my son," Rajiv blurted out. He shocked himself with the comment. Somehow, he felt safe.

"He not doing very good in the school. I worrying for him."

"Hmmm…."

"I meaning, is being better now. But I worrying he doing the badly again. I coming this country, my family, my brother, saying having better life for childrens. How to having better life if he no being good in the college?"

Rajiv saw that Pablo was staying quiet. It made him uncomfortable, so he decided to be quiet as well.

"By better life, you meaning having *dinero*? The money, right *señor*?"

Rajiv nodded his head.

"*Señor*, it is important that your son is happy as well."

"He will be being happy if he having the money."

Pablo sighed and shook his head. "Okay, well *señor*, think about when you were his age."

Rajiv thought back.

"Are his chances for having more money than you better or worse, even if he doesn't do great in school?"

Rajiv allowed a smile to creep onto his face. "He should be being better, like my brother or my other son, Sanjay."

"Well, *señor*, everyone is different." Pablo threw both hands into the air and shrugged his shoulders as he spoke.

There were a few moments of silence.

"You've told me about your other son and all the awards he is getting, but what's so special about your brother?" asked Pablo.

"Oh, he having very much money. He being very wealthy," explained Rajiv. "His idea being coming to this country. He telling my uncle and father, is being no room for him to making money in India, he doing better coming here. He also tell them that I being there to look after them. My brother, he feeling free. I having all responsibility. Everybody telling me what study, what read, what spending time doing. Nobody saying anything to him. He being free. Since young he reading about this country, getting exciting about this country. I say I giving him money for coming here. Is being family duty."

"That was good of you. What is he doing now?"

"He making some business here. He giving the money to small business, after when growing he selling the business and making much money. He very clever such things. I not so clever such things."

"You never talk about him much. Do you guys get along?" Pablo asked.

"He doing some mean things. Also, my uncle being mean to him. My uncle, always stealing the money from my father. I seeing this also, but I knowing better. I cannot saying anything. My brother, he complaining, he telling my father about my uncle stealing. The next morning, my uncle, he hanging him from a tree upside down, rope being at his ankles."

Pablo let out a laugh. Rajiv noticed Pablo tried to contain himself and restrain from laughing. Seeing his reaction made Rajiv laugh a little and they both chuckled together.

"I'm sorry, *señor*. I don't mean to laugh, but it is kinda funny," said Pablo, sheepishly. Rajiv had to admit. There was a comical element to it.

"But my brother, he getting even with my uncle. When coming back to India after he studying and after working and sending money, he say to my uncle 'I sending no more money, I studying more'. My uncle yelling at him, trying to beating him. My brother, he grabbing my uncle by the neck, saying many bad things to him. I remembering he say 'you no owning me anymore'. He then giving the money back he taking from me for his schooling and he leaving. He never speaking with my uncle or my father since then. My father passing away already, my brother never speaking with him before he dying."

"Wow, so he paid back the money you gave him for his school and then he forgot about everybody," Pablo confirmed.

"Yes. And then he spending many times with women. He marry woman from here. He never telling me this."

"Wow, does he have kids? How are they with your kids?"

"Oh he having no children. Maybe the God is punishing him."

Pablo looked at this friend. "So you agree there is more to life than just money."

Rajiv became lost in thought.

CHAPTER NINE

April 2007

It had been a month since the incident. Radha had suggested that Arun maintain a routine. It was hard for him, but he agreed with her. He knew it would make him feel better and he was eager for life to return to normalcy. All he ever achieved with the cruel machinations he had put himself through earlier was to temporarily displace the pain. It was merely a detour. Try as he would, he was never able to replace it. There were no alternate routes to get to his destination. He soon realized that like a tightly wound knot of muscle, or twisted ball, it needed to be pounded out. He had to think of himself as a baker – he had to knead it out as if it were dough with lumps.

It was hard for him. Trivial daily functions seemed almost futile. How could he add milk to his coffee or spread jam on his toast? It seemed so meaningless in light of what he was experiencing. He would stop himself and wonder – *hey, didn't a bomb just go off? Shouldn't I be in panic mode? Aren't there things I need to do – urgent matters that I need to resolve? How can I be wasting my time with this?* But, he forged ahead. Soon such activities became as commonplace as they had been in the past.

Arun had finally gotten tired of seeing his suit jacket on the arm chair in his bedroom. It had become a fixture, as things inevitably do when one's life becomes wholly consumed by crisis. Before he went for his walk that morning, Arun lifted it up. It felt heavier than normal. He began feeling around for the pockets and found his cell phone inside the breast pocket. The battery had died. He went to re-charge it and as soon as he turned it on, he heard a beeping sound indicating messages. He listened to five messages, three of which came from Andy. A part of Arun was sad that more people weren't reaching out for him, but he quickly stopped thinking about that as he listened to the messages. The messages that weren't from Andy related to GoWire business and were outdated. The first two from Andy were generic, asking to be called back. The last one, left four days ago, was cryptic. "I have a gift for Nandini's birthday. Sorry I missed the party. When can I deliver it in person?" Nandini's birthday wasn't for several weeks. Arun knew Andy was aware of that because he had come to Nandini's prior birthday parties and had always commented on how it was within two days of his wife's birthday. On instinct, he called Andy back. Arun only got his voicemail. He left a message. "It would be good to meet to get Nandini's gift."

During his walk, Arun thought back to when he had first taken the job as General Counsel of GoWire Systems, when he had first met Andy. His motivation for taking the job was clear enough. He wanted the money. It wasn't a matter of having a salary - he was earning that. No, he wanted to cash in big. He wanted the huge stock option grant that would bring him millions. Arun felt like he needed to make apologies for it now. He had already been comfortable enough. He was providing a good living for his family, better than the one he grew up with. *Why did he have to strive for more?*

At the time he got the job, he would craft clever arguments about how he wanted to contribute to growing something small into a large entity, how he wanted to feel a part of the process of building a company, how he was tired of assisting others to do it and he wasn't doing it himself. These were all lies he needed to tell to get the job – potential employers hated hearing the truth even though it was greed that fueled their own desires to be where they were.

As Arun struggled with himself to justify his lust for money, the excuses of "I wanted the money" or "I needed the money" just didn't seem to cover the issue. What was the truth? Arun thought hard. He tried to identify what he was feeling. He began listing what was troubling him as he walked that morning. He was tired of the constant comparisons that his parents made between him and his Uncle Arjun. He was tired of his uncle always being right and Arun always being wrong. Somehow, Arun felt that if he could prove himself the way Arjun had, by having the wealth Arjun did, maybe the comparisons would cease and they would be pleased with Arun. They respected Arjun so much. *It had to be about the money*, he reasoned. Arun concluded that he had been compelled to accomplish the immigrant manifesto for himself, in order to earn his parent's respect.

At the time, he talked to different friends that were in the Internet industry. "So where do you think that someone like me could fit in?" he asked.

They unanimously questioned his desire to make the move. They then looked at him with a wry smile and asked, "It's the money, right?"

With his good friends asking the question, it was hard for Arun to lie. He had to smile in response.

"Well now we have a basis to work from," they affirmed, a knowing sparkle in their eye. "You need to spin a good story."

"Ask your uncle to help. He is a venture capitalist, right?" Steven had made the obvious suggestion when Arun mentioned the job opportunity to him. Arun knew he had a point. Several of his other friends had brought Uncle Arjun up.

"Yeah, I kinda wanted to keep him out of it," Arun replied.

"Hmmm..."   Steven was the one person who had witnessed the most of Arun's interactions with his family, so he knew not to press on the issue.   Steven opted to caution him. "Are you sure you want to step out of your comfort zone?"

"Don't immigrants do it all the time?   Like them, I can get accustomed to another area.   My comfort zone won't give me the *material comfort* I am looking for," Arun insisted.   After he hung up with Steven, Arun muttered to himself, "Or the material comfort I need to prove my worth to my family."

● ● ●

GoWire was the fifth company with which Arun met.   He remembered being thrilled when they called him with the offer.

"Mom, Dad, I got the job at the technology company I was trying to get into," Arun shrieked with excitement.

"Oh," said Meena.   Rajiv was quiet.

Arun held his expression of joy for a few minutes.   It came crashing down like glass falling from a table.   "Dad, haven't you been hearing about how great all of these Internet stocks have been doing?" pleaded Arun.

His father was silent.

"Isn't this exciting for you, all of the money I am going to have?" urged Arun again.   He had been sure his mother would be moved by that.   There was continued silence.   Arun continued to talk.   He described the offer for them.

"You should being talking with your uncle," Rajiv responded plainly.   "He telling you if good or bad."   Before Arun could respond, Rajiv added, "Okay."   Arun knew that it wasn't a question.   Rajiv wasn't waiting for Arun to affirm what he was saying or to agree with it.   Rajiv then left the phone conversation with only Meena on the phone.

"Is it really you get more the money?" she attempted to confirm.

"Yes, I am going to be making more money," said Arun, some excitement coming back in his voice. *At least they asked me one question*, he thought to himself. He hung up the phone.

"I should've called Radha first," he admonished himself under his breath.

Arun considered heeding his father's advice and calling his uncle. But he couldn't bring himself to do it. He knew why he was reluctant. He didn't want to hear his uncle criticize the opportunity. It had taken Arun some time to land the position. He also couldn't help but feel that his uncle went about his business unfettered, so why did Arun have to go through all of this?

Arun accepted the offer from GoWire. After two days he got a call from Uncle Arjun. Arun had avoided calling him all this time. *It looks like my parents have intervened on my behalf*, Arun thought to himself.

"You shouldn't do this," was Uncle Arjun's first comment.

"Why do you feel that way?" Arun asked, attempting to glean some insight. He hated how smug his uncle was. Arun wondered what it would feel like when it was his turn. When he could be arrogant and dismissive with his parents. He knew it for sure; when he got his money, his parents would respect him, listen to him. He didn't mention to his uncle that he had already accepted the offer.

"I insist you don't take this job," said Arjun.

Arun thought to himself that he might be more apt to heed Uncle Arjun's advice if he would offer to look into some of his investments or ask around on Arun's behalf to try and land him a job. He hated that Uncle Arjun never wanted to assist him in establishing connections. Isn't that what uncles are for? Don't normal families behave this way?

"Look, even if you go beyond the fact that their technology is a has-been, keep in mind that they don't really need a General

Counsel and when things go south, you will be one of the first few to lose your job," reasoned Arjun.

Arun was really upset. *Why couldn't he ever be happy for me?* thought Arun. *But then again, he seemed to take greater joy in putting me down.* It was hard to avoid one nagging truth that was staring Arun in the face. He knew that his Uncle Arjun was not stupid and that what he was saying made a lot of sense. He wondered the same question – *why would a company this size need me?* He decided not to think about Arjun's warning. He proceeded to take the job. He wanted his chance at getting the money that he craved. Uncle Arjun had his. Why shouldn't Arun have a shot?

"If you think it is a good move, then do it," Radha had told Arun when he discussed it with her. Arun was thrilled that she was supportive. He thought about how she had always been very supportive of him. *At least she trusts my judgment,* Arun reflected.

"My friends who have made similar moves are now sitting on boatloads of money," Arun pointed out in an excited tone.

"Yeah, but that's not why you are doing it, right?"

"Uh, not completely," said Arun hesitatingly.

"What do you mean?" Radha pursued.

"The money is so alluring, look at how much they have made. It's not like the work is all that exciting. Getting the money is the only reason to do this," rationalized Arun.

"So is this where I recount a childhood fable where the moral of the story is not to blindly follow others?" asked Radha.

"You could try," taunted Arun, "but there isn't a high probability that I will pay attention to you."

"What does the company do?" asked Radha, resignedly.

"I'm sorry?" asked Arun.

"I was asking, 'What does the company do?'" Radha's voice began to show some concern.

Arun thought that maybe Radha had found him out. Arun knew that Radha was aware that when he didn't know the answer to a question, he always asked for it to be repeated so he could have some time to think of some kind of answer. Arun felt exposed. *I think she knows that I don't know. I suppose I have to try to say something.*

"Well… it's communication equipment…to connect diverse equipment…in a more…efficient way…saving people time and money…when they need to communicate," offered Arun. The last person he convinced was himself.

Radha's eyes grew large, "Are you kidding me? You sound worse than a first-year law school student trying to prosecute a case!"

"Look…" he continued, "the thing to keep our eyes on is the fact that some of their competitors have had their stock prices go up by a factor of five or six times. Isn't that jump in valuation great?"

"Correct that," Radha rectified. "A first day law school student."

Try as he might, he couldn't really get a more favorable response from Radha. Her silence was a sign that she was trusting, but had some concern.

She turned to Arun and placed her hand on his arm. "Please be careful."

• • •

The head of GoWire Systems, Chet, was very technically oriented. A geek in all senses of the name. Arun thought he had seen his official name in some press release as Chester. It was very antiquated, thought Arun when he first heard it.

"My mother named me after my grandfather," clarified Chet, during Arun's interview.

Chet lacked most social graces. He spoke with a nasal tone, which he would insist was attributed to some sinus deformity. Arun lost interest before he could fully follow what Chet was saying when he tried to explain it. He used a bunch of visuals, seemingly flailing his arms about, that Arun pretended to recognize, but in actuality, he had no clue that a sphenoidal sinus looked like a peninsula and had not been enlightened during the course of the conversation despite the images that Chet tried to create, poorly, with his two hands.

The man who managed the day-to-day operations was Chet's friend from high school, Derek. Derek had no understanding of technology and pretended he knew how to operate a business. It was clear that he had strong-armed Chet into giving him a great deal of responsibility. Derek's experience with business stemmed from managing a family-owned pizza chain (he called it a chain, but there were two stores) and running an Internet start-up several years earlier. The start-up had failed. If his former colleagues were asked, they would mostly admit that it was because Derek ran it into the ground.

"Could you imagine the two of these guys in high school?" Arun asked Radha one day.

"Derek would do the used car salesman pitch to girls for the two of them after Chet ran a logarithm to determine which two girls would be the most likely to go out with them!" Arun exclaimed gleefully to Radha.

Derek felt remarkably insecure about not being savvy with technology. He would show this in his being a control freak. He also acted as if Chet had saved his life by hiring him. It was true. He had been doing nothing for nine months after his prior firm blew up. People would complain to Chet about Derek incessantly. Derek would have so many other employees at GoWire running around in circles for him. It was almost as if he needed it to prove his superiority.

"He's your boss," would be Chet's response, typically delivered with a shrug of the shoulders.

There was nothing that Derek would say no to. Arun's challenge was that he cringed at the thought of wasting time and effort pursuing fruitless endeavors, something that Derek was always more than happy to see him engage in. Derek would be very confrontational with Arun and other employees. Most people would allow him to do it because he was Chet's good friend. In meetings, he seemed to take particular pleasure in embarrassing people in front of others.

● ● ●

Arun got a call back from Andy. "Why don't we meet at the Starbucks at the mall?" he suggested, "I'll bring the gift with me."

Arun felt strangely relieved to see his old colleague again.

"While you were away on business, on that last trip you did, Derek had many meetings with the guys at Smith and Jannsen."

That fact didn't surprise Arun. GoWire retained that law firm on a number of issues and Derek was known to interact with them.

"Including Phil Roslyn."

Arun was shocked to hear that name. "Phil's my chief contact there. I am the one that sought him out. Phil told me he had never met Derek before."

"Exactly. It gets weirder," Andy commented, "I saw Derek in the copy room one of the days that Phil was in our offices. I thought to myself, when do we ever see Derek in the copy room?"

"When he is doing something highly confidential that he doesn't want others to know about." Arun completed the thought.

"Precisely. I mean the guy is paranoid of his own assistant! Anyway, I tried to catch a glimpse of what he was copying as I engaged in a conversation with him."

"And?" Arun was becoming increasingly more intrigued.

"I could tell he wanted me to go away, but I didn't want to."

"Right. Did you see anything?" Arun was growing impatient.

"Yes. I caught sight of a page with a series of signatures. You know, the typed names below it, with the line and the space for the actual signature?"

"Okay..." Arun was looking intently at Andy, his head leaning forward.

"Well, the space for yours was occupied. With your signature."

"But I was away," argued Arun.

"Exactly."

Arun thought for a few seconds. "Can you get your hands on those documents?"

"I was just waiting for you to ask."

• • •

Radha had grown accustomed to seeing her husband wander about the house listlessly. It was good to see him be active once again, conducting calls from his study. She could tell by the cadence of his voice and the volume with which he spoke whether he was talking with a lawyer or with someone from whom he was trying to mask the incident, playing it off as if everything was normal. "Oh, yeah, I left GoWire." "I'm on to greener pastures." "I have something lined up; just waiting for kid number three to pop out, then I'll dive in." Her heart ached for him the most when she heard these phrases. She knew the torment he must be going through in pretending that all was well. However, the worst of it was when he spoke to his family. And then there was the e-mail he received from someone in India claiming to be his cousin. Radha had convinced Arun to ignore the person; it usually meant they wanted to visit and she and Arun were in no mood to entertain visitors.

• • •

Arun caught sight of Radha sitting on the edge of their bed, staring into space. "Why don't you talk to my father?" Radha asked Arun abruptly. Arun knew then that she was pretty desperate. Arun didn't respond.

"Okay, talk to your own father," suggested Radha.

That drew a laugh from Arun. He half-suspected that it was the reaction that Radha had in mind.

"You need to call somebody," said Radha.

And that's when he did. He called his friend Steven. Steven arrived the next day. They went for a walk. It was nice to have someone else to steer the direction of the ponderings going through his mind, charting a course that he may not have plotted on his own.

Arun explained the incident to Steven. "Radha thinks I should tell my parents."

"She must be desperate for you to get help," reasoned Steven.

"Yeah, Steven, but you know them. They aren't going to react well to this."

"No, they won't," admitted Steven.

"They aren't going to provide much support either," reasoned Arun.

"No, you'll likely just have to be responsible for their feelings," said Steven.

"I know."

"They will make you feel guilty," added Steven.

"That's what they always do," lamented Arun.

"If they even talk to you at all," worried Steven.

"You are right," Arun stopped walking and looked at his friend. "I'm afraid," Arun finally admitted.

"Of?"

"Uh…you know…everything. What Chet, Derek and the GoWire people are going to do to me. The torture they will put me through," proclaimed Arun. He suddenly felt self-conscious of his response.

Steven paused for several minutes. "Yes, but also you are afraid of your parents. The former will dissipate, but the latter you are stuck with for life unless you do something about it."

Arun stared at his friend. Sometimes it took someone completely detached to identify the problem.

"You know what? You should face your parents," declared Steven. "You *need* to face your parents. Tell them what is going on. Don't worry about the consequences."

"These aren't people I can turn to for help," pleaded Arun. Tears were beginning to roll down his face.

"I'm not saying that you should do that. Just get over your fear of telling them. Who cares how they will react? You are so worried of what they might think of you or what they might do. Imagine how much you could ease your burden if you just got it off your chest," reasoned Steven.

Arun created a deep furrow with his forehead. As if a hundred stones were being skipped into a pond simultaneously.

• • •

Anjali was surprised to see Steven when she came to the house the following morning. "Oh, hello."

"Hi," he responded.

"It's been over ten years," commented Anjali. She thought to add, "We met when Radha married Arun."

"That's funny, I remember it as Arun marrying Radha," Steven quipped.

They both laughed together.

"Yes, I remember meeting you when *they* got married," said Steven.

Anjali smiled in acceptance of his revision.

Nandini bolted into the breakfast nook. "Hello *Ma-si*, hello Uncle Steven. I'm so hungry!"

Steven sprung to action. "Well, come and sit here," he said. "Both of you," as he smiled to Anjali. "I'll get the cereal and the bowls." When Steven came out, he sat down next to Nandini at the table. He poured Nandini her cereal and milk. Clumsily, Nandini dropped her spoon on the floor. She went to reach for the one Steven was going to use.

Arun was entering the breakfast nook at that moment.

Steven grabbed Nandini's wrist. He had a smile on his face as he spoke. "No, no, no, young lady. That is not appropriate. Your parents would not be happy about that. Just ask me for another spoon and I will get it for you." Steven was getting ready to stand-up.

"What the hell do you think you are doing?" demanded Arun.

Steven's mouth fell wide open. He was still holding Nandini's wrist. She began squirming to get him to release her arm.

"Arun, why are you getting so mad?" asked Anjali.

"Let go of my daughter!" shouted Arun.

Anjali was shocked to hear her brother-in-law scream like that.

"I…I didn't mean any harm…" said Steven. "I was just trying to do what I thought you would…"

Arun cut him off. "You thought wrong. Don't ever touch my child again."

"Arun. Arun!" Anjali had stood up from her chair and tried to get Arun's attention. She was getting agitated that he wouldn't look over to her.

After a few seconds of silence, Arun told his friend, "I think it's time you go."

"Arun, that's ridiculous," Anjali protested.

"No, Anjali, it's okay," said Steven, "if that's what Arun wants, I'll go." Steven gathered his things and left within minutes.

● ● ●

Arun didn't feel well. He went for a walk again that morning. The reality was that coping with the incident was a slow, and at times painfully slow, process. This was a bomb where it would take years to see where all the damage had been, when it had all finalized, where all the shrapnel had ended up, the dead bodies, the debris. There was no rushing it or escalating it.

Did he really alienate his friend? The one who came to help him? Arun stopped searching for that avenue. He wanted to find another street.

It was so hard for him to cope with not knowing what the future might be. Was it okay for him to do this or do that? How could he plan for something that he had no comprehension of?

He knew that re-engaging in those seemingly trivial daily functions had provided him comfort. It gave him a sense that he could survive this, that there would be a time when he wouldn't have the aftermath of the incident hanging over his head. That there might be a time without fear.

He despised fear. He saw it in his parents all of the time. Arun's life had been different. In many regards, it had been a mission of his to eradicate fear from his life. He hadn't shied away from things that were different, unique or outside of his comfort zone. He had resolved his fear of the unknown through pro-activity. Striving to understand the world and the people in it was his salvation. But how could he apply that to this situation?

He reflected on the last few weeks, all that he had gone through. Music and tears helped soothe his pain. Blood shot eyes, somber music as a catalyst and marathon solitude - these helped chase the fiend of fear away. That was when he allowed the tears to drop. Those falling tears were acid on the dense metal in his body. Each drop corroded more of the metal of those shackles away, fear and the pain dripping down like drain water. It was as if the sobbing took down the roadblocks, dissolved the fence, opened the gate. It allowed him access to the road he needed to be on. He knew that one day the tears would flow like a waterfall and that they would dissolve the shackles away in their entirety.

It was like any other process; once it began, it ran its course. Soon marathon solitude was not needed. The swift current of tears had washed away a majority of the shackles. He could even tuck it away at times and pretend it wasn't there for awhile. He found he could move about again without experiencing the same excruciating pain and fear. He found that when his mind was occupied, he was better able to cope with the fear. Compartmentalizing it helped him cope. He knew Nandini's birthday was coming soon. That was his perfect excuse; the perfect walkway about which to pitch a tent, and preclude him from crossing those paths that he would rather avoid.

● ● ●

Arun contacted an attorney. Being a lawyer himself, he knew how to seek out an expert criminal lawyer. During his first meeting with him, Arun explained the situation in great detail, expanding on the phone conversation that he had with the attorney earlier that day. The lawyer took copious notes.

"Isn't your uncle Arjun Gandharni?"

"Yes, he is," responded Arun without emotion. From time-to-time Arun encountered people who knew his uncle. By the look on the lawyer's face Arun could tell that he was expecting Arun to be proud of the fact and not to respond in such a desultory manner.

"Do you know him?" asked Arun, sensing that the lawyer wanted to continue on the topic. He was concerned briefly, and then he recalled attorney client privilege and felt more at ease.

"I know of him," replied the lawyer. He was then quiet for a few moments. "You know, I did some digging prior to your arriving here. Your uncle has roughly twenty-five million dollars in recorded real estate assets. Plus an additional fifty million in publicly traded stock," said the lawyer. "And that is just what he has to disclose."

"He has done very well for himself," remarked Arun coldly.

"And his wife is a leading criminal defense lawyer," added the attorney.

Arun stayed quiet and simply looked at him.

"Yet, you came to me." The lawyer was silent for awhile as he observed Arun. "It would strike me that a man with an uncle like that doesn't really have a problem with people asking him for money. Whether you took it or not, you could pay these guys off, likely dodge a criminal record and move forward with your life."

Arun looked at his attorney again. He could feel the tension forming in his own forehead. His facial muscles actually began hurting as he held that frown for several minutes. He realized he had been doing it too much lately.

"That's not a viable solution." Arun spoke with an even tone. And then he walked out.

CHAPTER TEN

Late 1989 – 1993

Arun graduated Wharton salvaging his GPA as much as he could. When he went on the interview circuit for a summer internship before his senior year, he was amazed at how much of a challenge it was for him. Nobody called him back.

That fall, he continued to interview as aggressively as he could for a permanent position working his way through the maze, but he was unnerved. He was a bit further taken aback when he was not called back for subsequent rounds of interviewing. It disturbed him in the beginning and then it gnawed at him. He became scared. "What will people say if I can't find a job?" He heard his mother's voice when he asked himself that question. He imagined her having a conversation with Dipti. "My Vijay just finished his residency. How is your Arun doing?" He began searching for what would provide him greater security. He thought of approaching Arjun again about this, maybe even to solicit his help? It killed him to have to turn to him. It was always advice at a heavy price. It was only euphemized as advice; advice with the expectation that it be followed lost that identity and became a command. If Arjun said it should be done, Rajiv demanded that Arun follow through on it.

Meena had become vocal again. She was beginning to drop hints and make demands that he ought to re-consider pursuing medicine.

Much to his father's chagrin, Arun was about to graduate with an eighty-thousand-dollar degree and no sense of where he was going with it. Rajiv made his concern for Arun very clear, repeatedly, in every phone conversation.

With Steven's nudging, Arun recalled his fond love of debate and decided to apply to law school while looking for a job. At the end of the year, he had no job offers, but an acceptance at Columbia Law School.

Rajiv was distraught that there would be more fees to be paid. The matter reached a climax when Rajiv made clear to Arun one day, "I having no money for your lawyer university fees." By the way his father reacted to the news, Arun could tell that it troubled his father very much. Arun knew his father would have to ask Arjun for the money. Arun wondered if it had challenged his father's manhood. Maybe Rajiv was beginning to feel as if Arjun were the elder brother and not the other way around.

Arun wasn't sure how to react. There was a quiet strength that seemed to swell within him, taking root in his chest. He thought he should feel fear, that he should be concerned. Instead, Arun felt a sense of relief. It was as if he were re-entering his comfort zone. Shouldn't his family be happy for him? He shrugged it off. There was another cause for his relief. By enrolling in Wharton, he was head-to-head with his Uncle Arjun. It sank into him that this was not a competition that he wanted to engage in for the rest of his life. He felt that at this point, there was no way he could win. He knew that he had to branch out on his own and make his own mark. He was relieved to have a different path and a chance to carve out his own identity. He resolved that he would find a way to pay on his own.

Arun's grades through Law School were not stellar, but they were sufficient for him to earn his degree. When he graduated he took a job with a law firm in New York called

Sangdon & Langley. It was a mid-size law firm, but one with an international presence with offices in Europe and Asia. He focused on transactional work.

The workload was grueling for him in the beginning. However, he began to grow accustomed to it. He didn't have much time initially for social activities. He was in the office almost constantly. Over time things slowly improved.

• • •

"Hey," said Raj on the phone.

Arun recognized his brother immediately. "Hey. How's it going?" he asked.

"Badly," said Raj.

"Why? What's going on?" Arun enquired with concern.

"The car had a problem," said Raj.

"What kind of a problem?" asked Arun, tentatively, realizing that his brother might be up to one of his antics.

"It ran into the side of my friend's garage," said Raj.

"Uh-huh," said Arun.

"While I was driving it," finished Raj.

"And you are telling me this why?" asked Arun.

"Well, it's not really for me. You see, the guy at the collision repair place refuses to fix it."

"Why?" asked Arun.

"Because I don't have any money to pay him," said Raj.

"When did you become such a wise-ass?"

"When did you become such a hard-ass?"

"Okay, whatever, how much?" asked Arun.

"A thousand seventy-five. Better say eleven hundred fifty to cover tax."

"How are you going to get this fixed without Mom and Dad knowing?"

"They went to Uncle Arjun's for a few days," said Raj.

"Wait a minute," said Arun, "Why were you driving Mom's and Dad's car without a license?" He remembered his own experience of his parents not allowing him to get one at that age.

"Oh, I got my license," said Raj.

"You did?"

"How are you paying the insurance?"

"I'm not. Dad is."

"Dad is paying your insurance?"

"Yeah. Like I have any money," said Raj.

"I see," said Arun, "I'll send you a check." Arun hung up the phone. He didn't bother to say bye to Raj. He knew it didn't matter. Raj would recover.

● ● ●

"Hey," said Sanjay into the phone.

Arun recognized his brother's voice. "Hi, Sanjay."

"So, what do you have going on this weekend?" enquired Sanjay.

"We have a firm outing to Vegas," said Arun.

"You realize how pointless that is, don't you?" asked Sanjay.

"Well, I didn't decide to go there, I am going there with a bunch of other people from my firm," retorted Arun. He wondered why he bothered to give so much supporting detail to defend his position. Did he really want his brother to respect him that much?

"The statistics are never in your favor," said Sanjay.

"Yeah, I know," said Arun.

"The house always wins."

"I get it. I don't plan on gambling that much anyway," said Arun.

"You are stupid if you play slots."

"Okay. I don't play slots. Was there a reason you were calling?"

162

"Yeah. Thanks to you, there is no money for med school."

"What?" Arun had the sound of disbelief on his voice. After taking three years off, Sanjay had decided to go back to school to become a doctor. Arun remembered with chagrin the joy that had erupted from his parents as a result of the news.

"Yeah. Because you wouldn't pay Uncle Arjun back for the undergrad degree he bought for you, he won't shell out any more money for the rest of us."

"Whatever," said Arun. "Have Dad talk to him."

"That's what he told Dad."

"First of all, I never knew he was paying for it until I was in the middle of college, secondly, I didn't know I was supposed to pay him back, and lastly, I paid for law school on my own." Arun sensed his defensive self taking center-stage. He tried to keep in mind he was talking with a family member.

"Well, Uncle Arjun paid Dad back, so he expects you to do the same. Anyway, med school is more expensive."

"I didn't know Uncle Arjun paid Dad back. Dad never mentioned that," said Arun.

"Yeah, he did." Sanjay stayed quiet. Arun sensed he was doing it deliberately.

"Hey, wait a minute, Uncle Arjun paid for your undergrad degree too, are you planning to pay him back?" Arun was beginning to get more frustrated with his brother.

"Well if you didn't, why should I?"

"Do you realize your reasoning is circular?" asked Arun.

"Of course I do," said Sanjay. "Remember with whom you are speaking."

Arun rolled his eyes. "So what do you want me to do about it?" asked Arun.

"Pay Uncle Arjun back."

"If I do that, you'll have to do that."

"Then pay for my med school," said Sanjay.

He knew what my response was going to be when I made my earlier comment about him having to pay if I pay.

"Sanjay, I love you, but I'm not paying for your med school," Arun commented.

"Okay, well, you are just forcing me to join the army."

"I am not forcing you to do anything."

"You don't want me to go to med school?"

"I never said that, Sanjay."

"Mom wants me to go. You never fulfilled her dream so now it all rests on me."

"She only had that dream when she found out her friends had that dream," said Arun, exasperated.

"You still didn't fulfill it," said Sanjay.

"Look, I have to go," said Arun. "What is this army business?"

"If I go ROTC, the army will pay."

"That's what you are looking into?"

"And then I have to serve with them for a few years," Sanjay explained.

"Why don't you just talk to Uncle Arjun again? Tell him you'll do it as a loan."

"Why don't you talk to Uncle Arjun?"

"Okay, forget about it," said Arun, "I'm hanging up the phone."

During the entire Vegas trip, Arun had a hard time getting the conversation with Sanjay out of his mind. He suddenly felt guilty. He didn't know why he felt guilty. He didn't think that he should have to feel guilty. But he did. He couldn't help but feel that he had negatively impacted his brother's life. It bothered him.

What was wrong with his brother? Why did he have to come after him that way? *No matter what, I don't think Uncle Arjun would have ever talked that way to Dad. Or maybe he would have? I can't believe he won't help Sanjay out. He has so much money. Why doesn't Dad make Uncle Arjun do it? I guess the same reason I can't make Sanjay do anything. God, it is so frustrating. I didn't know that Uncle Arjun wanted me to pay it back. Had I known, I could have done something about it earlier. I don't care if he paid Dad back, that was his choice. Now they all think of me as the bad guy.*

• • •

Shortly after the Vegas outing, Arun flew to Hong Kong for work. He had no interaction with his family prior to leaving. He was still hurt by his parents, uncle and brother. The gutters were overflowing in his mind and the pathways were full of mud, refuse and sewage– there was no chance for him to think clearly. How could he be held responsible for what happened to Sanjay? Why did that hang over his head? He tried calling his family from Hong Kong, realizing that he was having trouble concentrating. He couldn't get through. One night after binge-drinking, he sought out companionship. Lately, Arun had been dating and was steady with someone most of the time. This was his first recent instance of seeking out the random, one-night stand. That evening, Arun kept holding the woman he had found at the bar close to him and attempted to kiss her face and back. She kept pulling back, resisting, almost becoming disgusted at his attempts to elevate their congress from sport to an amorous act. Seeking meaning in it seemed to disturb her.

A few weeks later he went to Brazil. He didn't speak with his family again during this period. He had a similar experience there. His woman of choice was a bit more accommodating, but she also realized just what a farce it was.

Arun continued his international deal exposure and received an assignment to be posted in India, where one of the firm's clients was based. It was the first time he had made a trip there.

Raj had called Arun asking for money the day of his flight to India. Arun explained about the trip. Within two hours, in one of the few instances in his life when it transpired, Rajiv called Arun.

"You must being visiting with your family there," said Rajiv.

"Dad, I'm not going to have much time."

Rajiv's voice became more forceful. "You must being going!"

"Dad, can I just get over there and see how things go. You know, see how much time I will have?"

"Why you no understand? You going. This is being final." Rajiv hung up the phone.

An hour later, Arun had another call. It was his father again.

"Everything being set. You taking the train. Your cousin and uncle being meeting you there," Rajiv explained. He spoke evenly, laying out his instructions.

Arun knew that he was powerless to resist. He was too afraid to defy his father. He agreed to go. While there, Arun received a cold shoulder during his visit. Rajiv argued with Arun that he didn't try hard enough.

"What did you want me to do, Dad, they kept insisting that there was no time to take me to the fields!" argued Arun.

"Why you no giving more time?" demanded Rajiv, clearing his throat. "You being disrespecting your family!"

"I did no such thing. I had limited time and I went to meet them. It's not my fault they were too lazy to make an efficient trip for me, Dad! I took the train and nobody was there to receive me. I had to stay in a hotel one night. I had to make someone else take me to the house. And then I had to go back." It was the first time Arun had spoken out against his father. He never raised his voice in the exchange, but he had the audacity to defend himself.   Arun felt tremendously guilty.

Rajiv hung up the phone.

The fiasco with his father's family aside, Bombay had been a mind-blowing experience for Arun.   He was shown around by his client's son, who was roughly his age.   His client was a very well-to-do family in India.   They had a palace on Malabar Hill and the son had his own place on Marine Drive.   The son partied a lot and kept Arun up all night going to parties and discos.   Arun mixed with the Bollywood set.   He was enthralled with this lifestyle.   When he was inside the various clubs, he felt as if he was in New York, London or Hong Kong.   He was amazed. There was another feature which he relished: women were noticing him.   He found it great that he was the center of attention.   He was always jealous of his American friends who would have girls fawn all over them back in the US.   In the US, Arun felt that the color of his skin was a barrier for him, in India, he had no such hurdle.   There were no tollbooths, no roadblocks, no detour signs – it was an open highway ready for him.   Arun felt like a king.   He became attracted to a woman working for his firm's client.   It was the first time that he had ever dated an Indian woman.   The identity conundrum didn't seem relevant – they were both in India, so it seemed to settle the matter.   But before he settled on one woman to date steadily, he spent a week where he took a different girl back to his bedroom every night.

"I know what it feels like to be John F. Kennedy, Jr.," Arun said to his host.

"Like whom?" was the response.

While his relationship didn't last, Arun found himself keen on Indian women for the first time.   When he came back to the US, he tried seeking them out.   He found that they were very different in the US than the girls he met in Bombay.   He seemed to remember that from high school and college.   They were far more guarded in the US. After a few months, he wrote an e-mail to his host in Bombay – "I need to come back; the Indian women in the US are so reserved."

He remembered calling a girl out on that issue and she had meekly responded, "That's how we are raised." The Indians in the US had become more conservative than those that stayed in India. *I suppose that's what happens when displaced immigrants strive so hard to preserve their culture – they have a tendency to overshoot.*

After he was done with his various trips to India, there was a renewed energy about him. He was getting more aggressive in the deals he worked on and more aggressive with the senior guys at the firm in terms of vying for more power. He began looking around to compare his economic well being to others around him. He noticed that his peers that were on Wall Street were doing a little better than him in terms of their financial well being. This gnawed at him.

"Maybe I can take Uncle Arjun on," he muttered to himself.

● ● ●

Rajiv met with his friend Pablo again.

"So, *señor*, we go for the meal that I would eat when I fell in love with my wife," exclaimed Pablo.

"I no understanding. While eating you falling in love with your wife?" asked Rajiv. He couldn't help himself, he blushed a little bit. The western concept of love was very foreign to him.

As they drove to the restaurant, Pablo explained. "My wife, Rosita, was a waitress at this Mexican place I am taking you to. I would go in there everyday and order the same thing."

Rajiv smiled. He couldn't help but be moved by this.

"It was chicken with mole sauce. They say the mole sauce is an aphrodisiac."

"What is being this?"

"It makes you fall in love," Pablo proclaimed. He made his voice soft as he explained this to Rajiv, as if they were two schoolboys about to engage in mischief.

Rajiv couldn't help but get red again.

When they arrived at the restaurant, Pablo ordered. "*Un pollo mole para mi* and for my friend, the vegetarian, please grill some vegetables and serve it with mole sauce on top."

Rajiv smiled. It was nice to be known. He felt very comfortable with Pablo.

"And how about you, *señor*, how did you meet your wife?"

"Oh it is being a very long story. Also is not being as nice as your story. Your story being very nice." Rajiv tried to smile for his friend.

"We have time, my friend. Please tell me."

"Okay." Rajiv waggled his head and cleared his throat.

"Before I telling how my family being in sugar cane…"

"Uh-huh"

"Meena's family also being in sugar cane. My family and her family making small numbers of the sugar cane. Together they making bigger numbers. My uncle and her father working together, making believing they are being one farm. Selling many numbers, bigger prices. Government thinking they are so big, cannot abusing them. If smaller and separate, government abusing, forcing much lower prices. My uncle and her father thinking making one big family. So, I marrying Meena."

"That's not so bad a story, *señor*!"

"There is being sad news. Actually Meena supposing to be marrying another. That boy's father getting very angry. His older son marrying Meena's older sister many years earlier, so wanting to keep in family. He getting so angry, he telling police about making believing one farm. Police coming and arresting my uncle and Meena's father."

"Oh for colluding, *señor*?"

"I not knowing this meaning, but government not being happy two families pretending one family."

Rajiv noticed Pablo smile and nod his head.

"My uncle saying you bring Lakshant, he my father's cousin, who saving me after tractor injury, to sitting in the jail. My father agreeing.   This was being very sad for Lakshant. After being five years in the jail, he coming out, nobody talking to him, his wife, his childrens.   I telling my father, not being nice, he no doing wrong things, why no one talking with him.   My father saying this is being the way.   If one family member going down, whole family cannot be going with him.   Must respect family.   Family first, individual second."

"Wow.   *Señor*, this is very harsh."

"It is being how things are doing there.   I thinking is worse for Meena and Meena's father.   After Meena's father coming back, he agreeing continuing with marriage to me.   Later he getting news his older daughter die.   Her family saying burning in accident.   But they knowing the truth.   This happening many places in India, her family putting her to the fire. Locking the door so she cannot being coming out."

"Oh my, *señor*.   This is a very tragic story."

"After I telling my brother, 'Bad things happening to families when there is being trouble, especially being with the law.'   My brother he saying back to me 'Bad things happening when you are being too close to family.'"

CHAPTER ELEVEN

April 2007

Arun called his brothers to invite them for Nandini's party. Usually it was Arun who would have to initiate any form of communication with them. Sanjay and Raj tended to be very involved in their own lives. Sanjay ended up practicing medicine. After completing college at Harvard, Sanjay eventually went to the University of California at San Francisco for medical school. Although Raj had attended UCLA, he was working at odd jobs. He seemed to always be involved with restaurants, but Arun didn't know what career that would constitute.

"We are throwing a party for Nandini. You should come," Arun informed Sanjay. He thought he would start with him first.

"Why don't you call Sujata to let her know?" Sanjay asked in a limp, disinterested manner. Sujata was his wife.

"Because I am calling you," retorted Arun. Sometimes his brother really upset him.

"Yeah okay, sure," Sanjay responded.

"Okay, bye," said Arun. There was no further comment from his brother. Just the line going dead.

Arun tried Raj next. He had to leave Raj a message.

Later in the day, Arun's cell phone rang. "Hello, this is United Airlines calling," said the person on the phone.

"Yes?" said Arun, curious as to why they were calling.

"I am calling to inform you that your next flight has been upgraded," indicated the agent.

That's funny, thought Arun to himself. All of his business travel had been cancelled. He also had no personal trips planned. "Which flight is that?" asked Arun.

"Yes, you will be traveling on a private jet with the president of the airline. He has a similar routing that day and he would like to be able meet his best customers," said the agent.

It occurred to Arun that perhaps all of his flights had not been cancelled. "Um, this trip was not cancelled?" asked Arun.

"No sir, it was not."

"Well, this flight should have been cancelled. Also, I don't think I will be flying that much anymore."

The voice on the line changed. "Why not?" It was the sound of his brother Raj's voice.

"You are such an ass," said Arun.

Raj began laughing.

"I hate how I always fall for this crap. You are too good," said Arun. This was the latest in a long line of practical jokes his brother had been able to play on him and on others.

"Oh, for my sweet little princess! I can't believe she is six already. Okay, I'll be there. I'm bringing Anthony," responded Raj when Arun told him the reason for the call.

"It's going to be mostly family," indicated Arun.

"Anthony is like family. Mom and Dad have been seeing him for years. He's practically a fourth son."

"Okay fine," said Arun. He was actually indifferent whether Anthony, Raj's roommate, were to come or not.

● ● ●

Arun's lawyer phoned him.

"I spoke with the people at GoWire," his lawyer said. "They also sent over a letter."

"What did the letter say?" asked Arun. His heart began beating a little faster. He began looking for his wallet.

"If you wire two million dollars to them in the next forty-eight hours, they will consider this a closed matter," said his lawyer.

Arun opened his wallet. He looked at the photo of his wife and kids.

"Arun, do you have the money?"

"No, I do not," Arun replied.

"What about your uncle…"

Arun cut him off. "I suppose the matter is still open." Arun hung up the phone.

● ● ●

Arun weighed the pros and cons of telling his parents and uncle. He couldn't remember a time when he had felt more conflicted. He knew that they were the ones he was supposed to be able to turn to in a crisis. They were supposed to help him. The money from his uncle could get him out of this mess. But would they help him? He had a long list of experiences that would suggest otherwise. And wouldn't there be dire consequences as a result of telling them? They would shut him out. Forget the pain he would experience, how would he explain it to the kids? *The relationship was just too fragile*, Arun thought to himself. He knew how they would react. He was afraid of their response, fearful of breaking that tenuous bond. He sensed that only heartache and pain could come of his telling them. Radha was right in encouraging him to pursue family in his time of need, but he didn't have a sibling like Anjali or a mother like Parvati to whom he could turn.

What should he do?

● ● ●

Andy met with Arun once again.

"I have copies of those documents," Andy said.   He was waving in his hands a yellow letter-size envelope.

"Are you sure nobody saw you?" Arun asked, his tone hushed.

"I think it's okay.   I did it late at night, around one in the morning, when I knew nobody would be around," Andy said.

"Good.   Let me see these."

"Oh.   This is some fascinating reading, let me tell you." Andy continued to wave the envelope and had yet to hand it to Arun.

"Okay, let me see."

"It's going to blow you away," Andy reiterated.

"Give me the damn envelope," Arun demanded.

"Oh right…sorry…here."

Arun opened it to see a series of wire transfer agreements. They had his signature on them and Derek's.   "These are a bunch of transfers to an account at a First Heritage Bank.   The account has my name on it."

"Yeah.   My guess is they are trying to say that you forged Derek's signature."

"I should try contacting this bank," said Arun.

"Done it already.   The account has a zero balance."

"You pretended to be me?" Arun asked Andy.

"Hey, if these jerks can do it, why can't I?"

Arun smiled.   "Where did the money go?"

"To an off-shore account registered in the British Virgin Islands.   Also, under your name."

"And from there?"   Arun's heart was beginning to beat fast again.

"From there it disappears, as does US jurisdiction to find out where it goes."

"Unfortunately for me, there is enough to incriminate me already," lamented Arun.

"Uh-huh."

"Can you get your hands on the company's original bank statements?"

"Yes."

• • •

"Why do you say loo instead of bathroom?" asked Nandini of her Anjali *Ma-si*.

"How do I explain to you my little one?" Anjali bounced her around in her arms as Nandini giggled in delight. "The long answer is that we are all far, yet near. We are Mother India's offspring – foster children spanning the globe, divided by a common heritage."

"What does that mean?"

"When your grandparents decided to leave India, they each chose different places to settle. Your parents grew up with different backgrounds, but we still share a togetherness."

Arun walked in. He grabbed his daughter in his arms and continued with the same antics that Anjali had been performing.

"Are you going to be smart like your Anjali *Ma-si*?"

"Yes-s-s-s-s, Daddy-y-y-y-y-y," squealed Nandini joyfully.

• • •

Derek decided to call Arun. *He couldn't help himself*, Arun later thought. Derek knew that Arun had a lawyer, but he chose to call Arun directly.

"We have informed the US Attorney," he said to Arun.

Arun's first reaction was, *How many victory laps is this guy going to take?* And then his heart started to beat so fast that he thought it would leap right out of his chest. Arun couldn't find his breath. *Why do these sensations repeat themselves? I thought I might be done with them after coming to terms with them the first time they occurred.* Arun felt nauseous. The world spun around him. He felt like he was at the center of a carousel, but instead of horses spinning around him, there were people's faces. All of them were laughing at him, taking such joy and pleasure in his misery. He saw Derek's face, he saw Chet's face. He passed out, hitting the hardwood floor of his den with a thud. It was the last thing he remembered.

He eventually came to and he found himself in a cold sweat. He shivered. His shirt was completely drenched.

It was the waiting time that became the most agonizing. The not knowing. The going through life without the ability to plan for the future with any assurance. There was a freedom he was missing. He would look around him at the faces he would see on the street. *Are they going through something like this? What is the misery in their lives?* He wasn't so naïve to presume that he was the only one in the world suffering; he knew better. Was there someone, anyone, who could help him cope with what he was going through? Somebody who could just say with confidence that no matter what, everything would be okay? He tried to derive that from within himself. He would convince himself every day. He would remind himself that every day the sun rose, twenty-four hours passed, and the next day started again. One could rely on that. It had happened everyday for the last forty years of his life. It would happen tomorrow. Time would pass, and the landscape would change. Circumstances would change. This too would pass. It became a daily prayer for him. He longed for so many things, but chief among them was his desire to plan for the future without having to worry about some disruptive, injurious, external factor.

Arun's agony extended beyond the fear of the unknown. He still didn't have a firm sense of what to do with his parents and uncle. He debated, stressed, debated, worried, debated, sought refuge. He was so conflicted with what to do. *Either they believe me or they don't*, he thought to himself, trying to reduce the decision tree to its most fundamental possibilities. *Don't believe me.*   He had trouble saying it.   It was what made him most afraid. He was so afraid of it because it was the most likely outcome. He had to face it as if it could be a reality.   It scared him so much to think of that.   He thought about his own kids and their activities – what if Zubin or Nandini were in a situation like this? Wouldn't he implicitly believe them?

It was those thoughts that entered in the quiet moments of doing something else that were the most troubling and that he struggled to beat away.   The demons that would enter when there were a few minutes without concentration or distraction. Stopped at a traffic light, riding an elevator, waiting in line to pay at the store.   If only he could control those demons.   They would enter in those subtle, quiet moments, and then they would consume him.   They would lead him down an avenue that he would otherwise strive to avoid.   He would have to constantly, wittingly, actively snap himself back to reality.   In times past, he would saunter down happy lanes during this time.   How long before he could return back to those locales?

As he went round and round, his circular reasoning always brought him to the same point.   Arun needed to be surrounded by people whom he could seriously rely upon.   He held his wallet.   He looked at the photos.   He knew whom he could rely on and the pain of relying on the wrong people.   He realized that it wasn't just about him anymore.   There would be pain that Radha and the children might have to suffer through as a result of comments from his parents or their negative actions.   The decision was clear.   He had no idea what the future would bring with GoWire, with Chet, with Derek.   One thing he was certain of.   He would do everything he could to keep the news from his parents.   He was sure, the instant they knew, they would flee. He would struggle through this on his own.

•   •   •

It was a rare occurrence when the whole family was able to get together for an event like Nandini's sixth birthday. Radha's parents were visiting from the UK. A good family friend who had married a Hollywood actress was celebrating a birthday party and Radha's father insisted on being there. Arun's brothers would be coming; Sanjay would be bringing his wife. Arun's parents came down from the Bay Area. Rajiv had just come out of the hospital; nonetheless, he and Meena insisted on driving down. Uncle Arjun was in town for business. The only one missing was Radha's sister Pooja.

In addition to the immediate family, the guests that evening would include members of the Gandharnis "extended family" in the US. These members included those non-Indian origin friends, neighbors, classmates, roommates, store owners and business colleagues with whom the Gandharnis had befriended and from whom the Gandharnis had learned how to become American. If they weren't themselves immigrants, they would think of themselves as the *"hosts"*, for inevitably, most viewed it as *"their country"*.

This distinction inevitably surfaced with the query "where are you from?" Foreigners, or visitors, would quote another country. Hosts would cite another city or state within the US. For those children of immigrants, the question posed an interesting dilemma.

Arun was attempting to purge his negative thoughts to try to focus on enjoying himself for his daughter's party. He didn't want the event to be affected by the incident or for his family members to glean that something was not right. He didn't have the patience to deal with their barrage of questions if they suspected that all was not well.

As Arun drove up to his house that day of the party, he thought about all of the things he could have done to make Nandini's birthday a grander affair – he could have rented a hotel banquet hall, or at least a restaurant. This was his precious little girl. The reasons why he was forced into not doing it were poignant. Unfortunately, they were also significant. It bothered him how the incident had to dictate his actions, another example of how his family had been victimized. All that he had suffered through in the last two months flashed through his mind and in that omnipresent psychosomatic relationship that is the mind's way of exerting its dominance, and superiority, over the body, it culminated into a focal point of physical pain over his heart. He had the knee-jerk reaction to put his right hand on his chest where he felt the pain. He felt foolish afterward for doing it – that wasn't going to take it away. Oh that dreaded, fear-induced pain. He was trying his best to maneuver down another side street.

On most days that he would come home, Nandini would watch him from the window and expect him to do stunts for her. He did this in the hopes of making her laugh. Nowadays that notion was lost on him. He hadn't done it for her in weeks, since the incident. He had either been distracted while coming home or he had been sitting in the house all day. Today when he looked up at the window, he saw that Nandini was there. She was looking at him. He wondered how many times in the last few weeks she had looked out for him and Arun had forgotten to look up at her. He tried to conjure a stunt, but he couldn't make it happen. *She must know something is off*, thought Arun. It troubled him that she was missing out on something on account of the incident. He felt a sudden pain in his heart again. How do I provide my darling girl with a quiet, secure street where she can be free and protected?

"I must try to make it up to her somehow," Arun muttered to himself.

As he attempted to put his chest forward, as he had done in the past, he found he couldn't bring himself to do it. Arun

Gandharni was damaged. No chest would stick out for some time. No stunts would be played for awhile. While the incident no longer paralyzed him, and he had become active once again, it hadn't completely removed its tentacles on his emotions. He had climbed out of the hole in the road, but he was still on the block. These fleeting thoughts were the pace cars that ushered in a whole race track of other musings. While most of his mental meanderings were whipping around his mind, he always felt a slow motion, frame-by-frame crawl as he thought about his parents, brothers and uncle. He was going to encounter all of them this evening. He wished he had a familiar face in the mix. He then realized that in fact, they were all familiar faces – what he really wanted was a familiar soul. He had agreed with Radha beforehand that they would say his new job was going great. She had not been happy when he told her that he had concocted a story about leaving for another job. She was even unhappier when Arun continued to insist that they not tell Anjali or her parents. He had a suspicion that Anjali was already attune to things not being right.

Arun took awhile to get his uncle out of his mind. *He could find out about this through his work channels,* worried Arun. There was that risk. GoWire was similar to some of his uncle's investments. Word could get out to him. He then thought about the advice his lawyer had given him. Arun reasoned that it would be a disaster if his uncle found out. The whole point of going to GoWire, Arun recalled, was to try to outdo his uncle, for once.

He knew he had to come up with a clever cover in terms of his new job. He had to think about who it was he was working for, where they were located, what he was doing. He had to conjure co-workers' names, the product that the company made or the service it provided and a history of the company, all to support the pretense of being employed. If his Uncle Arjun began asking questions, Arun risked being exposed.

After opening the front door, Arun first saw his ten-year old son, Zubin. Zubin moved towards him at a quick pace and, as he had done on each day of his father's returns prior to this one, he stood a few inches short of his father with his hand shyly placed over his mouth and waited for his father to approach him. As Arun embraced his son, having not completely shifted his thoughts away from his parents, he remembered the praise his mother had given him for having a boy first. While he had found it to be irrational, that praise somehow made him feel good at that moment. He held his son even tighter than he typically did. It was a rare instance in his memory of his mother saying something positive.

Hearing that her father had entered the home, young Nandini came bolting down the stairway from the window where she had been watching him. Arun caught sight of her. Nandini never stopped short; she dashed right to her father and if he did not time it right to move his body in position to swoop her up, she would tug at his pants legs impatiently until he released Zubin and picked her up. At six she was still eager to bask in the attention and doting that Arun provided her. Arun was elated that he never ceased to be the biggest presence in his daughter's life. *I am the center of her universe,* he thought to himself. He held her tightly, more tightly than he had held Zubin.

Radha, coordinating the food preparation for the evening's festivities in the kitchen, continued with her concentrated effort, but spared a moment to stick her head out from behind the wall.

With a smile she quipped, "Sustained."

Arun smiled at her, knowing that his clever wife was utilizing her wit to get a point across to him, her mild approach to saying she wasn't happy. He was pleased to be back in the rhythm of doing that.

Without waiting for Arun to respond, Radha continued, "The children have an objection to your tardiness." She was playing up her British accent.

"Yeah! Yeah!" shouted Zubin and Nandini.

"And you are going to support them?" asked Arun of his wife.

"They can be relied upon to be to be mindful of the time," retorted Radha.

Arun winced at her comment. He knew that this was his typical behavior. He was suddenly very sad as he thought about how he had sacrificed so much time with his family for his job, all for nothing. *I think she has been forced to go through enough on account of me*, he thought to himself. He thought of saying something to defend himself. He usually staged a huge argument to justify why he wasn't there earlier. Sometimes, Arun could simply not help it, at least that was how he pleaded his case with Radha. Defense came naturally to him; debating was his strong suit. When under fire, he was typically quick to resort to it. He would step down, however, when he became cognizant that it was his wife. On this occasion, in light of all that they had gone through, he decided to be particularly gentle with her.

"How do you plead, Mr. Barrister?" trumpeted a mildly triumphant Radha when she saw that Arun was not about to mount a defense. Arun knew that she was saying it this way because she was aware of how Arun would get when she pushed points with him. She understood him. She understood that after pointing out a mistake he made, she ought to ease up on him and end the discussion quickly. The word *barrister* was still a remnant of her upbringing. She continued to put groceries in the *boot* and take the *lift* in a building.

"I like spending time with my dear Nandini," Arun replied, continuing to hold his daughter and snuggling his nose to her face. He decided to dodge his wife's line of enquiry.

"That's okay, Daddy," chimed Nandini. "You are here now." She was always so forgiving to Arun. *I am very fortunate to have that*, he thought.

"At least one of the women around here is soft on you," said Radha.

"No chance of getting both?" asked Arun as he moved in to kiss his wife.

Radha covered her face with a paper towel. Arun smiled at how his wife was still playful after so many years of marriage. "No chance whatsoever," she responded as she lowered the paper towel and kissed him on the lips. There it was again. "*Shance.*"

In response to his wife's rebuke, Arun praised her earlier dialog. "We ought to get you on *Law & Order*".

"They called," responded Radha. "I start next week." Arun loved his wife's rapid-fire sense of humor.

"By the way, some fellow saying he is your cousin from India called. Didn't leave a name."

"Oh," said Arun, "he's probably the same guy that e-mailed me. I think we should continue to ignore him."

His thinking was interrupted by Nandini approaching, dragging the large paper bag Arun had brought home with him into the kitchen.

"Daddy, Daddy, what's in the bag?"

"Oh, those are the gifts that your grandparents sent," stated Arun.

"How come's they sent them before the party?"

"Uh…they wanted you to feel excited."

Radha gave a knowing smile to her husband. Arun could see, it was laced with pity.

"I'll get ready," Arun said firmly as he walked out of the kitchen. In his heart he knew he was referring to his emotions as well as to his attire.

CHAPTER TWELVE

May 1994 – May 1995

Arun and Radha first met on one of his business trips to the UK. He had often heard of his mother's friend Parvati Bhardpuri in the UK and her husband Kishan, the politician. While she was not a blood relative, somewhere in the family tree there was a cousin who lived next to their second cousin's daughter back in India, hence under the definitions of the new Indian diaspora, they were friends, practically relatives. It was considered rude in Indian culture to refer to a friend of one's parents by their first name. Even the name "Mrs. Bhardpuri" would create a distance that seemed inappropriate. The term Auntie or Uncle would have to be used. They were throwbacks to the cultural heritage of being Indian. One of the few trademarks that those alienated from the land attempted desperately to hang onto, as they grappled with their identities.

Kishan Bhardpuri had recently been elected as a Member of Parliament from the district in which he lived. Arun's mom was even more insistent that Arun visit with them, although Arun knew that most of the insistence came from Dipti. When she heard that Meena knew someone in Parliament, Dipti insisted that Meena get to know them better.

"You take sweets to their house. You no go with nothing," Arun's mom told him.

He let out a deep sigh as he stood outside of his boarding gate at the airport. He had ignored her first three calls; he thought he better pick this one up. "Where am I going to find that? I told you I am going for work, Mom."

"In England Indians is all places. You can be going to Southall. All Indians there, isn't it?" retorted his mother.

As he shook his head in disgust, he caught a duty free shop in his gaze. There in the window he spotted his solution, a box of Godiva chocolates. He quickly placated his mother. "Don't worry Mom. I'll find the sweets to take to them."

"Why I worry? You must do means you must do. Also you say *namaste* when you meet ..."

Arun could feel the darts flying. "Okay, Mom."

"Also, you should bow down to touch feet. She is like sister to me, isn't it?"

Arun recalled how she was just an acquaintance prior to her new status as Mrs. MP. Arun didn't even remember his parents sending her family a holiday greeting card. He had done the custom of touching an elder person's feet many times before. It required him to bend down and make a motion from their feet to his own forehead with his hands, a sign of respect. He recalled that it was typically done only with relatives. He had done it with his Uncle Arjun and his own parents. He was waiting in line at the store with the box in hand. "Sure, Mom."

"You buy nice sweets. Get bigger ones. No cheap ones. You get big numbers also. I don't want any bad talk. Peoples always saying bad talk. We never do enough. Dipti says make sure this never happen. Take few boxes, isn't it?"

"Yes, Mom," said Arun as he signed the credit card slip. "Mom, my flight is boarding now. I have to go," he attempted to conclude.

"Also, don't you forget..."

"Sorry, Mom, I'll call you from there." Arun hung up the phone.

He liked flying for work; it allowed him to fly business class. He enjoyed how it made him feel better about himself – as if he were somehow more deserving or had earned a place amongst more important people. It gave him a natural rush to head to the front of the plane.

Arun decided to get the visit to the Bhardpuris out of the way early in his trip. After settling in at his hotel, he went down to the taxi stand and gave the driver the address. It was nearly dark already so he did not have the best view as he drove. He let his mind wander with thoughts of work as he approached the house. He was hopeful he could finish here soon so he could go back and find a nice bar to go to for the evening.

Arun rang the doorbell. A girl answered the door. She seemed to be in her late teens, not quite twenty. Arun thought to himself, *If only she were older*.

She remained quiet, observing him.

Arun asked, "Are your parents home?"

"Yes. Yes, indeed," she replied and remained standing there.

Arun chuckled and said, "May I see one of them?"

"Which one would you like?" She gave a slight smile, one that hinted at her acknowledging the joke but also showed a reluctance to let up. There was a bit of a bratty element to that smile of hers, but there was also warmth that revealed that she would be gentle in her torture. She must know, realized Arun, that she was being a little difficult and being allowed to get away with it because everyone, like him, was now coming to pay respects to her parents.

Then it dawned on Arun, *that's right*, he thought. Auntie Parvati had three daughters. Arun saw an elderly woman approach the door from the back and say, "Don't mind her, *behta*, she likes to be childish. Run along, Angel."

"I'm not being childish, Mum, I am simply answering the gentleman's questions," the girl protested.

"Oh thank you, Auntie. No it's not a problem. Nice to meet you...Angel." Arun emphasized the nickname with a pejorative tone that indicated that her conduct was actually quite the opposite.

"It's Anjali, as a matter of fact," she responded with a distorted smile, indicating that she was pleased that the visitor got the irony. "It is only family that calls me Angel."

Arun nodded to her with a smile and proceeded to touch Auntie Parvati's feet.

Parvati commented, "I am impressed that even in the US you remember our traditions."

Trying to think of something clever to say, he quipped, "Well you know what they say, you can take the Indian out of India but you can never take the India out of the Indian."

Arun heard a giggle, but it came from the background. He knew it was generous; what he said was not that funny. Arun followed the voice to the top of the staircase. There he saw what he had asked for: *the girl who answered the door, only older.*

"That is my eldest daughter, Radha," stated Auntie Parvati.

"Hello," said Arun with as broad a smile as he could muster.

"Hello," replied Radha, tilting her head to one side.

What a ravishing British accent, Arun thought to himself. He had only heard her say "hello", but he kept replaying it, over and over again, in his head. He suddenly felt a wave of gratitude for his mother. He decided that perhaps she had her plus points. The group retreated into the living room. Arun watched, somewhat longingly, as Radha went into the kitchen. He met yet another daughter, Pooja. He noted at the time how she looked different than both Radha and Anjali. Radha came out from the kitchen and served everyone tea.

Like a series of emergency vehicles suddenly appearing on the horizon, disrupting the relative harmony of the day, Auntie Parvati's husband, Kishan Bhardpuri, stomped into the room like a fire engine with sirens blaring, turning a corner. He sat down opposite Arun and didn't say a word.

"Your daughters are lovely," offered Arun in an attempt to start a conversation. He noticed how Radha and Pooja turned a little red, smiled shyly and looked down. Anjali was transfixed on her father, awaiting his response, a seeming glint of hope that turned into a focused inquisitiveness.

"Oh, they're alright. I tolerate them," replied Kishan with a dismissive chuckle.

Then it was Anjali's turn to look down. Her lips also made a smiling motion, but it was more an indication of disappointed resignation.

Arun was taken aback by the response. At first he didn't quite know how to react. Thinking that perhaps the old man was fishing for Arun to be insistent in his compliments, he decided to retort with, "No, they really are lovely."

Rather than hearing additional lines of false humility, Arun received from Mr. Bhardpuri a glance that felt like an affront and that seemed to scream, *Are you trying to tell me something about my family*? Kishan locked gazes with Arun and asked him, "So what brings you to our great country?"

Arun decided that a change of topic was probably a good idea and responded with some earnestness, "Well, I am here on business. One of our UK based clients is interested in expanding into the US and -"

"Why on earth would they want to do that?" Kishan cut him off. "Don't they know that the business climate is much better here?" Both Radha and Anjali were quick to look at Arun, with almost a look of apology, on behalf of their father. Pooja continued to look down.

Arun faced a dilemma. *How do I continue this without pissing the old curmudgeon off so that I can spend more time with one of his daughters?*

"Well they made that decision. I'm just helping them execute." Arun decided that the safest approach would be to try and end this portion of the conversation.

Parvati walked in. She gave a pointed look at Kishan. "Be nice to our guest," she commanded.

Arun was taken aback by her statement. It looked like there was someone who could tame the pit bull. He looked over to the daughters. They didn't react to their mother's comment to their father. Arun wondered if his mother would ever do that to his father. And then he realized that Meena exercised her control through action and Rajiv showed his acquiescence through his inaction. This inertia propelled them through life.

Arun was relieved that Aunti Parvati had interjected like that. Kishan changed the topic once again. "So, where did you study?"

"Oh," said Arun, thinking that this would be an opportunity to impress the old man, "at the University of Pennsylvania for my undergraduate degree and then Columbia University for Law School."

"The American system of education is inferior to the British. You know that, don't you?" Kishan challenged.

Arun was at ease when Kishan did not pause for a response. Arun still wasn't sure whether or not he was being facetious with his aggressive character or if this was genuinely how he behaved. By the embarrassed look on the daughters' faces, he sensed it was the latter.

"For someone to become a lawyer here they don't have to waste four years in college and then another three in law school. They start learning what they need to know right away. I am a Cambridge Man myself. Pembroke College."

"I suppose it is a different approach," replied Arun, praying for the conversation to end.

"It's inferior," retorted Kishan.

Arun responded to Radha and Anjali's looks of sympathy with a look that suggested – *I pity you for having been born to this monster.*

"Pembroke is a great college," said Arun. He had learned something about the college system of the UK universities.

"Don't you think I know that?" replied Kishan.

Right, of course. How silly of me. His thoughts and the need to continue the torture of the conversation were relieved by Auntie Parvati making a suggestion. "Arun, maybe you would like to have a walk in the garden?"

Pooja remained seated and both Radha and Anjali sprung up.

Arun was thrilled at the prospect of ending his torture interrogation session.

"Anjali, perhaps you can help me in the kitchen?" asked Auntie Parvati.

Anjali first looked at her mother quizzically, but soon understood what her mother was doing and agreed. She made one final look at Arun, this time a mischievous grin creeping up on her face.

"You are right, dear. I need time to make my calls before dinner, and I don't need any further distractions," Kishan declared as he got up from his chair with a commotion.

● ● ●

The Bhardpuri residence was an atypical British home. Most houses that Arun had seen were the cookie-cutter red brick façade track houses – each one looking exactly alike. This one was slightly bigger and stood on its own. There was an expansive lawn in the back, and it was clear that care had been taken to make it look as regal and as grand as possible. There was a verandah with pathways of concrete. The property was not huge, maybe three-fourths of an acre, but it was well laid out. And for the region of Surrey, to the Southeast of London, that size land cost a fair amount. There were several lampposts and three benches. After strolling through the whole area, Arun settled on the bench that was furthest from the house and invited Radha to sit with him. He was amused at how all the benches were in plain sight of the house. He was further amused by the fact that Mr. MP, rather than having a phone to his ear, could be seen periodically looking out of the window.

"I thought all houses from England were made from the same mold. I thought the whole country had one architect," noted Arun.

This made Radha laugh. She seemed happy, and even a bit relieved Arun detected, that Arun had made an attempt to get her to laugh.

"I like your bit of a modern take on the tradition of presenting Indian sweets," said Radha.

It was a shortcut, Arun thought to himself. She didn't need to know that, he decided. "Thank you. I thought I would get something more reflective of us and our generation, you know, not being in India and all," Arun offered.

"Have you ever been?" she asked Arun. Arun's heart skipped a beat. He loved that high note she hit as she said *"been"*.

"I actually just went for the first time. It was an incredible experience. How about you?"

"We were there every summer," she told Arun.

"Wow, how was that?"

"Those were great experiences. It was a delightful time. I enjoyed it thoroughly, really I did. I feel really close to our culture because of it," she commented. "I can identify with the language, the people - you know what I mean?"

Arun understood that this was a rhetorical question. His British friends would say it all of the time.

"My sister Pooja really feels at home there," Radha added.

"You know," said Arun, "whenever I talk to my cousins over the phone and I use Hindi, they always start sneering and laughing at me. It is so demoralizing and frustrating. It makes me want to give up on the language and the culture altogether. I mean, I never make fun of them when they speak English in an accent that sounds ridiculous to me."

"It's all about the accent, you see? You've got to get that absolutely right, otherwise they will all have a laugh at your expense," Radha indicated, as she laughed to herself lightly. "I can help you with that - if you'd like." There was a meekness to the way that Radha spoke that Arun found endearing. Every time she said something she would look to him for affirmation that Arun understood what she was saying. It seemed more like she wanted to be sure that Arun had heard her. She moved her head with a delicate grace. Arun thought of morning rays of sunlight pouring into a room when the shades were opened slowly for the first time that day.

"That would be lovely," said Arun. He suddenly realized that he was beginning to sound like her. He was amused by that. He was also intrigued with how her suggestion pre-supposed that they would be sharing time together in the future. *I wonder how far her thinking has progressed*, thought Arun.

"Your father," Arun chuckled. "He is really pro-England."

"Yeah," said Radha. "He has a bit of a complex about it, actually. It comes from his having been alienated by all his brothers in India. They all clung together and left him an outsider. Papa had a rough go of it, actually. He scrambled for identity and being a haughty, almost scornful, nationalistic English gentleman suited him just fine."

Wow, thought Arun. He was impressed equally with the cleverness of her analytics as he was with the manner in which she articulated her findings. It stirred something in him. He was being seduced by her intelligence - her intelligence with respect to emotional matters.

"Those are such astute observations," said Arun to her. His tone showed the wonder that he was feeling.

"Well, I've had many a year to watch him," she said. Arun liked how she was being humble. She looked around the garden. She lifted her two hands up, looked at her two thumbs and then the rest of her nails and put her hands down again. She looked at Arun.

Arun could see the tenderness with which she thought about her loved ones. "And how about your mother? How would you describe her if you had to, succinctly?" Arun asked her.

Radha looked over at him. She smiled softly. "Mum is," she began, "really strong. She allows all of us to anchor ourselves in her. Unlike my father, all of her ambitions relate purely to the family and our collective success. She is very selfless in that regard, you know what I mean?"

If he had to, he could respond to that rhetorical question, thought Arun. He could sense how loving she was. Arun was touched that Radha described her mother with a passion and a compassion that warmed his heart. He could tell she wanted to be just like her mother. "That's great," said Arun.

Radha turned to him. "And how about you? What of your parents?" she asked him.

Arun suddenly felt like he should have sensed it coming. He hadn't prepared for the question. The honest answer was that he had no idea how he felt about his parents. And he certainly couldn't present an articulate summary of his feelings.

"Well…"

Arun agonized for awhile. He scrunched his forehead in deep concentration.

Radha seemed to be moved by this sight and shifted a bit. It looked like she was about to say something.

Arun decided to speak up. He didn't want her to feel like she had to rescue him. "You know...my relationship with my parents isn't the best. We don't really relate or talk very much," offered Arun. He felt like he stumbled through it. He was in a bit of shock that he had chosen to be so brutally honest. She seemed to cull it out of him.

"Perhaps you haven't got an understanding of how they are?" Radha suggested timidly. She shifted again and looked at Arun with an earnestness that seemed as if she wanted to be sure she wasn't upsetting him.

That's for damn sure, Arun thought to himself. Radha had stood up and started to walk. Perhaps she felt suddenly shy about being so straight-forward. He got up at a quick pace. He didn't want her to stop.

"Maybe they don't understand me?" Arun offered. He realized that it may have come across as him trying to be clever. He felt remorse. *Maybe I should have re-phrased that* he thought to himself, *I am not trying to be standoffish*. But he was genuine in his sentiment and his tone captured his frustration.

"Parents will always look to their children as kids. They provide as much support as is needed throughout their kids' lives. They parent as well as they are capable of doing. But they also are the sum of all of their own life experiences - strengths, weaknesses, triumphs and fears," Radha expounded.

Arun listened intently, absorbing what she was saying. He didn't expect to be getting this; somehow he felt like he needed it. It was therapeutic for him to hear.

"The onus is on the child to understand the parents, why they are the way they are. And ultimately, it is for kids to forgive their parents, if they feel there are any shortcomings. It's the only way to become a better parent ourselves. We can replicate those things we agree with and modify what we don't, accordingly," Radha suggested.

Arun stopped walking. He looked at the woman in front of him with an expression of dumbstruck reverence. He tried to think of something to say, but he wasn't prepared to respond. Radha tilted her head to one side and crossed her arms in front of her. Arun looked straight ahead. They continued to walk.

"So, I suppose you have been on many such 'walks'," Radha asked after several minutes had passed.

Arun woke from his thoughts. He felt like he was on a roller coaster ride, in free fall, his heart at his feet and the contents of his stomach on the verge of being seen again. He observed Radha. He was glad for the change of subject. He had a flash of insight that maybe Radha sensed that Arun needed the change too. That realization made him excited. She had rescued him, steered him clear to a thoroughfare where he was happy to stroll.

Arun thought he detected a little glint in her eye, a sparkle to punctuate the question with an exclamation mark, a little sign where she conveyed that she knew she was asking a pointed question, designed specifically to elicit information from him that she was eager to know.

"No," said Arun, smiling broadly, "I never walk."

"Oh, you just jump in, do you? How wonderfully American of you!"

They both laughed.

He looked over to Radha, who looked slightly disappointed. He laughed out loud.

"Okay, I'll give. This has been the first one arranged by my parents."

Radha seemed surprised. She shifted her body a bit.

"And you? How many have you been on?" asked Arun.

Radha laughed. "I knew I wasn't going to be able to escape that easily."

"No," said Arun, smiling broadly again. He loved the extra emphasis she placed on the word "*that*".

"There have been a lot of potential suitors that have come to the house," Radha revealed.

Arun turned to face her. He almost stopped walking and then remembered that he should continue. He didn't want to show too much alarm, or concern. On the inside he felt devastated. It was as if she had ordered a call to arms, rang a five-alarm fire, or triggered sirens announcing a breach of security.

Radha seemed to enjoy Arun's response. *Was there a little bounce in her step?* Arun wondered. She continued with levity, "But nothing has really been settled."

Arun looked away first. He didn't want her to detect his relief. He then turned to her and deciding to be sly, stated, "Well that's good to hear."

Without her looking up, Arun could see a smile creeping up on her face. Arun couldn't help but phase in and out of the discussion with Radha and his own thoughts. He was amazed with what he was feeling with this woman. It was as if she were inviting him to be honest and open. He felt a strange sense of implicit trust with her. The kind of trust that it takes months, if not years, to develop with some people. And then he felt a strange closeness, an intimacy that typically had a longer timeline for him than trust. He didn't believe in instantaneous affection, but unwittingly, the phrase "love at first conversation" popped into his head.

When they came back from their walk, Arun heard Kishan playing Gilbert and Sullivan's "He Is an Englishman" from the study.

Arun postponed his return back home. He took the last remaining vacation days he had available to him. He tried his best to work remotely to extend his time even more. He went into the firm's offices in London for three days to buy himself another week. But as much as he wanted, he couldn't drag his time out any further. He knew he had to go back. When he went to the airport, he had an inspiration.

"If I exchange my business class return for a coach seat, how much money would I get back?" Arun asked the woman at the counter.

When he got the answer he lifted his eyebrows. "Is that enough to buy a round-trip coach ticket?" he asked.

This time he lifted his eyebrows and his eyes became bigger. "Great. Get me a ticket to come back in one month."

When Arun went back to the US, he and Radha began a regular cross-fire of communication. It started with daily e-mails and occasional phone calls, which grew to daily phone calls. He re-structured his day so that he could be available to make calls to her when the time difference worked out. He bought a new watch that showed dual time zones. That way, at a glance, he would always know what time it was for Radha.

● ● ●

After Arun left the UK, Radha would think of him often. Anjali walked into her room one afternoon. Radha was holding a pillow to her chest.

"You're thinking of him, aren't you?" demanded Anjali.

Radha was shocked slightly, as if waking from a daydream. When Anjali repeated the question, Radha simply smiled.

"Most of the blokes coming through here have wanted someone to cook and clean and take care of their ailing Mum and Dad, or they have political ambitions and want to get close to Dad," Radha explained, "Arun…he listened to my thoughts. He was interested in what I was saying, almost moved by it."

Anjali smiled to her sister. Then she gave her a hug.

● ● ●

When Arun was planning for his second trip, he had his assistant call the Bhardpuri house and ask for Anjali. Arun then spoke with her. "I need your help," requested Arun.

"Okay."

Anjali called him after he had landed in the UK and was within the vicinity of the Bhardpuri house. "She's gone out. You can come now."

"Thanks for your help," whispered Arun. He then realized he had no need to be whispering, there was nobody around him. Arun went into Radha's bedroom. He left her a single rose on her pillow - unbeknownst to him the same pillow that she held when thinking of him - with the message, *Roses are meant for those who are beautiful*.

● ● ●

Arun had a hard time getting Radha off his mind after those first two visits. Unfortunately, several months had to pass before Arun was able to visit a third time. He and Radha had built such a strong dynamic over the phone and through e-mail during those months of separation. It was like a mini-series or a chain that formed a part of one great, long conversation. They fell into the rhythm of it very quickly. It turned out to be a little awkward to be in each other's company once again after that.

Their first in-person conversation in months started like their first one ever, when they first met, with the posturing. There was propriety, strategy, defense. Comfort set in, massaged by the ease of words, the seduction of their meaning, and the sweet lullaby of voices spoken softly. Intimacy bloomed once again. There were glimmers of safety, Arun detected. The space was no longer foreign or incomprehensible. It suddenly felt like an extension of him. His surroundings didn't begin or end; his body didn't begin or end. He became one with space, it was of him, he was of it. Liberation made Arun feel weightless, like a gossamer dress. Assurance strode along next to him, arm over his shoulder.   Confidence grabbed his hand firmly.   And then, in the quiet recesses, compunction died.   There was no thud to announce its passing; it went surreptitiously.   Barely did he notice that it was gone, and he experienced the alarm of forthrightness emerging.

"I feel so close to you," said Arun.   The words fell from his lips with such effortlessness that he surprised even himself. *Did I want to say that?   Did those words jump out or did I want to be that honest?*   He felt like a delicate baby, dangling over a mountain chasm with no safety net.   Observers - he, Radha - stood in awe. Neither breathed.   Silence screamed.   *Don't touch it - it is so fragile, so pure, so exposed.*   Being without clothes would be easier. Shelter was sought.   Arun found solace in resolving to take action. Arun breathed a sigh of relief followed by a deep intake of air.

He kissed her.

Both marveled at the feat.

He grabbed her hand and placed it over his heart.   His heart thumped heavily.

"See what you do to me?"

Radha was so moved that she shivered.   Arun could feel her hand trembling underneath his.   She couldn't look into his eyes anymore.   She looked down.   Seconds passed.   He lifted her chin up.   She still wouldn't make eye contact.

"Will you marry me?"

Arun got his response from the moisture that collected in one corner of her eye taking shape with each passing second in the form of a teardrop.   She looked him in the eye and smiled.   He kissed her again.

● ● ●

Arun and Radha were married eight months after Radha agreed to be Arun's wife.   The Gandharni clan and their closest friends, including Steven, invaded the United Kingdom for the wedding.

"Since we are halfway, maybe we being visiting India as well?" Rajiv had suggested. Rajiv had already spoken to a travel agent. The ticket cost would have increased by another eight hundred fourteen dollars. He weighed this in his mind. He had been with his company for over twenty-five years now. He had saved enough vacation time to be able to make a lengthier trip. He had actually seen to it that he would have enough time. He had written down the phone number, address and a contact person for the travel agent's London office.

"Well…the marriage taking much time…I no think there is chance," protested Meena.

When Rajiv raised the thought of a trip to India with Arjun, he received a similar lackluster response.

"I wouldn't worry about it," suggested Arjun, shrugging his shoulders as he spoke.

Rajiv was holding the number for the travel agent's London office in his hand. He threw it in the garbage with emphasis.

During the evening prior to the wedding, Radha's family hosted dinner for all of the out-of-town guests. There were over fifty people at the event. While everyone was enjoying their meal, the phone rang. The butler came running into the dining room.

"Sir, it is the Prime Minister on the phone," he said.

B.P. jumped up, nearly choking on his food. There were gasps from all of the guests – some of genuine shock, others of astonished admiration. B.P. quickly quipped to his guests, while chuckling, "Oh he does that all the time."

He picked up the phone and said in a loud, booming voice so that others might overhear him, "Good evening, Mr. Prime Minister, so kind of you to honor me with your phone call."

On the other end he heard, "Hello Uncle. Raj here. I just wanted to say that I will be coming a few minutes late. Is everyone else there already?"

• • •

The following morning, a Hindu priest officiated the wedding. While he was performing all of the ceremonial rites to bind Arun and Radha in matrimony under the Hindu tradition, he kept getting interrupted by messages from his wife. They were mostly questions such as "What shall we have for dinner on Tuesday?", "Do green beans still give you gas?", "Did you wear matching socks?" The messages kept being relayed by a little girl whom his wife was sending from an adjoining room. The little girl would get the priest's attention and blurt out the question in front of everybody. Finally, Arun got upset with all of the interruptions.

"Mom, can you tell her to stop sending messages for awhile?" demanded Arun.

"What is matter if she send message?" protested Meena.

Arun knew better than to ask his father to do it. Arun decided to get up himself. When he went into the room, he saw the woman who appeared to be the wife of the priest. She suddenly stopped moving.

"Are you the priest's wife?" asked Arun.

There was no response. Suddenly the little girl who had been delivering the messages to the priest came to the room. Arun posed the same question to her.

"No, that's Raj under there."

Arun pulled away the sari to reveal that in fact, it had been his brother Raj, dressed up in woman's clothing, pretending to be the priest's wife. His face was covered with the end of the sari, so nobody could tell who it was.

Arun stood still briefly, his mouth slightly open. He felt a sudden piercing in his heart, as if he were receiving an injection of anguish. Arun didn't say a word to his brother, who looked up at him with restrained glee as if he were waiting for Arun to join him in uproarious laughter. Arun quietly walked out. He detected a mild expression of guilt on Raj's face, but Arun reminded himself that it was most likely satisfaction at the joke he had played.

I hate how miserably unreliable my family is Arun thought to himself as he walked back to the area where the ceremony was taking place.   When he got there, he saw his brother Sanjay begin to laugh as he noticed Raj walking behind, still dressed in the sari. Meena began hitting Raj for wearing women's clothing and their father just watched the episode with apathy.   Arun's in-laws and he were the only ones not happy.   Arjun shook his head, pulled out his cell phone and began dialing a number.

Arun muttered under his breath, "What have I done to deserve this?"

While the family was waiting to have photos taken after the ceremony, Arjun was taking a phone call.   The crowd waiting for the photo was getting restless; however, Arjun kept holding up one finger indicating that he would be right there.   Arun could see that Radha was getting uncomfortable.   She looked like she did not want to remain standing in that position.   Arun approached his uncle, "Can we just take some quick photos and then you can get back to your call?"

Arjun looked at him with a scowl.   "I'll be right there," Arjun reiterated.

By then, almost all of the guests had arrived.   Naturally, they were mostly on Radha's side of the family.   They began asking for her and Arun.   Their entrance was being delayed as a result of waiting for the photos to be finished.   Arun grew increasingly more agitated with his uncle.

"Dad, why don't you tell him to come, it will only take a few minutes," Arun suggested to his father.   His father looked over to Arjun listlessly.   He turned back to Arun and tried to calm him by moving both hands up and down in front of his stomach, as if pushing down air and then allowing it to rise again. Arun found it condescending and patronizing.

"Mom, can you just get him for a few minutes? He can go back to his call after we are done!" he pleaded.

"He coming, you worrying too much," Meena insisted.

Arun looked at the exasperated expressions on his in-laws' faces. He also saw the tension building in Radha's eyes. He was beginning to feel embarrassed that his family was behaving in such a callous manner. More than twenty minutes passed.

"Let's just get started," instructed Arun.

"No, no rushing," emphasized Meena.

Arun looked at his brothers and asked them to go encourage their uncle to join them. Neither moved. Arun approached his uncle. "We are running out of time."

His uncle cupped his hand over the phone. "I'm coming."

When he went back to where the other members of the family were, his mother began harassing him. "How come you don't being more understanding?"

Arun looked at his father bitterly. Finally Arjun showed up. He made no apologies to anyone. Arun kept tight-lipped about the matter.

●　●　●

Later that evening, during the reception, Anjali approached Arun.

"You have such a screwed up family. They are so insular!" she proclaimed.

"What do you mean by that?" asked Arun.

"Look at them now. They aren't really mingling or talking to anyone," she pointed out.

Arun observed his parents. It was true. They looked a bit out of place. Arun thought to himself that usually his mother was talkative. And then he recalled that she would mostly do it when her friend Dipti was around.

"They are kind of always like that," Arun admitted.

"I know," said Anjali. "Life seems to happen to them. They don't seem to make life happen. That's a problem. Also, the men in your family are particularly screwed up."

"Great," responded Arun. "I'm not sure I want to hear this."

Steven rounded the corner. "You know, I have been telling him the same.thing for years. Your father, Rajiv," Steven began talking to both Anjali and Arun and was pointing his finger towards Arun as he spoke, "had tons of pressure dumped on him and always had to excel and please; your uncle never had the pressure but did something great with his life and ended up impressing the heck out of Rajiv; Arun, you have the pressure and can never end up pleasing your father or your uncle. And because of that they seem to have this indifference towards you. They don't give a damn if you are happy or not, suffering or not. They aren't able to take your feelings into consideration."

"When the hell did you learn all that?" Arun asked, mildly upset but mostly in a state of wonder.

"Years and years of observations," said Steven, putting his arm around Arun.

"What were you going to say?" asked Steven, turning to face Anjali.

"I was going to take a guess on the whole indifference bit. You really brought it into perspective, confirming it for me. I had only observed minimal clues," Anjali revealed, with a look of amazement.

Steven smiled at her.

"I did?" asked Arun, dumbfounded. He hadn't realized he had done that. He then realized that she was directing her comment to Steven and not to him. Somehow, his reaction still seemed valid, and he didn't bother to retract it or clarify the fact that he thought Anjali was making the comment to him.

Arun was impressed with how perceptive Anjali was. The fact that she blurted it out to him was impressive also, in a way. He was taken aback slightly by her straightforwardness. He was much more accustomed to Radha and her more subtle approach.

"And what do I do about that?" enquired Arun, directing his question to Anjali in an attempt to insert himself back into the conversation. He was hopeful that if she was so perceptive in her diagnostics, she would have some talent in knowing how to solve the problem.

"Oh, I have no clue. That's going to take a customized solution." She chuckled to herself. "Good luck. You'll have some work cut out for you."

That's depressing, thought Arun. He didn't want to dwell on it, but Anjali had such an aptitude for identifying what was wrong. *If only she knew how to fix it*, he thought. *If only I knew how to fix it*, he clarified.

• • •

"My daughter just had herself a son. I'm a Grandpa!" exclaimed Pablo to Rajiv.

"Oh, that is wonderful news. I am most happy for you."

Rajiv was grinning from ear to ear.

"Hey, maybe you'll be grandpa soon yourself," suggested Pablo.

Rajiv blushed a little.

"That's right," said Pablo. "You just got back from your son's wedding. Tell him to hurry on up."

Rajiv laughed.

• • •

After Radha and Arun got married, they spent the early years of married life getting settled in Los Angeles. Three years passed quickly. In no time, or so it seemed for Arun, Zubin was born. When Zubin was a few months old, they purchased a home. Radha suggested that they do a Hindu prayer ceremony. Arun recalled this from his childhood.

"Oh right, we did one of those when Mom and Dad bought their first house," recalled Arun.

"What kind of puja was it?" asked Radha.

Arun had a perplexed look on his face. "Aren't they all the same?" asked Arun, naively.

"No. Different *pujas* have different meanings," explained Radha.

Arun had a blank expression on his face.

Radha continued, "For the purchase of a home it is called a *grah pravesh*. It is performed to ward off any bad luck from the prior owners or dwellers and to wish for happiness and prosperity for the future for the family coming in."

"I see," said Arun.

It seemed to make some sense to him. It no longer seemed so mysterious or odd now. Arun thought that he might even like doing it. He wondered what other interesting thoughts or tidbits he had been made to miss out on while growing up.

● ● ●

Arun continued to be pleased with his position at his law firm, garnering much success. He closed large transactions, including some of the biggest that the firm had ever worked on. He was even bringing in some of these on his own.

Nonetheless, Uncle Arjun was still out there as a benchmark. Additionally, Arun would have weekly discussions with B.P., who would attempt to pry into every detail of Arun's work and attempt to make recommendations. Arun found this very stifling.

"I think he is jealous that you had a boy," reasoned Anjali, when he explained his plight to her.

Most significantly, however, he continued to feel that the compensation he was receiving was not commensurate with the work that he was completing for the firm in terms of bringing in revenues. It made him feel as if he was missing out on what a lot of his peers were experiencing.

Arun would take notice of and watch his friends where it seemed they were making so much more than him. That troubled him. He felt that he had been educated as well, if not better, than they had. He also thought that he was smarter than them. As if the pain of comparing himself to people in investment banking or private equity was not painful enough, he began to feel even more insecure as he began hearing about some of the Internet phenomena and the amount of money that some of those peers were beginning to make as they sold their tiny businesses to larger entities. Arun decided that he needed to jump into that mix.

CHAPTER THIRTEEN

Early May 2007

Rajiv and Meena were the first to arrive at Nandini's party. They had driven down from the Bay Area two days prior and were staying at a local friend's place.   It was the first time that they had come to Arun's house in years, keeping their distance during the "silent years" and being lukewarm in their affections for the three years after that.   In his heart, Arun knew his parents were staying at their friend's place to keep some distance.   It hurt him, and he knew it bothered Radha, but on the surface, Arun played it off as if the arrangement suited him fine and Radha pretended that she was actually pleased.

Rajiv entered with his characteristic quiet demeanor, greeting his son and daughter-in-law with seemingly equal aloofness.   It was with his grandchildren that he really lit up, especially with Zubin.   Since Rajiv was hospitalized the first time, nearly three years ago, Arun had asked Zubin to stay close to his grandfather whenever there were family get-togethers.   The years of silence hadn't really impacted Zubin.   He had been four when it started and seven when the marathon of non-communication ended.

"*Que pasa*, Zubin?" asked Rajiv.

It shocked all of those within earshot.

Arun turned to Zubin.   "Why are you teaching your grandfather such phrases?"

"It's not me!" shrieked Zubin.

"Where are Uncle and Aunty?" asked Arun, with a nervous prognostication of what was to come. He was referring to the people with whom his parents were staying; although not related to his parents, it was an important sign of respect to refer to them as if they were related.

Meena was quick to snap, "They will be here later."

In the background, Arun could overhear his father telling Zubin, "We came down on Interstate Five so we could see all of the fields of food that had been planted."

Arun watched as Meena took a survey of the room.

"Why you call us here before everyone? You expecting us we help?" she demanded of Arun.

Arun thought he could hear the sound of a tire deflating inside his chest. He certainly felt the sensation. He didn't think his mother would get started this early. Arun remembered when his mother used to be more easygoing and was not quite so caustic.

"Mom, you yourself are early. Anyway, this makes you more like the hostess – don't you want to be that for your granddaughter?" retorted Arun.

He was sure to look around gingerly to be certain that Radha was not within earshot. Not that Radha would have given him a hard time; he just didn't like the idea of diminishing the credit to his wife when he knew that his mother would not be doing a thing to play hostess.

Meena continued, "Why you see your father twice only while he in hospital? The man who do everything for you, and you do no things to help."

Arun preferred the times when she would invoke God in every other statement she made. Since her return from her trip to India a few years ago, she was a changed woman. Arun had grown accustomed to these recent diatribes; he cringed because he knew what more was coming.

"Your Uncle Arjun coming three times to make visit," said Meena. There it was. He wanted to say so much. *That's because he lives twenty minutes away.* But the words didn't come out. They *never* came out. He swallowed his suffering.

Rajiv was silent during Meena's invective. Arun didn't even get a glance. Defense would have been too much to hope for. Arun felt trapped with no way out. He thought to change the subject. He wondered if he should mention the cousin whom had been reaching out to him, but he decided to wait on asking about that.

"Mom, I think I settled the last of the hospital bills. Let me know if any others turn up," Arun offered.

"Where you settle all? Yesterday another showing up for twelve hundred dollars," said Meena.

"Well, Mom, that's why I'm asking."

Before his mother could get another word out, the doorbell rang again. It was Sanjay. Arun was relieved. He let Sanjay and his wife in.

Arun turned to his kid brother. "You have mom duty."

Sanjay gave Arun a quizzical look. Sanjay's wife, Sujata, who had been born and raised in India, raised her eyebrows. She always seemed to have a hard time understanding Arun's colloquial accent. She leaned into Sanjay.

Arun overheard her asking. "What is he asking of us to do?"

Sanjay would usually oblige her with a multi-second, multi-minute if need be, explanation of what had just transpired. This would all occur under hushed tones, much to the discomfort of whomever was in the vicinity. This time, he shrugged his shoulders.

Meena saw the two enter. "What you two whispering? Come and sit by me," said Meena.

Sujata quickened her pace and sat next to her mother-in-law, the pink in her cheeks becoming a few shades richer in color. Sanjay obediently followed the women in his life.

After a few more minutes, Radha re-entered the room.

Meena commented, "Looks like the Gandharni family knows how to be on time."

Radha replied with, "Papa just called, he needed help with directions. He is not used to driving in the US."

This seemed to quiet Meena. Radha had brought Nandini in the room with her. She told Nandini to go sit next to her grandmother. Arun overheard this. He was surprised that Radha was doing it. Radha had grown concerned in recent years that Nandini would believe something bad that Meena might be saying about Radha.

"I don't know what to do," Sanjay was pleading to his mother.

Arun overhead the conversation. "Regarding what?" he asked.

There was a period of silence. Arun had become accustomed to those awkward silences. He stood and waited. He decided that he had no intention of making it easier on them by shifting his feet, changing the subject or walking away. Standing there, staring at him, was like a challenge.

"Dad wants me to possibly go to India to look into the property matter," he finally said. "If Uncle Arjun doesn't come through for him." He never looked at Arun as he spoke, rather, he directed his voice towards the floor.

"You've been through ROTC training," commented Arun, not knowing what else to say. "You can tough it out in India."

Sanjay didn't respond to Arun. Arun knew why. For some ridiculous reason, he was still blaming Arun for their uncle not offering to pay for his medical school.

Arun thought it was odd how his brother, the quietest, nerdiest, most socially awkward of all of them, would be asked by their father to do this. Arun stayed quiet for awhile. He then decided to address the issue. It lingered in the air. He was tired of everyone just staying quiet about what was bothering them. Shouldn't problems be aired out and resolved? "Why do you still harbor resentment towards me?" asked Arun.

Sanjay was quiet.

Arun didn't want to end up in that rut again. "Listen, damn it, answer my question," Arun insisted.

Sanjay stayed quiet.

Arun looked at his parents. "Make him answer the question!"

They were quiet. "You calms down, Arun," Meena said.

"Don't give me that crap, Mom." Arun grabbed Sanjay by the arms and turned him so that he was facing him. "Give me an answer!"

"Why does everything have to be about you?" asked Sanjay.

"What?" asked Arun in disbelief.

"Everything is always about you!"

Arun was getting frustrated. "Do you just say the first thing that comes to your mind? You are so damn smart, how come you never think before you talk?" demanded Arun.

Sanjay stayed quiet. He had this look of disgust on his face. Arun knew that there was no way that Sanjay was going to say anything to him. Arun let go of his grip on Sanjay. Arun looked around. *It's a good thing only family is here,* he thought to himself. Arun avoided talking with Sanjay the rest of the evening.

Shortly thereafter, Anjali arrived. When she saw who else was there, she looked at Arun with a pleading facial expression that showed hesitation. Arun responded with a helpless look. Anjali rose to the task and dove into the conversation mix. She attempted to come up with conversation topic after conversation topic, the weather, the Indian prime minister's visit, traffic, but slowly and painfully ran out of things to discuss. Arun saw her look at her wrist repeatedly as he darted around continuing to set the home up for the guests. Soon Arun noticed that she looked to the door repeatedly. Arun then thought he saw her lips move, counting numbers.

"So are you still divorced?" came the comment from Meena.

Oh, said Arun, *she was counting the seconds until my mother asked the inevitable question.*

"Yes, Aunty," said Anjali forcing a smile, "things like that don't change."

She said this last part in such a hushed tone that Meena had to ask her to repeat. Anjali was spared when the doorbell rang again. She was relieved when she saw some white faces come through the door. Arun laughed to himself as he approached the door. He knew why Anjali was so happy. Indians would always be on their best behavior when Americans were around. Anjali knew that she would be spared.

The neighbors from across the street had arrived with their two young children. So did Meena's good friend, Dipti. Arun felt like he could now relax a bit. Dipti would keep his mother occupied.

.Steven was also at the door. Arun was shocked. But, he wasn't angry; he was relieved. "How did you find out about..." Arun began to ask.

"Nandini is like a daughter to me." Steven smiled as he spoke. "Plus, Anjali kept me in the loop." Anjali seemed particularly pleased to see him.

"I see," said Arun. He was happy that she had. After letting a few seconds pass, Arun finally spoke up. "Look, I am sorry about fighting with you over the whole Nandini situation."

"I am sorry for not being more respectful," offered Steven.

"No, it's okay, really.   I have a tendency to overreact when it comes to such issues, especially when it involves my daughter."

"I know."   Steven smiled.   "No harm done, my friend, no harm done."   He leaned in to give Arun a hug.   It left Arun deep in thought, particularly after the episode with Sanjay.   *Some friendships can be stronger than family bonds.*

● ● ●

Shortly after that, Radha and Anjali's parents arrived. Arun detected Anjali being more at peace having their familiarity present.   Her shoulders were more relaxed, her voice a little louder.   She seemed to still be on edge with her father; anxiety occupying her face when she stood next to him.

First Anjali embraced her mother, then Radha did.   Arun greeted Parvati after that.   He liked to tease his father-in-law. He extended his hand and proclaimed, "Good evening Mr. MP!" It was not lost on Arun that his father-in-law always had a huge smile when Arun said that, and it would certainly soften him up. Arun chuckled to himself as he thought about how B.P. would spend the rest of the evening ensuring that all other attendees at the event were aware of his title too.   B.P. simply nodded at his daughters.

Nandini approached B.P.   She was about his legs, ready to tug on his pants.   He didn't make any attempts to hug her.

"Parvati?" asked B.P.

There was no response.

"PARVATI!" he shouted.

Parvati had just finished embracing Meena and had given her usual *namaste* greeting, from a socially acceptable distance, to Rajiv.   She approached B.P., composed as she had been before the comment.   As she smiled and picked up Nandini, she said through her teeth, "Don't ever do that again."

A PERMANENT EXILE

Arun was within earshot. He scanned the room looking for Radha. His eyes caught Anjali's; she seemed to be enraged with the episode.

Parvati returned to talking with Meena.

"How are you?" asked Meena of Parvati. The concern that Meena was expressing was moving. He hadn't heard that sweetness in his mother's voice for a very long time. Arun knew that this was a facet of the old Meena. She had been terribly upset when she had heard the news about Pooja.

Parvati looked at her two daughters. Tears were beginning to develop in all three sets of eyes. Parvati went to them and spoke in a hushed tone. "Today is for Nandini. Don't forget that. And you think of your little one." She patted Radha's stomach. "You can't be crying like this whilst you are carrying."

Radha held her stomach and she looked at Nandini. Arun caught sight of her emotion. He knew why she was tortured even more than what her mother was witnessing. If only it could be shared, thought Arun. But it couldn't be that way. If Arun's parents ever found out that Radha's parents knew before they did, there would be severe repercussions. They would certainly cease talking to him then. He caught himself thinking these thoughts. He suddenly felt like a child again. It bothered him that he would feel this way. That he would be *made* to feel this way.

Arun noticed that Radha's gaze was still fixed on Nandini. She seemed to be spewing love from her eyes - as if there were a radiant beam emanating forth washing Nandini with emotion, nourishing her in the process, strength bestowed upon her, her mother crowning her with an inheritance of willpower that was the pillar of her mother's constitution. *I get my strength from her too,* Arun wanted to concede to his wife.

● ● ●

215

Raj finally arrived. "Ah, family get-togethers" announced Raj as he slapped his hands together and then moved them vigorously in a rubbing motion. "It always brings out the finest in everybody."

Turning to his mother he exclaimed, "Yo Meena! Wassup girlfriend? Gimme some skin!"

Most of those in the gathering responded with a snicker or a perfunctory giggle. Meena, who clearly thought her son had said something wonderfully savvy, was the only one who laughed out loud. She slapped her hands together and said, "It's so true, isn't it?" as she looked around searching for other people to acknowledge the intelligence of her son as well. Arun rolled his eyes. He hated the incessant affection his mother threw on his youngest brother, even when he was not deserving of it. It also upset him how he could get away with calling his mother by her first name. Arun imagined the repercussions if he were to attempt something like that. Raj smiled an embarrassed smile, one that seemed to reveal that he knew his mother was overdoing it and that the joke that he had intended was wholly and completely lost on her.

Uncle Arjun was the last one to arrive. Rajiv suddenly became noticeably more sullen. Arun could tell by how others altered the way they were interacting with him, that he did not command as much presence in his own house as he did prior to Arjun's arrival. It was palpable to Arun. He suddenly really resented his uncle for making him feel small.

Arjun's wife Sara seemed to be in a particularly jovial mood. She had not noticed Anjali when she arrived. The two saw each other. Anjali came over. Considering prior events, Anjali wanted to try and make nice with Sara.

"Look at us, we are the inverse of each other," Anjali commented.

Sara laughed, attempting to make it sound gracious, but it was more nervous than she wanted it to be, "Whatever do you mean, my dear?"

Anjali looked at her. She suddenly didn't feel as much guilt. "Well, you married an Indian. I married an American," Anjali illustrated, making a motion with her left hand to one side and her right hand to the other, as if she were making a comparison.

"Oh yes, dear, you are right," responded Sara laughing emphatically with a full backwards and forwards tilt of her body.

"Excuse me," said Anjali as politely as she could at the moment. Arun caught sight of Anjali as she walked away. She rolled her eyes towards him and blew out a deep sigh of relief. Arun couldn't help but laugh.

There was a noticeable tension between Arjun and Rajiv. Arun approached them, but stayed behind within earshot.

"Hello," Arjun said.

Rajiv smiled back.

They both stood together for awhile.

"You are coming from India?" asked Rajiv.

"Yes. I got back two days ago," stated Arjun. Arjun was flying to Bangalore and Bombay frequently for his work.

"Are you having any news?" asked Rajiv, seeming to be exasperated that he had to request the information.

"No, brother, I did not have a chance to follow-up on it. I will make some time to do it during my next visit," Arjun responded.

Rajiv looked straight ahead.

"Why you no understand?" Rajiv asked his brother Arjun, and only then did he turn to look at him. Rajiv cleared his throat.

Arjun did not give him a response. He carried a troubled look on his face. It was almost as if he was eager to roll his eyes but he was conscious of his brother looking right at him. After a few minutes Rajiv walked away quietly.

Arun found that he was staring at his uncle, who remained standing there. *He would probably know how to help me,* thought Arun, as he observed Arjun. *But no,* he realized. *He is the last person I could think of approaching.*

Like a light switch, Uncle Arjun whirled about and dived into another conversation. Arun knew his own father was likely in the corner sulking. Nobody was more gregarious and affable in the room, or in the family for that matter, than Uncle Arjun. He knew how to work a room. Arun would always find it fascinating how he would never exhibit this kind of warmth with his own family. It was like he lived two lives.

Sometimes he didn't understand his uncle. He had been worth millions for awhile now. Why would he come after Arun and pester him about that money so many years ago for his undergrad degree? Hadn't Arun's family done enough for him? It wasn't as if he had any kids of his own.

And then there was the ripple effect that drove a further wedge between Arun and Sanjay as a result of that. Arun felt that the damage between him and his brother was almost insurmountable.

There were several points in the evening where Arun wanted to break down and seek his Uncle Arjun's advice. Or just boldly ask him for the money. He was so desperate to hear some consoling words, some pearls of wisdom, or simply some comfort. He just wanted to hear one phrase, from someone who could be in a position of authority or who had maybe gone through something like this before.

"Everything is going to be okay."

He wanted to believe it. He needed to believe it. Couldn't somebody just say it to him? Could he hear it just once? He was brought back to his thoughts by a commotion he heard in the background. It was the sound of Anjali's voice followed by the crash of a plate hitting the floor.

"I am not an embarrassment. How dare you? HOW DARE YOU HATE US ALL OF OUR LIVES! YOU HAVE RESENTED US SINCE WE WERE BORN!" Anjali boomed.

Arun caught sight of his mother-in-law heading in the direction of the noise. Arun followed. He saw Anjali standing in front of her father. There was a broken plate of food on the floor.

B.P. looked at his wife, "You come here and manage your daughter!"

Parvati came to her daughter and hugged her. Parvati gave a stern look at B.P. He was about to say something more, making a motion with his hand and opening his mouth. Parvati spoke up. "You stay quiet." She spoke with firmness. It quieted B.P.

Radha approached her sister and with an expression of severe disappointment on her face directed towards her father –it was clear she had expected so much more – she walked her sister out of the room. It was only the second time that Arun had seen Anjali cry.

Uncle Arjun then turned to Arun. "It's a shame you left your company. GoWire's competition is having a hard time with its technology. It just came out in the news. GoWire stock is about to go through the roof."

Arun absorbed what his uncle was saying, but remained quiet.

"You shouldn't have left," he told Arun, his tone critical.

Arun looked at his uncle.

CHAPTER FOURTEEN

June 2001

Arun paid a visit to his family. He had not heard from them in several weeks. When he got there he saw that his brother was bedridden with a large mask of bandages covering the side of his face.

"What happened?" asked Arun.

His brother lay there quietly.

Arun asked him again. Still no answer. Arun went in search of his father. He could see him from the kitchen window. He was at his garden, seated in a lawn chair, staring out over it. Arun went in search of his mother. "Mom, will someone please tell me what happened?" Arun urged.

She turned to face him. She had been crying.

"He got an accident," she said after a long pause. There was an accusatory tone to her voice.

It put Arun on edge. "What kind of accident?"

There was another long pause. Arun felt like walking out.

"Army accident. He was in jeep."

"Why are you talking to me this way? What did I do wrong?"

After several minutes, Arun left. He approached Sanjay.

"I'm sorry to hear about your accident," offered Arun.

There was no reaction from Sanjay.

"I don't get you. Why are you bitter with me?"

By then, Meena had come down the stairs.

"It's your fault he in this military business," challenged Meena.

"What are you talking about?" demanded Arun.

"He ask you for the help and you no do it."

"That's absurd. Why didn't he go to Uncle Arjun? Why are you assigning the blame to me?"

"You had your help for your time. When turn for give help, you no help your brother," Arun's mother argued in front of him. She used that same accusatory tone that had agitated Arun earlier.

"What do you people think of me? That I have money pouring out of my ears? I paid for my own law school!" shouted Arun.

"Yeah but Uncle Arjun paid for your undergrad!" challenged Sanjay.

"And he paid for yours. So why don't you hate him? Why do you take it out on me?" demanded Arun.

"Yeah, but you were supposed to pay him back."

With that Arun walked out of the house. Thus began three years of silence.

CHAPTER FIFTEEN

Late May 2007 – July 2007

Arun arrived home one afternoon three weeks after the party and five days since the news appeared in the papers. He was occupying himself with household chores – getting groceries, dropping off paid bills, getting a replacement plant waterer for Zubin – anything to keep himself busy.

The phone virtually ceased ringing. Arun made a few calls the first two days after the article was published, but not a single call had been returned. Still, at the top of his mind, was the alienation from his parents, uncle and brothers. It troubled that they would begin anew another stretch of not communicating. He was willing to accept that they cared little for his feelings, but Zubin had become close to Rajiv – was there no consideration for that? Both Zubin and Nandini would notice the lack of interaction. And then there was another one on the way.

He changed his clothes quickly after stepping into the house and went to the front door. As he was reaching for his sneakers, he saw Radha.

"I am going with you," she said.

"No," said Arun, chuckling. "That's silly. I'll be right back."

"Either I go with you or you are not going," she told him.

Arun put the sneakers back.

Radha came to her husband and embraced him. "We are going to get through this," she said to him. "I need you to be strong," she added.

Arun stayed quiet. He held his wife. He looked up at the ceiling. Radha's head fit just under Arun's chin. It nestled there nicely. He moved his hand through her hair and stroked the back of her head. Arun wondered where he would get the strength from to fix this. He realized that he was holding part of the answer in his arms.

● ● ●

Andy called Arun.

"Arun, I am so sorry," declared Andy.

"It is good of you to call me," said Arun, relieved to hear from an old colleague. It was strangely endearing. He believed him, believed in him. Andy was a good man.

● ● ●

"Now what do I do with myself, Steven?" asked Arun.

"Take things in stride," suggested Steven.

"How am I going to support my family? Who will look after them?" asked Arun.

● ● ●

Arun knew the decision he had made and the conclusion he had reached. But now the news was out. It was troubling that he had not received any enquiries from his family. In his heart he still had hope, even though he knew how stupid and puerile that was of him. He knew they must know. At the end of it, he wasn't surprised that they hadn't reached out. Arjun followed all of this news very carefully. It was unfathomable that they wouldn't know.

Two weeks passed.

Anjali had come by the house on a daily basis. Her support was tremendous.

There was no word from anyone in Arun's family.

Arun thought to reach out to his parents.   He called with his cell phone.   He didn't get an answer.

"It's Arun calling.   Call me when you can," he left on the answering machine.

Another two weeks passed.   No response.

• • •

The paperwork arrived from his lawyer.   He saw the wording on the left-hand side of the page.

"United States of America vs. Arun Gandharni"

I have an entire country against me.

Arun couldn't remember a time when he felt so miniscule. It made it seem like a lopsided boxing match.

In this corner, the unchallenged, last remaining superpower, the richest, most powerful country in the world, unlimited resources, whose foreign policy makes everyone on the planet shudder, who can make or break the economic prospects of most countries, with power and influence stemming to nearly each of the two hundred sovereign nations on Earth and impacting each of its six billion inhabitants...AGAINST me.

His cell phone rang.   It was his friend Steven.   The weight of the words suddenly fell on Arun.

"I was just declared war upon," he told his friend.

He suddenly felt like Afghanistan, or Iraq, or Iran, or Vietnam, or Korea, or Germany, or Japan, or Terror, or Drugs. Any of the other countries or evils that the US had declared war against.   *I am now an enemy of that same ilk?*

"I'm dead," he told Steven.

With how many people would he do battle?   From how many people would he be alienated?

My father has quietly toiled in his job to make some already rich American more money.   My Uncle Arjun does nothing more than make already wealthy Americans wealthier.   Sure they made money in the process for themselves.   That was the point wasn't it?   The land of opportunity.   Everyone has to be happier here than where they came from right?   It was the American way.

What had this country given to him?   Sure, he was a citizen, but he never felt like he belonged here.   *First generation Irish, Italians, Germans, French or Brits are considered American if born here.   But me, I'm like the Chinese, Japanese, Koreans, Mexicans, Central and South Americans born here, I am always my ancestral origin first.   That's what people see.   Isn't that why the Japanese were interned during WWII and not the Italians and the Germans?   People from such areas are automatically called Indian-American, Chinese-American, Japanese-American, Korean-American, Mexican-American, etc. but you never hear of French-American, German-American or British-American.   You only had it partially right, President Reagan, when you said, "You can't go to Germany and become German.   You can't go to Japan and become Japanese.   But you can come to America and become American."   Maybe you should have kept talking Ronnie.   You left out, "If your skin color matches."*

This battle had been fought before.   This great melting pot.   *What about the content of my character?*   Wasn't that the dream of a great American hero, Martin Luther King?   Centuries earlier, his namesake had fought for change.   It created a lasting impact nearly half a century ago.   Dr. King won it for his people.   *There is irony*, thought Arun.   *His inspiration was Gandhi, who stamped out the prejudice in his own homeland.   Am I a part of that?   It didn't feel like it with my pidgin Hindi.   My cousins laugh quickly at me every time I tried to speak it.   My mannerisms, my speech, not fitting in.*

Arun often thought about this speech when skinheads would shout out to him, "Go back to your own country!"   *Intelligent people, aren't they?   Where am I supposed to go?*   He would marvel at how the same people in that crowd would be sporting nose rings.   He remembered fondly how he called out to them once, "Don't you know that that trend originated from where I came from?"   They appeared more taken aback by his accent, or lack thereof from their perspective, rather than the sudden insight into world cultural fashion trends.

He preferred talking over the telephone. There was anonymity to it. People assumed he was "American." Whenever he would say his name, they would ask *"Aaron?"* Ninety percent of the time he would just say "Yes." It was the same at Starbucks. He could see the look of incredulity in their eyes. *Hey, maybe I just have a really good tan,* Arun would think to say to them.

• • •

Radha attempted to convince Arun that he can't continue not speaking with his parents. She was struggling, seeing him mope about, his forehead being forced into the image of a comb's bristles.

Radha approached and put a hand on his arm. He looked up at her, startled, waking up from his thoughts. His forehead became smoother as he observed his wife.

"I think you should call your parents. Or go over there," Radha encouraged. "You don't want a repeat of last time. Three years of silence was so hard on you. The children are grown now. They will feel the impact. You know that the onus is on you. They won't act. Just accept it. You must make the first move."

This time, rather than responding, he just walked away. Radha could see the muscles in his forehead tense up as he walked away.

• • •

"I have some additional information that might be of interest to you," mentioned Andy, calling Arun again.

Andy asked to meet him. Arun went.

"So remember how we had been spending $150,000 a year on marketing studies to see what competitors, like LogicNet, were coming up with?"

"Yeah."

"Remember the one group that we hired that said they weren't doing anything competitive to us and then we got surprised at the trade show when LogicNet's product had more features than ours?"

"Yeah."

"And then the other group that came out with the doomsday scenario, saying that LogicNet had three new products they were launching, but there was actually nothing to worry about."

"Andy, where are you going with this?"

"Oh, well, we're not doing that anymore."

"Not doing what?"

"Our budget for market research has gone down to zero."

"No money on market studies?" clarified Arun.

"None."

"I wonder if it's because they are selling the company," considered Arun.

● ● ●

The worst encounter with Derek happened the day the company lined up its biggest customer. Everyone had been scrambling for weeks. The customer was very demanding. They wanted to draft a lengthy supply agreement and have that in place before they entered into the arrangement.

Arun was responsible for drafting the agreement. He would rely on input and direction from Chet and Derek. Arun attempted to present a document that was thoughtful, but that did not require a thankless number of hours to complete. Derek complained that terms were left out or were not explained in sufficient detail. Additionally, Derek was being overly generous with the financial terms. Arun was able to see that Derek was being too generous. He would highlight this to Derek.

"Derek, we are giving up the ranch here, buddy," quipped Arun, attempting to be lighthearted about it. Arun thought that he would empathize with Derek in order to keep Derek from getting defensive. It didn't work.

"It's not your ranch, so mind your own business," retorted Derek. Chet was within earshot.

Arun paused a few seconds, expecting Chet to say something. Chet missed the cue, or he simply chose to ignore it. Arun would always be disappointed in Chet at times like this. *Where are your leadership skills?* Arun would wonder. He imagined himself grabbing Chet by the neck and shaking him back and forth violently. He envisioned a cartoon image where Chet's tongue flew back and forth in the air and spit landed everywhere. The mental image calmed Arun down. He was glad for that.

"Look, Derek, I am just trying to do what is good for the company," said Arun affirmatively. He nodded his head in Chet's direction to try to solicit his support. Chet remained quiet.

"You just draft the documents like you are supposed to," said Derek.

There was a bit too much "instruction" in Derek's voice, Arun decided. "You aren't my boss, Derek, we are working on this together," Arun pointed out. Arun's composure provided him with a quiet strength. Otherwise, he knew that his face would be getting as red as Derek's was turning.

"Look, I cut this deal with them, OKAY? I am bringing in all of this great business for the company and I don't need you to screw it up!" Derek was screaming. He started to pant at the end of his sentence.

Arun just looked at him. "Great way to exercise your control, tough guy. Do you do that with customers when they say they don't want to buy from us?" Arun questioned. He immediately regretted it after saying it.

He certainly regretted it now.

• • •

Zubin came to his father and asked him for some additional help for a science competition that he wanted to enter.

Arun looked at his son as he spoke. Arun's eyes were bloodshot and his head had been hurting for several days now. When he stood up he would feel dizzy and would have the need to sit immediately. He smiled at his son. He thought about how it might be a nice distraction for him to have something to sink his teeth into.

"I'd like to do it on plants," Zubin commented.

"I see," said Arun. He didn't want to be obnoxious to his son. Any other person, and Arun would have been rolling his eyes.

"Maybe I can get Grandpa's help?" asked Zubin, hope in his voice.

Arun felt as low as he had ever felt when thinking of his parents. His forehead went into a deep furrow. "Let's see how far we can get on our own first, shall we?" he managed to say.

• • •

Andy phoned Arun again, "Can we meet?"

Arun agreed.

"I don't think they are selling the company," hinted Andy.

"Why not?"

"They just signed a lease for a bigger space. It's like sixty percent more space than what we have currently."

"Wow. You actually saw this lease?"

"In Derek's office."

"Maybe they are buying someone else," mused Arun.

• • •

Rajiv came by Pablo's nursery again. They had agreed to meet for lunch for the third time that week.

"How is your family doing?" asked Pablo.

They both sat down to a meal of vegetarian burritos.

Rajiv was quiet for a few seconds. "Everything fine," he finally managed to say. "Tell me of your family."

"Oh they are doing very well. My little granddaughter said *Abeulo* or grandfather on the phone yesterday. I was so proud."

Rajiv became quiet again.

Pablo turned to him. "Isn't your son expecting another one?"

"Yes," started Rajiv, "Arun…" Rajiv cleared his throat. There was a long period of silence.

"Is everything okay?" asked Pablo.

● ● ●

As Radha began her labor, Arun called Parvati. Anjali was with Radha.

"We are on our way," Parvati said.

Arun instinctively opened his phone again and was about to dial his parents. He stopped short. He looked up in the air. He thought about not calling. He went ahead and dialed. There was no answer. He thought about whether to leave a message or not.

"We are going into labor."

There was a few seconds of silence.

"We are at the same hospital where Zubin and Nandini were born."

He quickly hung up. Should he have asked them to come, he thought? No, that was silly. It was understood. Given the current circumstances, should that have changed anything? He couldn't see why it should.

● ● ●

Within six hours, Radha gave birth to a baby girl. Arun was so proud. For the first time in months he had tears of joy running down his face. He held his daughter. He sobbed with

230

a jerking motion of his shoulders. Radha worried that he might drop the newborn. But he held his child so close to him.

"I won't ever abandon you or cease speaking to you, my precious girl," he whispered in her tiny ear. His comment ushered a torrent of tears.

As he held his daughter close to him, he turned to Radha.

"I think we should call her Sapna," Arun said.

Through her fatigue Radha smiled at her husband.

Anjali came over to observe her niece. "She does look like a dream," Anjali confirmed.

• • •

Parvati arrived by the following morning. B.P. was not with her. "He had some work to do," she explained. Her lack of conviction came through loudly, as it became apparent she had intended, and each of Radha, Arun and Anjali knew what the real issue was.

Arun gave his mother-in-law a hug.

She pulled him away and looked him in the eye. "Everything is going to be okay." She spoke with certainty and reassurance. Yet again, the three of them understood what she was referring to.

Arun walked out to the waiting area. He called his parents again, this time using the pay phone in the lobby.

He heard his father answer the phone. "Hello?"

"Dad, it's Arun, Dad."

Arun waited for his father to acknowledge. He never did. After five seconds, Arun heard a dial tone.

CHAPTER SIXTEEN

———

May 2004

Arjun called Rajiv angrily.

"How could you make the decision to not grow on all plots?" asked Arjun.

"It is being the right thing. You must resting some of it. We are not getting nice fruit," explained Rajiv.

Pablo had suggested it to Rajiv as a way to revitalize the grapes that were being grown.

"Do you know how little money this thing is making?" demanded Arjun.

Rajiv was stunned that his brother spoke to him that way. He was at a loss for words.

"Don't go back to the vineyard! Just leave it alone! IT DOESN'T BELONG TO YOU!"

Rajiv didn't say anything to his brother.

"You haven't even paid me back for the down payment I gave you for your home and on top of that, you are screwing up my other investments!"

Rajiv hung up the phone. He drove home. A few days later, he suffered a mild heart attack, his first.

• • •

Rajiv was elated when he saw Pablo enter the hospital room.

"I called your work and they said you were in the hospital. What are you doing to yourself, *señor*?"

232

Rajiv smiled. It was the best he had been feeling for awhile.

Pablo opened the plastic bag he had with him. He pulled out two mangoes.

Rajiv smiled in excitement. He motioned to his friend to sit close to his bed.

"I thought maybe I would be meeting your family here."

"Oh," said Rajiv as he cleared his throat, "they coming later."

"Okay."

There were a few minutes of silence that passed between them. Rajiv felt very comfortable in the silence. The presence of his friend was wonderfully therapeutic for him.

Rajiv heard those last words from his brother again and again: it doesn't belong to you. "Why he no understand?" he asked of Pablo. "In India, whatever is being in the family is belonging to everybody. Here everyone is being alone."

"I bet you didn't think this would happen to you when you came to this country."

Rajiv looked at his friend. "I having being thinking much thoughts about time I coming to this country."

Pablo smiled.

"On day we coming here, my uncle getting very angry because he trying to finding me but cannot. Taxi waiting, Meena waiting. I being in the field. I taking a photo with my friend camera – I no having a camera and then I taking a canister and I putting it inside there the soil of my home."

Rajiv looked at Pablo. There were tears in his eyes. The sight made Rajiv cry as well.

●　●　●

Dipti had found a bride for her son in India. The girl came from a part of India that was close to where Rajiv's family had come from. Naturally, Dipti invited Meena and Rajiv.

Meena was excited to go back. She hadn't been to India in many years. Rajiv was excited about the prospect of going as well. There was still a great deal of unease he felt about Arun's visit to the family. "I not knowing how that boy being offending them. I will having to fixing matters with my uncle," lamented Rajiv.

Rajiv looked at their financial situation. Not all of the costs for the medical expenditures from his heart attack had been covered. He made a determination that he would not be able to make the trip with Meena. "You must being visiting my family," Rajiv insisted to Meena. It was the first time that he had ever been insistent on something.

"Not have much time, isn't it?" Meena commented. Her friend Dipti had so many places that she wanted to go together with Meena.

For weeks before her departure, Rajiv insisted that she go. Meena eventually agreed.

Rajiv overheard a bit of her conversation with Dipti when Dipti came over later that week. It was not intentional. She must not have known that Rajiv was in the dining room while she talked with her friend in the living room.

"I know there is problem," Meena said to her friend, "but I needs to be going. Rajiv is too much saying I must go."

"Oh, it's going to be so boring without you there. I planned on doing so much shopping and introducing you to all of my fashionable friends," Dipti responded.

"I am knowing. I rather be with you. He is thinking, maybe we living there later," Meena lamented.

Rajiv was troubled by hearing this. His wife must not know he can hear what she was saying. He didn't care much for Dipti.

"Oh you should never let your husband get away with such decisions. You must control him!" insisted Dipti.

Rajiv wasn't sure if he should feel relieved or not by the fact that Meena wasn't responding.

"I must going," reiterated Meena, her voice getting a bit anxious. The hint of anxiety suggested the tension she must have been feeling. Rajiv sensed that she was concerned about maintaining her friendship with Dipti and didn't want to do anything to harm Dipti's view of her.

"If you must, you must," Dipti responded grudgingly, with a slight tinge of condescension.

"I am worried. I no feel so good living again in India. Maybe is no possible for me." After a few moments of silence, Meena added, "Maybe is good I going. I see where all money for so many years is being spent, isn't it?"

Rajiv was troubled to hear this. He had also wanted to go back. He thought his wife felt the same way.

"Yes, of course, you must always know where the money is going! If it isn't spent on you, you should direct how it is spent!" proclaimed Dipti.

Meena laughed out loud.

She stopped as soon as Rajiv cleared his throat.

Six weeks later Rajiv dropped her off at the airport.

● ● ●

After a week, Rajiv got a phone call with a crackling sound at the end of it. It was his uncle. He was calling to inform Rajiv that Meena had been most disrespectful and that neither she nor he were welcome in the house again. Rajiv did not know what to say. He apologized profusely to his uncle.

"I'm sorry," he said. "You please, not banishing us from being coming to the home; there is being answer for everythings. I will learning what is this."

It took him over forty-eight hours to find Meena. He tracked her down through Dipti's husband. Rajiv's anger in that period had not abated any. He was prepared to be incredibly fierce.

When he got a hold of Meena on the phone, he got as far as saying, "Where being you?" His mind was racing. He thought maybe she did something similar to Arun and upset them because she didn't want to go back.

And that's when it began. Meena had not shed a tear since she had heard the news. Now it all came out. She cried solidly minute after minute.

Rajiv kept asking, "What is being wrong, what is being wrong?"

She couldn't respond. She finally managed to say, "They sold it! THEY SOLD IT ALL!"

She described for him how Lakshant's grandson, the man whom Rajiv's uncle R.K. had sent to prison, gave her a ride through the fields. He covered about a tenth of a mile and turned around to head back to the house. Meena asked why they were turning back – she remembered that it took a few hours to cover all of the territory that her husband's family had owned when she took this tour as a newlywed. The driver informed her that all of that land had been sold. Rajiv's younger brother, Lal, who was in real estate, had systematically sold off the land, bit-by-bit.

Rajiv had no idea what to say. He suddenly understood everything. Everything that had been going on. He quietly put down the phone. There was so little for Rajiv to go back to now.

● ● ●

Rajiv went to see his brother Arjun in his office. Rajiv in his dark brown pants, used shoes looking tired, in bad need of a polish, and white shirt looked out of place in the plush offices of Arjun's venture capital firm. Arjun was sporting a French cuff shirt with Ferragamo loafers.

"What we going to being doing about this?" Rajiv pleaded with Arjun.

"I don't think there is anything we can do," responded Arjun, appearing a bit perturbed.

"We must being doing something, must being doing, we must," reiterated Rajiv.

"I don't think it is going to be possible."

"I sending so much money. So many years. What is being happened to my the money?" Rajiv was getting more and more agitated.

Arjun jerked his head back slightly, surprised at his brother's reaction.

"You have been sending money?" Arjun asked again.

"Yes, since I coming here, I sending money. I sending your share also," said Rajiv, almost combatively.

Arjun had a look of shock and dismay on his face. "I had no idea..." Arjun started to say. "If you had told me, I would have told them to go to hell for both of us."

Rajiv maintained his pleading look at his brother. He felt conflicted. In his mind and heart, he knew he would never have wanted to say that to his family. Now, his sense of betrayal was so strong.

Arjun was quiet for awhile. He looked out his window. He leaned back in his chair.

"Look, Rajiv, you are settled here now. Why do you worry about back there?" Arjun asked him.

Rajiv looked at Arjun. A sadness entered his face.

"Well, it's not like you are going to go back." Arjun pointed out.

"Why you no understand?" Rajiv asked.

● ● ●

A week after Meena got back, she got a call from Rajiv's work.

"It's your husband. He is in the hospital," said the woman.

Meena rushed to the hospital. She called Arun.

"You come here now," she said, in between her tears. It was the first time she had spoken to Arun in three years.

Arun arrived first. Arun did not quite know how to console him. Arun felt so bad for his father. He knew that he had sent money back home every month. Deep down, in a place that he hated to admit existed, he was secretly scared that an expectation rested on his shoulders to do the same. Arun wondered if his brothers felt similarly.

Radha came with the kids later in the day. Rajiv opened his eyes. He first reached out for Zubin. Zubin looked frightened. It had been so long since he had seen his grandfather.

Arun pushed his son towards his father. "It's okay, go," Arun said.

Zubin ran to his grandfather. Zubin hugged him intently. He began to cry. "What did you do? What did you do?"

Rajiv held Zubin as best he could. He had tubes, needles and monitors running criss-cross over his body. It was a clumsy grip, Zubin was practically falling off the bed, but he was able to touch and be touched by his grandfather.

When they were leaving that evening, Zubin stopped in the corridor to the hallway. "We need to get Grandpa a plant," Zubin said.

Arun, who was holding Nandini in his arms, was exhausted. "Come, Zubie, we'll talk about it in the car," Arun said.

Zubin didn't move.

Arun yelled out to him, "Zubin, let's go."

Zubin didn't move.

"Okay, we'll get a stupid plant. Get in the car."

"It's not stupid, Daddy."

"Okay, Zubie, it's not stupid."

"Can we go now?"

Arun looked at Radha.   She nodded her head.

"Okay, Zubie, we'll go now."

When Zubin presented the plant to his grandfather, Rajiv looked more animated than he had since his attack.   Arun even noticed a tear in his eye as Zubin handed to him a canister that he had taken from his grandparent's house.   Arun made a mental note to ask Zubin about that later.

Rajiv recovered quickly after that.

●   ●   ●

Upon Meena's return, most of Arun's interaction with his mother was caustic.   She was always yelling at him.   For some reason Arun could do nothing right anymore.   His mother picked at everything now.   Arun was sad that his mother had become a different person.

"Since when did Mom start hating the world?" Arun asked Sanjay.

Sanjay made a face that revealed he did not understand Arun's question.   "That's silly, Mom doesn't hate the world." Arun didn't bother pursuing the topic with his brother.

Meena called Arun after a week.   "I plan Sanjay's wedding with girl I meet in India."

Arun had overheard Dipti encouraging his mother to throw herself into some task or project to help her forget about what his father's family in India had done.   He never expected it would be this.

"Why are you arranging his marriage?   Hasn't he found anyone on his own?" enquired Arun.

"With what you did to his face, how is that poor fellow going to find a bride, you tell me," challenged Meena.

"I did nothing to his face, Mom," insisted Arun.

There were a few moments of silence.

"Why do you accuse me of stuff like this?" demanded Arun. He never received an answer from his mother that evening.

Later that night, he posed the same question to Radha. Before she could get an answer out, Anjali interjected.

"Because you let them," she pointed out.

"What does that mean, I let them," Arun sought clarification.

"You let them walk all over you. You never say anything, so they think they can continue to get away with it," Anjali pointed out.

Remarkably lucid, Arun thought to himself. He thought about her response. He wondered if there was merit to it.

He recalled how in the past when his family would alienate him this way, he had sought comfort in a woman's arms. He looked at his wife, who was juggling two children. *Where did she have the time?*

●　●　●

The doctors said that the heart attack was mild enough that he could travel for the wedding; nonetheless Rajiv had decided not to go to India to see Sanjay marry Sujata. It was the first time Arun had ever sensed his father embellishing what was actually going on. His health condition, according to him, was much worse than what the doctor indicated was physically wrong with him. He kept alluding to this pain that he was experiencing in his chest, but all of his EKGs came out normal.

Meena was prepared to send wedding invitations to Rajiv's family in India, although she did this with a heavy heart. It was Rajiv who told her not to send them.

After the wedding, all came back at the same time, Sujata, Sanjay and Meena. Sanjay had purchased his own place not too far from where his parents were living. They spent a few weeks getting settled, and Sanjay returned to his work.

Sujata answered the phone one afternoon. "Hello?"

"Yes. I need to speak with Ms. *Sue-jadda Gan-dare-knee*," said the voice.

"This is her speaking," said Sujata.

"Ma'am, I am calling from the US Immigration and Naturalization Service. There are some irregularities with your paperwork. I'd like for you to schedule an appointment to come in," said the person on the phone.

Sujata didn't know what to say. She asked if her husband could call him back.

"No problem," said the man on the phone. "This is Agent Joseph King."

Sujata quickly called Sanjay to explain what happened. He insisted that everything had been done properly. When Sujata gave the Agent's name and number to Sanjay, she was shocked to hear his response of, "I'll kill him."

"I think that is a bit harsh. He spoke to me properly. He was friendly on the phone," said Sujata.

"A little too friendly; that was Raj. He was Joe-King. *Joking.*"

• • •

Rajiv called Arjun.

"We no can being letting them getting away with this," he insisted, after clearing his throat, "I wishing to being having my property."

"What if I gave you the money that you sent over there? Would that calm you down?" Arjun asked in exasperation.

"It is not being about money. It is about being having our home. About losing our home."

Arjun was silent.

"Why you no understand?" demanded Rajiv.

• • •

Rajiv was one of the last few to arrive at the wedding reception for Sanjay and Sujata that was being thrown in the US.

Rajiv looked physically weaker than he had at any time in the past. His second heart attack had had taken a heavier toll on him than the first.

Uncle Arjun had a pretty heavy hand in determining the guest list. He had not had any kids of his own, so he took the initiative with his nephews. He understood the importance of inviting the right people to such important family functions. His contacts now ranged wide and deep. He knew all of the important people about town, about the US and about the world. The range of attendees he had invited included high-net-worth individuals, business leaders, politicians and even Bollywood actors and actresses – mostly off the B list, but it still inspired the same level of awe that Arjun was seeking.

Arjun greeted an attractive woman at the door. Arun watched the exchange with interest. She reminded him of the women he would see in Bombay. She had a model-like beauty, lots of make-up and glamorous hair. She was five feet six inches tall, had almond-shaped eyes and an overly-defined jaw line. She seemed hungry to Arun. The shape and duration of his uncle's smile seemed to suggest that he liked her excessive coquettishness, but received it with the healthy distrust of a man who knows that he is not being singled out to receive this false affection, but is merely one of a long-line of men who have and who will experience it. Arun observed the spectacle. He knew his uncle had seen all types from his days at Berkeley until today.

Arjun introduced her to Arun. "Please meet my nephew, Arun." Arun turned to face her, pretending that he had not noticed the exchange between her and his uncle. "Arun, meet Meenakshi." Being in her presence provided exhilaration for Arun. Her cover girl beauty struck him and he found he was unable to breathe for a second. When he came to, he bellowed, in a voice a few octaves lower than was his usual, "Why, hello."

"Hello, back," replied Meenakshi. She seemed like a woman who had just dropped the heavy article she was lugging around in exchange for something lighter and less burdensome. Arun amused himself in thinking that she had found another toy that she decided she liked more. Arjun walked away.

Arun thought to himself, *Wow, a strong command of English and witty too. I think she's even flirting with me.*

He had a knee-jerk reaction to look for Radha. Perhaps it was to remind himself that he was married, but he soon realized that his intentions were not that pure; he wanted to be sure she was not witnessing his interaction. When he did catch sight of her, she was engrossed in carrying Nandini and trying to get Zubin to eat. He thought about how long it had been since they were intimate.

Arun managed a smile and said, as his mouth opened into a grin, "You seem awfully familiar."

Meenakshi displayed an expression on her face indicating that were she talking, she would have said, 'well, duh.' Arun realized that she had probably gone through this a hundred times, and by the way she altered the expression on her face to resume her previous inviting composure, it appeared that she had decided to suffer through it yet once again. Arun did note that she made a cursory glance at the rest of the party. *I guess she can't find anyone better* thought Arun. *No recognizable producers or directors. Let's see if she decides to just pass the time with me. Maybe I need to show her that I can offer her some dividends,* thought Arun. "I know," stated Arun, "you're a model." Arun actually had no idea. But she seemed like she was, or at least could have been, and he was eager to win some points.

"You probably recognize me from television," she finally said. "I am an actress." She dropped the line with as much dreaminess and star struck wonder as she seemed able to muster. She was excessively "breathy". Arun decided that it was working;

it certainly did create a mystique. She looked up at Arun through the upper corners of her eyes, attempting to evoke an almost pouty look. She held her body with her hands on her hips and her shoulders thrown back. She was putting herself on display. The stance shouted, "Admire me!" Arun nodded his head and smiled. She looked up in the air and threw her hands up letting out a sigh of satisfaction. She looked like she felt relief that she still had it in her.

"I have been to Bombay," offered Arun.

"Oh really?" asked Meenakshi. She asked it with a qualified tone, as if she didn't know whether his trip there would be an engaging twist or if he just sat in someone's house while visiting family.

Arun was working hard trying to remember the names of some clubs. He started speaking, hoping for the best. "I stayed at the Oberoi."

Meenakshi's interest seemed to be piqued. She had an earnest look about her now, perhaps she had decided to help him out. "Did you go to the club Insomnia?"

"Why yes," said Arun. "That's the one at the Taj."

Meenakshi's eyes lit up a bit. "Very good, Arun." She patted his shoulder lightly. "And what is it that you do?"

"Well I'm a lawyer," said Arun.

Meenakshi looked dejected. *Looks like she had been hopeful that I might have some affiliation with Bollywood or acting in Hollywood* thought Arun to himself. *She must have hit a real low point in her career,* thought Arun. Radha usually kept the Indian channels on in the background at home, and Arun had a habit of noticing the faces of the women; he didn't recognize her from anything recent. *I bet she is eager to have some new prospects turn up for her.* After a few more pleasantries about Bombay, Meenakshi excused herself. *I guess I have exhausted my allotted time with her,* thought Arun. She probably wanted to get a sense of who else was around. Arun didn't want her to leave so he thought quickly of something to say.

"I have some producer friends," Arun offered.

"Oh really?" asked Meenakshi. She had already started to walk away. She seemed to sense that Arun was trying to make a last-ditch effort to keep her there. She appeared to be flattered by it; although she maintained the distance between the two of them, she did turn her whole body around to face him.

"Yes," said Arun. *Damn*, he thought to himself, *I wish I had something more to say.* He just couldn't think of it fast enough.

"What type of work do they do?" asked Meenakshi.

Damn again, thought Arun, *she is trying to see if I am lying.* "I'm sorry?" he asked.

"Why don't I see you in a little while," suggested Meenakshi. She leaned into him and placed her hand down his front jacket pocket. He sensed that she left something in there. She turned to walk away without waiting for Arun to respond.

Damn a third time, thought Arun. *Oh well, I couldn't do enough to keep her.* He pulled out of his pocket a card with her number. She had placed a number of Xs over the "i" of her name. Arun knew they were meant to be kisses. By then, Radha came by, holding Nandini. Arun quickly put the card in his pocket. *Good timing*, he thought to himself.

"Hi," said Arun, turning to face Radha and Nandini. He took his daughter in his arms and played with her. He felt guilty about the thoughts he had earlier. He had a sudden urge to throw out the card in his pocket, but he knew he would not be able to do it inconspicuously.

Anjali had settled her divorce shortly before the date of the reception. Anjali was not up to attending, but Radha insisted that Anjali come to the event. Radha was trying to get Anjali to take her mind off of what had happened so that she could get her life back on track.

Sara arrived after Arjun. When she presented herself, she was dressed in a sari. And she had something new that she had on display – she had gotten a nose ring.

"Well I just felt that most of the Indian women in Arjun's family have it, so it would be a good idea to do the same." She laughed as she spoke. Arun overheard her talking to a crowd of people, showing it off. There was a bit of nervousness as she spoke. Sara caught sight of Arun and Radha. They had stayed quiet as she talked and they hadn't really reacted to her proclamation. Arun felt obligated after several seconds had passed.

"I think it looks great," said Arun. "What do you think, Radha?"

"Yes, it's very nice," said Radha.

Sara saw Anjali. Radha had explained to Sara on the phone what was happening.

"Oh you poor little thing," Sara said to Anjali. "You come here." Sara embraced Anjali. Anjali cringed.

"I can only imagine how devastated you are, you poor dear," Sara said. "My family is originally from the UK and they were stationed in Calcutta during the Raj. Sometimes my fellow non-Indians can't appreciate all that you Indians have to offer. You are such a wonderful group of people. Matthew should have just worshipped you."

Anjali's face began turning more and more red. Arun noticed that and grew concerned. He knew that Anjali had already been through her weeks of crying and talking it out with friends. Arun knew that she really wanted to be moving on.

"I can only imagine how devastated YOU are," said Anjali, her tone taking a more aggressive posturing.

"Whatever do you mean, my dear?"

"Give it up. How desperate are you to be accepted and fit in to our culture? What's the deal with the nose ring? Stop trying so damn hard.   Is this some kind of crazy guilt you are still feeling from what your family did in raping and pillaging our country?"

"Now, now, you are just upset," said Sara, her voice showing more anxiety.

"Stop trying to atone for their sins.   We are over it.   We don't care anymore.   Why can't you get over it!"

Arun stepped in.   "Why don't we get a drink," he said to Anjali, pushing her in the direction of the bar.

"I'm really sorry," said Radha to Sara.   "I think the nose ring is really nice," Radha added, making every effort to try to get Sara to be less upset.

• • •

Two days later, Arun was back at his office.   He answered his phone.   It was his mother.

"Hey, Mom.   How are you?"

"Why you no care more for your brother?"

"What are you talking about?" asked Arun.   "Also, which one are you talking about?"

"You only buy plates for marriage."

"Well, it's a whole dining set.   Radha and I thought it was significant," responded Arun.

"No.   You must do better.   You are elder," she scolded him.

Arun's head began to hurt.   He hated when his mother got this way with him.   It had only been a few short months since they began communicating again.   He couldn't understand why the standard with him was so high.

"What did you get him?"   Arun asked the question with a flash of insight.

"We are parents.   We no need to get him anything." Arun heard his mother raise her voice.   He knew she was reacting to him being insolent.

"I have to go Mom, someone is entering my office." Arun hung up the phone without waiting for her response.

As he was placing the phone down, he noticed a folded card that he had stuffed in his pocket a few days earlier. He had hid it under his wallet at home and ended up bringing it to the office. He held Meenakshi's number in his hands. He had to admit; he had been thinking about her. He could us the "pick-me-up"; he knew that, although not genuine, she would say all of the things to him that would boost his ego.

He called her. She answered the phone after one ring. After the initial greetings, Arun began, "So my producer friend is interested in casting an Indian female lead." He paused deliberately for a few seconds. "Would you mind if I sent him your particulars?" asked Arun. The reality was that Arun had no such friend. He wished he had, however, in case she happened to ask any detailed questions about the industry. Regardless of her reaction, Arun was proud of himself because he had devised a way to see her again.

Arun felt a little self-conscious. Meenakshi seemed to sense that it was a ploy. Arun could overhear her giggling. Maybe she was amused because she thought it was clever, he thought to himself.

She asked him with seeming skepticism, "Where can I send my headshots?"

"Why don't we get together and I can collect them from you in person?" replied Arun. He said it with a huge leap of faith. He wanted to deliver it slowly, so that it seemed as natural as possible. He didn't want her to guess that he had contrived the sentence, pre-meditated it before the call.

There was silence for awhile. Meenakshi seemed to be thinking. Arun became a little concerned. *Maybe she is smiling to herself,* he thought. *Or perhaps she is reviled by my approach. She finds it childish and unsophisticated.* He decided that the very next thing she said would indicate if she were interested or not. He waited for what seemed like an eternity. He wouldn't bruise his ego, however. He was going to hold his ground and wait.

"There's a café down the block from where I live. Meet me there at four," said Meenakshi.

Arun felt a sudden rush of excitement. *Wow,* he thought to himself. *I suppose I still have some desirability in me.*

Meenakshi brought to their get-together a very revealing photo. Arun studied the photo for longer than he probably should have, he realized. Longer than would have been socially acceptable. When he looked up, feeling guilty, and knowing that he was carrying an expression of guilt on his face, she had a big smile on her face. Arun felt caught - as if Meenakshi had figured out that Arun suddenly had a strong desire of "wanting to be alone" with the photo. Her smile got bigger as Arun kept looking at her. Arun got excited by thinking that she found that to be a turn-on and that it excited her as well.

"So tell me more about your interest in acting," asked Arun. He kept going after she answered that. "What have been your favorite roles to act in?" he also asked. "If you could have your dream role, what would it be?' he asked, finally.

While he was asking the questions, every now and again he would look over his shoulder and scan the passers-by and those sitting next to them. Arun felt uncomfortable sitting there in the open-air café. It wasn't even appropriately blocked off. Quite frankly, he was worried about getting caught. He knew he wanted to sleep with her, and he sensed that because of the photo she gave, she wanted the same. He kept looking around to be sure that nobody he knew would see him. He had not taken that risk into consideration in deciding on a location to meet.

Meenakshi, perhaps sensing his sudden unease, placed her hand on his. "Why don't we go back to my place?" She leaned in as she asked the question and only looked into his eyes after she had asked it.   Arun pulled back a little bit, but he allowed a smile to slowly creep up on his face, signaling that he accepted her proposition.

He opened his wallet to pay the bill at the café.   As he did, he saw a photo of his wife and family.   He put twenty dollars on the table.   He turned to Meenakshi.   "I'm terribly sorry, but I need to go," he said.   He closed his wallet.   He got up and left without waiting for her to respond.

Since that day, he would always turn to that photo when he needed strength.

•   •   •

Arun went to his office after the Meenakshi encounter. He tried to avoid thinking about her by diving into work.   While he was on a conference call, his assistant called him.

"There is an Indian woman here to see you.   It's not Radha.   She says she knows you well," said his assistant.

Arun felt conflicted.   He acknowledged that he was excited about the prospect that Meenakshi was pursuing him. However, he remembered the photo and knew what he needed to do.   "Let her come in," he instructed.

Arun left his door open and kept his back towards it.   He continued with his conference call, putting it on speaker.

"How should we approach this?" asked the other party.

"Look, you guys have strung us along in the past and we don't want to continue to be jerked around," Arun said.   He stood up and looked out the window.   He wanted to maintain his composure.

"Well, if that's how you feel…," began the other party.

"That is how we feel.   And don't expect us to back down," Arun said with determination.   He hung up the phone.   He turned around and was shocked with whom he saw.

Standing before him was Anjali.   "What are you doing here?"

"I saw you with that other woman," Anjali said.

Arun's face fell. He went to the couch and sat down. Anjali sat next to him.

"Oh God, Anjali, that is such a ridiculous thing for me to be getting caught up in. Nothing has happened. I left her after I remembered Radha and the kids," Arun pleaded.

After a few second pause, with Anjali looking at Arun intently, she offered, "I believe you."

"Oh thank God."

"I won't tell Radha either," Anjali continued.

"You are a saint," Arun said.

"You know, how come you don't act the way you did on the call with your parents?"

"What?"

"You are so aggressive in your work. You don't take crap from people here. Why do you let your family give it to you?"

Arun just remained silent, looking at the floor.

"I think you are too much of a coward with your parents," declared Anjali matter-of-factly.

Arun was taken aback by her comment.

"You need to be more firm with them," she insisted. "That is the only way you can make progress with them. Otherwise, they just won't get it."

She began walking out the door. "Oh, and they are the reason you think of doing silly things, like cheating."

CHAPTER SEVENTEEN

August – September 2007

Weeks had gone by. He hadn't heard from any of his family. *I could be in jail right now*, Arun thought, *and they would never know. Why is there no concern?*, he lamented.

Why is there no desire to see my newborn child?

As he pondered these questions he noticed Anjali playing with Nandini out of the corner of his eye. Anjali had been great at occupying the kids so that attention could be given to little Sapna.

"*Ma-si* we are singing all of these Christmas songs in school," Nandini said.

"Oh that's fun, 'Jingle Bells' and all that!" exclaimed Anjali, showing her enthusiasm.

"There's even a Chanukah song," Nandini added.

"I remember that one. It must be about a *draedel*," Anjali commented.

"Yeah. It is," Nandini said smiling. Her face turned serious after that. "How come we don't sing any Hindi songs? For Diwali or one of our holidays?" she asked.

Anjali held her niece. Arun entered the room but tried not to be noticed by Nandini.

"Well, my astute young lady," began Anjali, "don't feel so bad about that. It's because a simple fact of life is that the desires of the majority are what prevail – I mean what most people want is what happens. Most of your schoolmates are Christian or Jewish.

If we were all in India, then we would be singing Indian songs and not Christmas or Chanukah ones."

"Ohhhh…How come we are not in India?" asked Nandini.

Arun was taken back by the simplicity of the question and the innocence with which his daughter asked it.

Anjali was quiet for a moment. Arun could tell she was weighing how to answer.

"For a lot of reasons, little darling, all of our parents decided that we would have a better life here. By that they were focused on matcrial well-being – I mean that they wanted us to have nice things and a nice education," Anjali explained.

"But because of that we have to learn to sing Christmas songs?" Nandini asked.

"Yes, because of that, we have to sing Christmas songs. There are more of them here," replied Anjali.

Arun walked away. He thought about Anjali's response. It was a shame his parents never understood that.

● ● ●

Andy presented a bunch of documents to Arun. They all were labeled with the word LogicNet at the bottom. They were plans for a prototype piece of communications equipment.

"These are all from GoWire's main competitor," observed Arun. "What are you doing with them?"

"These were lying around GoWire's offices."

"These are important trade secrets that GoWire should not have access to," Arun pointed out.

"Exactly," agreed Andy.

"The fact that they do have them indicates that there may be some foul play here," hinted Arun.

"Uh-huh," said Andy.

"No wonder they don't need any more market research studies. Do you think they are involved in corporate espionage?" wondered Arun aloud.

"Perhaps."

"Although, it is curious that their press release regarding the unacceptability of their product came out just two weeks ago," speculated Arun.

Andy smiled. "Something does seem off, doesn't it?"

Arun turned to his friend. "Can you look into this for me?"

Andy smiled. "I got your back."

• • •

Arun continued receiving e-mails from a young man in India who now indicated that he was interested in studying law in the US. Each time, he insisted, "I am your cousin."

Arun finally suggested that he send over a photo as Arun wasn't convinced. He had a striking resemblance to Uncle Arjun, Arun decided once he saw the photo.

Arun assumed it must be his Uncle Lal's son, his father's other brother.

In a subsequent e-mail, he indicated he was coming to the US and asked if Arun could pick him up from the airport. Arun felt shy that he was not in communication with the rest of the family, so he decided not to admit that to his cousin. Instead he agreed to pick him up.

"How will I get him to my parent's place?" Arun asked Radha.

"Well, just have him stay here for awhile and then you can take him over. I know I said it would be a nuisance, but maybe this will be an excuse to finally patch things up with your family," Radha suggested.

Arun decided he may as well since the whole family was being silent with him anyway.

• • •

Andy called Arun.

"So, I looked into the testing agency that released the results of the analysis condemning LogicNet's products," Andy informed Arun.

"And?"

"It turns out that it is owned jointly by the two VCs that each individually own GoWire Systems and LogicNet."

"Very interesting. I'm surprised that information never got out."

* * *

Arun was on the phone with Steven.

"How are you holding up?"

"Well, every day is a struggle," said Arun.

"I'm sorry to hear that."

"Well, I have made it through other times that have been difficult."

Steven was quiet on the other end.

"How is Radha holding up?" asked Steven.

"You know," said Arun. "She seems pretty strong, but I can tell she is affected by this."

"Of course," said Steven. "What about Zubin and Nandini?"

"They are okay. Hanging in. They are kind of oblivious to what is going on," remarked Arun. "You know," said Arun, "Radha gave me the most unique look yesterday."

"Uh-oh. Is she angry with you?"

"I don't think so. It was a look of appreciation. The last time she gave me that look was a few years ago when I threw her a surprise birthday party."

"That long ago?"

"Yes. It has been some time," mentioned Arun.

"Really?"

"Yes, I'm not kidding." Arun was wondering why Steven was not believing him.

"She must be feeling badly for you," said Steven. "She knows you're coping with a lot."

"Yeah, the criminal charges, my family…"

"Exactly," said Steven.

• • •

Arjun was making ever more frequent trips to Bangalore, focusing on his various investments in that city. He indicated to Rajiv that he had bought a place there.

Rajiv approached him. "Maybe you look into getting land back?"

Arjun told him that he would look into it.

When he arrived back, Rajiv accosted him.

"What is happening, what is the answer?" asked Rajiv.

"Uh, I didn't have a chance to get there this trip, but I will soon," promised Arjun.

"Why you no go?" demanded Rajiv.

"Things are busy with me, okay? I had matters to attend to and I couldn't just look into what is bothering you. Is that okay?"

Rajiv stayed quiet. "When you are going again?" Rajiv asked.

"In two weeks," Arjun answered.

• • •

Rajiv called Arjun as soon as he got back from his very next trip to India.

"Oh yes, Rajiv. Look, a lot of it has been sold off, but there is still a little bit of it left," he reported.

"Arjun, you are going there often. You must save that for me. I buy more land there. You don't let that land go. You, please, must save it for me," Rajiv indicated.

Arjun rolled his eyes. "Rajiv, are you sure this is what you want?"

"Yes, yes, you must save it for me," pleaded Rajiv.

"Okay," said Arjun, as he shook his head in dismay, "I'll do it."

But he never did. Arjun had two additional trips after that conversation, but he would come back and offer the same response. Rajiv became more and more frustrated with Arjun. Rajiv approached Sanjay. "You go to India for me. It is difficult for me going. Your Uncle Arjun not helping."

• • •

Arun received a call from his lawyer.

"The US Attorney wants to have a meeting," he said.

The apparition of fear came back, instantaneously. Arun felt his heart take a deep beat. Instead of the typical pump, it felt as if it fell to the ground and through the earth several thousand feet before it came back up to rejoin the rest of his body. He had the sensation that he was going to fall through with it.

"What are we going to discuss at that meeting?" asked Arun, after what felt like several minutes of silence.

"It's called a reverse proffer. They are going to present the evidence they have against you," his lawyer explained.

"Right. We don't do any talking, we just hear what they have to say and make a decision as to how to proceed from there." Arun completed the thought.

"That's exactly right," confirmed his lawyer.

• • •

"Remember what I explained to you earlier," Anjali said to Nandini, "We are like a bridge across an ocean between two lands."

Nandini looked at her aunt quizzically.

Anjali knew she had to explain. "To which land does the bridge belong?"

Nandini began to show a smile. "To both?" She asked it questioningly.

"Exactly."

● ● ●

Arun went to the meeting with the US Attorney.

There were an elaborate series of charts and diagrams showing a mechanism by which he had siphoned off over two million dollars. They had even turned to some slides that showed his signature on a number of documents.

A cold sweat began to break out on Arun's forehead, under his arms and on his back. He was soaked in sweat very soon. As he sat there, he felt a queasy sensation in his stomach. He reminded himself to think of his wife and kids. He pulled out his wallet. He looked at their photos. He proceeded to pass out. As he slumped to the floor, he hit his head on the desk.

● ● ●

Anjali was the one who came to get Arun from the Federal Building. He didn't want to face her when she first walked in.

"Better me than Radha," was the first comment she made to him.

He had to smile at her remark. He looked at her through bloodshot eyes. His shirt was still sticking to him. He looked disheveled.

"Oh, Angel, I need more strength to get through this," he muttered to her.

"No kidding," she responded with a flippancy that made the comment comical. "You'll find it," she assured him, attempting to balance the sting and irreverence of her earlier sentiment.

He suddenly felt very close to Anjali. At that time, at that instant. He gave her a hug.

"I know you didn't do it," Anjali said to him.

He unconsciously held the back of her head in his hand and massaged it.

He pulled away slightly and looked deep into her eyes with a romantic longing. He caught the expression on her face. Anjali looked down and attempted to make herself busy.

"I'm sorry," Arun suddenly felt the urge to say.

"Don't be," Anjali responded quickly. "It's the situation you are in. I know that. That's what you have shown before."

Arun knew that she was referring to Meenakshi.

• • •

Andy called Arun again. "I think I have some information that might be helpful. I got access to the financial records. Looks like there were a bunch of payments made by GoWire to this research company."

"That's normal though, isn't it?" Arun argued.

"Except the timing," Andy said. "I spoke with the testing place. They said all payments are made up front and testing a product costs around fifty to seventy-five thousand," Andy indicated.

"Uh-huh," responded Arun.

"The amount of the payments is close to two million dollars."

"The exact amount that they said I took," Arun pointed out.

• • •

Arun presented himself at the courthouse to enter his guilty plea. His attorney had indicated that it would be the path of least resistance, allowing him to come through this with the least punishment possible. If he were to fight it, he might not be able to have as lenient an end result if things did not go in his favor.

While they processed him, they placed handcuffs on him. He posted bail and was released within half an hour. Arun rationalized the experience so that he could stomach what was happening to him. As he thought about it, he kept coming back to the same question in his mind.   Thanks to his family, when had he ever been free?

CHAPTER EIGHTEEN

October – November 2007

Sam's son, Thomas, bumped into Arun at a University of Pennsylvania mixer. It had been months since the article in the paper. Arun was curious how it would feel to face people again.

"I am sorry to hear about your brother," Thomas offered.

Not wanting to look stupid, Arun replied, "Thanks, I appreciate that." Arun looked off into the distance. He was wondering what had happened and he wondered which brother.

"He was a good man and he will be missed," Thomas said.

Arun's face fell. One of his brothers was gone. He had no idea which one. His heart was beating very fast. He was desperate to ask Thomas which one it was. Whom did he lose, Sanjay or Raj?

"It's a shame about his wife," Thomas added.

Sanjay. Arun had lost Sanjay. Arun tried his best to maintain his composure, but he was not adequately able to hold back the tears that began flowing profusely. Thomas fidgeted about, clearly uncomfortable. Arun managed to put his drink down and walk out of the event. As he stood in the parking lot, he pulled out his wallet and looked at his family.

He thought about how the last time he had interacted with his brother, they had fought. He thought about the last five months and how his family had been ignoring him. He thought about how no one had congratulated him or Radha on the birth of Sapna. Nor had they come to see her. He thought about all of these things as he drove to the airport. He wanted to relay them to Radha over the phone. He couldn't get a hold of her and this was not something he wanted to leave a message about. He imagined her encouraging him to go to his parent's house.

"How did this happen?" Arun pleaded as he entered the house. He had not spoken with them since the newspaper article.

As usual, there was silence.

"What is going on, Mom?" he asked directing the question towards Meena.

She began to cry again. Arun looked around impatiently. His eyes fell on Raj sitting by himself, also crying.

"We've lost our brother," said Raj through a squeaky crackling voice.

Arun was stunned. Somehow hearing one of his family members say it made it instantaneously real. A loud deafening sound filled his ears. His heart was doing the same slingshot up and down that it had done before. Arun didn't want to believe what he was hearing. It couldn't be true.

"Where is Sujata?"

There were other thoughts on Arun's mind. *When did everyone find out? How come no one told me?*

Raj pointed with his head towards their parents' room.

He saw Sujata sitting there, draped in white, the traditional color for widows. Her eyes looked as swollen as the top of a mushroom with patches of pink on them. Did she have any more tears left, he wondered? Arun wished that he knew how to console her. He found that he could not come up with the right words. He also didn't want to butcher it by saying something erroneous in Hindi.

He opened his phone, this time getting through. "Radha, can you come? Sanjay died."

● ● ●

The reality was that Arun had no idea how to cope. He hated the last conversation that he had had with Sanjay. *No, he* thought, *that's silly to think about that, there was so much more that was wrong with the relationship.* It was so troubled, so damaged. But he loved his brother. He didn't want this to have happened. He always thought that his brother was just naïve about how the world worked. He was a bookworm; that was the world and the reality that he knew.

Arun always thought that he had time. He thought that after several years, they would be able to see more eye-to-eye, potentially even resolve the tension between them and possibly even begin to enjoy each other's company. In many ways, Sanjay filled an important void for his parents. At least they had somebody whom they could turn to. Even though it made it challenging for Arun at times, deep down, he realized he actually appreciated that. It likely had taken some of the pressure off of him.

Raj finally revealed to him that there had been an accident involving the jeep that Sanjay was using to get from the train station to the plantation. He fell out of the vehicle and hit his head on the pavement. He seemed okay for awhile but then lost consciousness, the driver had reported. They took him to the hospital. After several hours he died. The doctors said it was due to a brain hemorrhage. Arun recalled the accident that he had right before getting married. He felt guilty, even though it was irrational for him to feel that way. He knew somehow, his parents would blame it on him.

Arun felt selfish for being lost in his own thoughts. He went to Raj. Raj looked up when Arun walked in.

"We should check in on Mom and Dad and see how they are doing," Arun said to Raj.

Raj looked down. Arun went downstairs by himself.

He found his mother sitting in front of a number of Hindu gods and goddesses, a makeshift home temple.

He saw his father through the glass window. He was sitting in a lawn chair by the garden.

"I'll never be able to figure him out," said Arun out loud.

• • •

Andy called Arun. This time he was frantically excited.

"I have the bank statements that show the money that was wired! These were all done with Chet's authority. I found the doctored wire transfer request forms where they put your signatures. I've got the originals. The bank statements only show one set, not both," proclaimed Andy.

Arun met with Andy and collected the documents.

"I guess we should get this to the US Attorney right away?"

"No," indicated Arun, "let's get it to my parents."

• • •

Arun and Radha attended the funeral for Sanjay. All eyes stared at them as they entered. Nobody approached them. They clung to each other. Radha led him towards a quiet isolated area. Arun resisted. He took Radha by the hand and defiantly stood next to his father and mother, neither of whom looked at him or his wife for the entire ceremony. Prior to leaving, Raj came to his brother and sister-in-law and embraced them both. Arun and Radha left without uttering a word.

• • •

"You were always so cocky, so arrogant," started Arun. Arun was standing at his uncle's doorstep.

Arjun sighed as he looked at Arun. He had a look of shock and disgust on his face.

"What do you think you are doing here?"

"You judged me so harshly," said Arun.

"I think you should leave my house," Arjun commanded.

"I know all about your secrets," said Arun.   Arun signaled to the man claiming to be his cousin to come out of the car and approach the house.

"Papa!" he shouted.

Sara came to that front door at that moment.   Arjun dropped the stack of papers in his hands.   Arun's cousin hugged Arjun and called him "Papa" again.   Sara left the house in tears.

Arun walked away as well, feeling neither satisfied nor happy.   He felt resentment.   His life could have been so much better he thought to himself.   He never should have had the unattainable bar of his Uncle Arjun to surpass.

● ● ●

Arun confronted Derek and Chet.   They were both exiting the building.

"Why me?" demanded Arun.

"Wh-what are you talking about?" asked Derek.

Arun kept facing Chet.   "Don't talk to me you worthless piece of crap."

"Why me, Chet?" Arun demanded once again.

Chet had no words.   His face got very red.

"Let's get out of here, Derek," commanded Chet.

"I have some people that will want to talk to you first," Arun commented.

From behind Arun came a number of vehicles full of FBI agents.   They took both Chet and Derek into custody.

● ● ●

Arun and Radha decided to do a small diwali gathering at their place for family.   It had been a very trying year for them. They couldn't do anything lavish in honor of Sanjay's passing, but they wished to be with family.   It was meant to be a solemn gathering.

Rajiv and Meena came.   After seeking counsel from Pablo about whether or not to attend, Rajiv decided to come.

When Raj arrived, he shouted out, "Happy Diwali! Yeah, let's party!" Everyone looked at him askance. He seemed to suddenly remember what had happened and he bowed his head, as if in penance.

"Religion," commented Anjali, "in its most sublime, it is a therapeutic wellspring of hope; in its most generic, it is a sanctuary from fear; in its most mediocre it is a social gathering." Arun was the only one who heard her. He never ceased being impressed with her intelligence.

Nandini turned to her paternal grandparents. "I'm a big sister now. Come look!"

Nandini dragged Rajiv and Meena to the bassinet where her younger sister was sleeping. "You see!" she said gleefully. She then turned to them, "How come you weren't there for the birth of Sapna?"

Neither Rajiv nor Meena moved. They observed their granddaughter for the first time. Both began to swell with emotion.

Nandini repeated her question several more times.

There was silence from her grandparents.

Arun found that his heart was beating faster. He also felt a shortness of breath. "Answer her question," he told his parents.

There was silence.

He went in front of his parents. "Answer her question."

Continued silence.

He grabbed his father by the arms and screamed in Rajiv's face, "Answer her question!"

Rajiv came down on Arun with a hard slap on the face. Arun let go of his father. Through bloodshot eyes he observed the man who struck him.

Radha picked Sapna up. Zubin stood by, stunned.

"This has to be the nadir," mumbled Anjali.

Nandini started to cry. She first went to her father and embraced his legs. She then went to her grandfather and started tugging at his leg.

"Why did you hit Daddy, why did you hit Daddy? Why did you make angry with Daddy?"

Rajiv raised his right arm again. He was about to bring it down across the right side of her face and teach her the same lesson he had just dealt his son. As he attempted to bring his arm down, he was met with resistance. It was Arun.

"If you touch her, I will break it," said Arun.

Rajiv thought back to Arjun and his Uncle R.K. Rajiv put his hand down. A look of remorse entered his face. He remembered his friend Pablo's words. He moved to embrace Arun.

Arun wouldn't let him. "You need to get out of my house," Arun said.

"Son, what happening to you is not being good. I don't want you being going to the jail," Rajiv said in a meek voice.

"GET OUT OF MY HOUSE!" Arun screamed. There was a rage in his voice. Years of pent up anger and frustration came out.

Quietly Rajiv and Meena gathered their things and left. Sujata went with them. Raj was speechless.

• • •

Radha thought about the comment that Rajiv had made. Anjali had a confused expression on her face as well. They looked at each other.

Radha turned to Arun. "I don't think he knows that you have been cleared."

"How could he not know?" questioned Arun.

"Why did he make that comment if he knows? It doesn't make sense," Radha indicated.

"I think Radha is right," Anjali said.

267

"Why don't you talk to your father?" Radha asked Arun.

"Did you see what he was going to do to Nandini!" demanded Arun.

"He wouldn't have reacted to that if you had been discussing the problem with him or if he hadn't been fighting with Uncle Arjun. I don't think he heard the news regarding you. He would have focused on that instead," explained Radha.

"He can be silent like he was with me for all those months that I suffered, and I can't do the same with him! I'm so disgusted with the way he treats me, the way all of them treat me," Arun proclaimed.

"You aren't going to make progress this way," said Radha. "He's not well. Your father did not look well today."

"I think you should go after them," suggested Anjali.

Arun took Nandini in his arms and walked away. He whispered to his daughter, "I'll protect you, darling."

Nandini, still shook up by the events, touched her father's face.

CHAPTER NINETEEN

December 2007

Rajiv met with Pablo.

"It has been awhile, *señor*," commented Pablo.

Rajiv stayed quiet. He seemed content to just be in Pablo's presence.

"I am still so sorry about your son dying. It remains very hard, I imagine," Pablo said.

"I am regretting, my friend, I taking time to being seeing you," apologized Rajiv. He didn't want to dwell on that topic.

"Was that your other son - *en el periodico* - in them papers?" asked Pablo.

"Yes, it is being him," admitted Rajiv. Rajiv looked down.

"How have you been able to do anything to help him?" asked Pablo.

"What can I being doing?" asked Rajiv. He shrugged his shoulders.

"What have you tried?" asked Pablo.

"I no trying anything. What can I being doing? People thinking he doing the bad things. Is not being good for rest of family. We must keeping the distance," explained Rajiv.

"You have to do something! He is your son!" Pablo was very excited and very animated as he spoke. He took his hat off and seemed to be squeezing it with one hand. A cloud of dust blew up from his shuffled feet.

"But I having large family. Others being there to worry about. Family is being the first. Person in the family is being the second," said Rajiv.

"That is not the way, *señor*," pleaded Pablo, "You cannot leave him like that! What you do when plant gets *enfermo* – sick? Or when rabbit come and eat leaves?"

Rajiv continued to look down.

"You bring it back to life, *señor*," Pablo commented.

Tears began to swell in Rajiv's eyes.

"*Es tu hijo* - He is your son, *señor*, your son!"

● ● ●

"I heard about your son Arun," indicated Sam.

Rajiv was silent. He was looking down. He had just come back from lunch with Pablo. He was experiencing confused emotions.

"It's a damn shame when kids get led astray like that," Sam added.

Rajiv was still silent. He managed a smile for Sam.

Sam turned to walk away.

Rajiv called out to him. "Sam, my son being very good. He doing no things wrong," Rajiv shouted. He thought he felt the urge to clear his throat, but then he realized that he didn't.

● ● ●

"Arjun, Arun is being in the trouble and needing the help. Your wife needing being doing something. She is being lawyer. She helping in Arun's case." Rajiv had called Arjun.

Arjun replied, "Look Rajiv, although it is her area of expertise, she is very busy. Anyway, I have my own crisis here. She hasn't been around much. We are having problems. I don't think I can talk to her about it. Find someone else."

Rajiv, who had felt emotions all his life but was never able to put a voice to them, found that voice within him on that day at that moment.   He was so emotional that he couldn't keep from shaking.

"Why you no understand?" he demanded of Arjun.   For the first time in his life, he was shouting.   His voice had such a heavy weight to it, as if it were struggling to push a two-ton truck uphill.   His eyes had the hollowness of the deepest cavern.   The white of his eyes nearly gone, overshadowed by the red of blood vessels making him look like a map with routes identified in red. His emotion came from deep within.   Like an archaeologist, he had to dig to find them, excavating numerous layers.   Decades of neglect and poor nourishment for his soul relinquished his feelings to depths so far that he didn't know if he could ever tap into them.

He surprised Arjun and Meena.   Most of all, Rajiv surprised himself.   At that moment, to the outside world, people heard Rajiv clear his throat.   Inside, his surprise was followed by a sharp pain in his chest, a burst of warm air and stillness.

His throat was not being cleared, his body was clearing his soul.   Rajiv was no longer of this world.

● ● ●

Arun kept protesting to Radha not to call.   It had been two days.

"Arun, I love you, but I am doing this," she declared.

Arun watched as Radha picked up the phone and dialed. "Hello, Mom?"   Arun could hear screaming from the other side. He wondered if his mother was scolding Radha.   Feeling like it was unjust he got up to walk to the phone to take over the conversation.   He watched as Radha began to cry.   The sight made him more angry.   She cupped her free hand over her mouth.   When he was about to reach for the phone, Radha blurted out, "He's gone.   Your father's gone."

CHAPTER TWENTY

December 2007

The conversation with his uncle was later recounted to him. Arun felt miserable. He had always asked for his father to defend him. The day he did was the day he died.

Radha stood in front of her husband. "We've been through enough, already," she lamented. "Things can not go on like this."

Arun looked at her in silence. She was watching his forehead. There was no crinkling. It was as taut as a trampoline. It surprised her at first and then she felt relieved. He understood.

"We have to accept our parents' shortcomings, and love them in spite of it. Like Anjali and I do with Dad," Radha added.

"I know," he said. "I now remember the education you gave me the first night we met. Love at first conversation."

That night, before they slept, Radha was presented with a single red rose by Arun.

● ● ●

When Arun walked into his parent's house, he overheard his mother on the phone. She was speaking with Dipti.

"Of course Arun feel responsible. His fault for Sanjay having the injury to head. And then his father never arguing with brother if Arun make no trouble."

Arun had a surge of disappointment overcome him. "Mom, I'm here," he decided to shout out after a few seconds pause.

His mother quickly ended the conversation and hung up the phone. She had a sour mood on her face when he walked in and made eye contact. She was cold towards him as he embraced her.

"I forgive you, Mom," Arun said. To himself.

• • •

Pablo arrived at Rajiv's funeral. He approached Arun. "You must be Arun," he said.

"Yes," said Arun, a bit stunned.

"Hey, Zubin. *Como estas?*"

"*Hola*," replied Zubin. Zubin handed Pablo a program.

"*Dhanyibhad,*" said Pablo.

Arun was taken aback.

"Boy that tractor story was something, wasn't it?"

Zubin responded, "Oh, *si*."

"What are you two talking about?" Arun asked. Arun heard the story of his father from this man. It was like he was being told about someone for the first time. There were tears in his eyes.

"Your father's uncle R.K. was a piece of work, wasn't he?"

Arun heard the story of the family past. He had never heard these details before. He was finally beginning to understand his father.

• • •

After a few years, Anjali married Steven. Meena showed up and congratulated her. B.P. gave his daughter away.

Arun heard explosions in the background. This time, they were fireworks. B.P. couldn't help himself, Arun mused. Feeling scared, Arun instinctively reached for his wallet after hearing the loud bangs. He then remembered where he was.

He walked over to his family. "Group hug everyone. Everyone come and hug Mommy and Daddy."

He didn't need his photo. He had everyone in front of him.

• • •

Arun found a job providing legal aid to immigrants, particularly migrant farmers from Mexico. The joy and satisfaction that he felt was more than he had expected. He spent the balance of his time managing his uncle's vineyard, trying to follow in his father's footsteps with the help and guidance of his son. Over time, he bought his uncle out. His uncle told him he could just take it, but Arun was insistent on paying for it.

• • •

Years later, when Arjun passed away, he left a substantial sum of money to Arun, Raj, Zubin, Nandini and Sapna. Arun went to India with Zubin. The two of them took the money and bought a piece of land. It was close to where Rajiv had been born and raised. They purchased the property under the name of the Rajiv Gandharni Pvt Ltd Corporation.

Arun decided to go for a walk on the land. He asked Zubin to join him. Arun wanted to be sure to find a path that both he and his son could chart together. He had come to appreciate the importance of map-building with those whom you loved.

Arun handed a gift to Zubin. "It's from your grandfather."

Zubin had a quizzical look on his face as he held an old canister.

"Why you no understand?"

Zubin smiled as he looked at his father. Arun held his son.